The Ultimatum

By Dan Graziano

THE ULTIMATUM
I THINK SHE'S TRYING TO TELL ME SOMETHING

The Ultimatum

DAN GRAZIANO

AVON

An Imprint of HarperCollins*Publishers*

HarperCollins books may be purchased for educational, business, or sales promotional use. For information please write: Special Markets Department, HarperCollins Publishers, 10 East 53rd Street, New York, NY 10022.

FIRST EDITION

Interior text designed by Diahann Sturge

B+T 13.95 10/07

Library of Congress Cataloging-in-Publication Data

Graziano, Dan.
  The ultimatum / by Dan Graziano.—1st ed.
    p. cm.
ISBN: 978-0-06-084797-5
ISBN-10: 0-06-084797-2
1. Commitment (Psychology)—Fiction.   2. Marriage—Fiction.   I. Title.
PS3607.R399U44   2007
813'.54—dc22   2006037917

07 08 09 10 11   ❖/RRD   10 9 8 7 6 5 4 3 2 1

For Andrea,
who made all the decisions easy.

PART I

Saturday

One

He woke because he smelled French toast.

Oh, there was no mistaking it—cinnamon French toast. Lying in bed, he could just about see it. The big, thick slices his mother used to make on Sunday mornings. Heavy and yellow on both sides from the butter. Deep, brown rivers of cinnamon ringing their way through each juicy piece. The fleck of burned grease that would dangle off the corner, looking like stray crust and tasting, gloriously, of the bottom of the frying pan. Yep, that was the smell all right. Cinnamon French toast . . . and fresh coffee.

As he blinked his eyes open, Henry knew he'd arrived at the weekend. It was brighter and warmer in the bedroom than it ever was on weekday mornings. There was no alarm clock beeping at him, and the late spring sun had wrapped its fingers around the drawn curtains just enough to let him know it was out there, waiting for him, whenever he was ready. Henry rolled over onto his back and smiled. She was downstairs, waiting for him too. And she'd made French toast.

Still in his pajamas, he descended the stairs, knowing his footfalls would let her know he was coming. It was just after nine A.M., and she'd probably been up for more than an hour. She was always up before he was, even on the weekends.

He smiled again as he walked into the kitchen. Layla sat at the far end of their white rectangular table, still dressed in her running shorts and shirt. Her light brown hair was tied back in a ponytail. One perfect leg was crossed over the other as she sipped her coffee and looked up from her crossword puzzle. Her toes were painted pink.

"Good morning," she said.

"Morning," he replied, and looked over to the stove, where two fat slices of cinnamon French toast were sizzling. "You sleep okay?"

"Sure," she said, looking up to receive his kiss as he made his way to the refrigerator. "You?"

"Like a baby," he said, and wondered for a second why she giggled.

"That's good," she said.

He poured a glass of orange juice and walked over to the stove. He picked up the spatula and pressed down, slightly, on one of the slices. The grease bubbled up to the surface. He smiled again.

"To what do I owe this?" he asked.

"Just felt like something different," she said, back now to her crossword. "They're probably done, if you want them. I already had mine."

"And what? You were making these in case I came down right this second?"

"I kind of figured the smell might get you . . . eventually."

She knew him well, which was one of the reasons these mornings felt so good. Sure, they saw each other in the mornings during the week, but it was always hectic. She hustling out to work in the morning, he pecking her on the cheek as he began his own workday at the computer, already in his zone. But on these mornings, on Saturdays, it always felt more comfortable. Saturday felt like you'd made it to something—like the workweek was worth it. Saturday was a reward, and he enjoyed sharing it with her.

"So," she said, still looking at the paper.

"Mmm-hmm?" Henry asked through his first forkful of French toast.

"Do you know what next Saturday is?"

He did know, and as soon as he swallowed his food, he answered proudly.

"Jack and Gina's wedding," he said.

"Well, right," she said, looking up at him now. "But do you know what else next Saturday is?"

And he didn't. Not really fair, a quiz this early in the morning. And especially not if the French toast was a trap. He wasn't ready for this. Not fair to wreck a Saturday in the first few minutes. Not fair at all.

"What?" he asked, oblivious.

"Henry," she said, and she might have looked sad if she hadn't looked triumphant. "You really don't know?"

And he set his mind to a frantic scramble. June 5. What was June 5? Why was June 5 an important day? What was it about June . . . oh.

"Oh," he said. "Of course. June fifth."

It was Layla's turn to smile. Of course, she'd been fishing for this. It hadn't been a quiz at all, but a segue to the next part of her Saturday morning surprise. She'd just wanted him to get there on his own, before springing it on him.

"June fifth, six years ago," she said to him.

"I remember," he said.

"You took me to that little sandwich place in George-town, the one down near Wisconsin Avenue."

"Booeymonger's."

"Right. Booeymonger's."

"Our first date," he said.

"Our first date. Do you remember? You had to borrow money from your roommate?"

"From Brian. He let me borrow his credit card. He didn't have any money either, but he had something like a hundred left on this one card. He was a good roommate."

Layla chuckled a little. And now he was beginning to worry. She'd been sitting completely still this whole time, the pen lying across the crossword, the coffee on the table in front of her, her hands folded in her lap. She was looking him directly in the eye.

"Do you know why I bring this up?" she asked.

And he didn't know this one either. He was really getting his ass kicked on this conversation, and he couldn't figure out why. It had been years since they'd given each other gifts on June 5, years since he'd even sent roses. They always marked the occasion with a nice dinner for two, somewhere simple, and a bottle of wine. Last year they'd had champagne.

All he could offer was a blank look.

"Well," she said, making him wonder when she'd lapsed into her lawyer tone of voice. "I bring this up, Henry, because next Saturday will mark the six-year anniversary of our first date together. And Henry, I think it's about time we made it official."

Henry stared at Layla for a full, pregnant second before dropping his eyes back toward the plate. He looked at the remaining bites of French toast, swimming in syrup. They'd betrayed him. It was the French toast that had lured him into this, and he'd be damned if he'd ever trust another breakfast carbohydrate again.

"Henry?" she was saying. "Henry, look at me. I'm serious."

He did as she told him to do, but he could only look at her legs. Man, she had great legs.

"Henry? Okay, don't look at me, but I am serious."

And finally, he looked up and met her eyes with his.

"I . . ." he stammered. "I didn't think . . ."

"Right," she said. "You didn't think I wanted to get married. You don't want to get married, I don't want to get married, we have this perfect little deal set up where we live together, have sex, make each other breakfast and never get married. Right?"

Well, he thought, kind of. Yeah.

"Well, you're kidding yourself, Henry," she said, without letting him answer out loud. "And here's the deal. I'm sorry to spring this on you, but I feel like I need to shock you into action. Are you ready?"

Henry seriously doubted that he was ready.

"Okay . . ." he ventured.

"You have one week to get this figured out."

"One week?" he blurted. "You hit me with this on a Saturday morning and you're giving me one week?"

"Henry, it's been six years," she said. "Actually, five years and 358 days. That's how long we've been together. I'm going to be thirty years old in August. A lot of women need to get married by thirty, you know. And a hell of a lot of couples get married after dating for a lot less than six years."

"Yeah, but—"

"Yeah, but nothing." She was fully in charge of the conversation now. She didn't do this often—treat him as a hostile witness. But when she did, there was very little he could do about it. "It's one week. We're going to Jack and Gina's wedding. And Henry, if you don't make up your mind on this by the time she throws her bouquet, we're coming back in different cars. And when you get here, I won't be here."

"You're serious?" he asked, knowing the answer.

"Totally serious," she said, looking straight at him, locking him in. "Totally."

"I mean, about the bouquet and everything."

"Yes, Henry. That's your deadline. That bouquet hits the floor, or lands in some poor, desperate bridesmaid's hands, and you still don't have an answer for me, I'm out. It may not be fair. It may not be right. But this is the way it is."

"Can't we talk about this?" he asked.

She was up now, out of her chair for the first time since he'd come downstairs. She carried her plate over to the sink, sipped the last of her coffee, set down the dishes and turned to leave the room.

"Sure we can," she said. "We can spend the whole week talking about this. We can talk about this the whole way up to Maine, and all night and all day before the wedding if you want. I mean, Henry, I know what I want your decision to be, and I'm happy to help you make it. But nothing will change my deadline."

She had stopped in the doorway and was looking up at the wall, picking at a speck with her thumbnail.

"Wow," Henry said, looking down at the floor.

"So," she said. "I'm getting dressed to go meet Susan and Gloria for golf. You, my friend, have a lot to think about."

Henry said nothing as the love of his life kissed him on the top of his head and left the kitchen. He still hadn't finished his French toast, and now he didn't think he wanted to. He sat there for about ten minutes before finally getting up and starting to load the dishwasher. Her coffee spoon was still on the table, next to the completed crossword puzzle. And as he reached over to grab it, the word in the puzzle's bottom right corner, 60 across, caught his eye:

QUANDARY

Yeah, he thought. You can say that again.

Two

"So let me get this straight," Pete was saying. "If you don't propose to her by the time Gina throws her bouquet—"

"She's leaving," Henry said, looking at Pete's hands, which were busy filling in the right leg of a cartoon rabbit with a green crayon.

"Man," Pete said, his tongue poking slightly out of the left side of his mouth, his eyes locked on the rabbit. "That's messed up."

And for a second Henry thought this was somebody to talk.

Pete Gresham was a tall, skinny guy with curly, Mike Brady–type black hair, who almost always ate lunch at Friendly's. That last part might have been strange on its own for a thirty-year-old man with no kids, but what made it even stranger in Pete's case was that, in addition to eating at Friendly's, he always ordered off the children's menu. And in addition to ordering off the children's menu, Pete also required the waiters and waitresses in his friendly neighborhood Friendly's to supply him with the crayons and paper activity place mat they gave to the children who ate there. This had been going on for years, and all of the waiters and waitresses in this particular Friendly's knew the drill. What was funny was coming here with Pete when a new Friendly's employee met him at the door and asked, innocently, "Two?" and Pete said, "Yes. One adult and one child." That was funny. Well, funny and humiliating.

Pete almost always ate lunch alone. His days were generally hurried, since he was a very successful money manager whose clients were counting on him to steer their finances in a direction that would ensure the comfort and security of themselves and of future generations of their families. But he always found time for lunch, and he took his time there. He never brought work to lunch, because there was too much coloring to do. And when he went to lunch with a friend, as he did on this sunny spring Saturday, he didn't pay the friend very much attention. Not until all of the woodland creatures were colored.

But instead of pointing out his friend's issues, Henry chose to keep the conversation's focus on the issue he'd raised—Layla's deadline. That was the reason he'd called Pete at work on a Saturday morning (an emergency measure, since he knew Pete didn't like to be bothered on Saturday mornings), and it was the reason he was here now, watching Pete put down the green crayon, pick up the orange one, and set to work on the rabbit's fluffy tail as three waitresses stood in a corner giggling at him. Pete, as always, was oblivious.

"So, yeah," Henry offered, trying to bring Pete back from the rabbit hole. "You can see why I wanted to have lunch."

The tail completed, Pete put down the orange crayon and sat back to have a look at his artwork. The green rabbit with the blue eyes and orange tail was an unsettling sight, but Pete seemed as proud of it as he'd seemed moments earlier, when he'd circled STEP to complete his Word Finder puzzle. After a moment of self-admiration, Pete looked up at Henry.

"Yeah, man, absolutely," he said. "This is serious stuff. So now, what's the deal? You still going to the wedding with her?"

"Right now, yeah," Henry said. "I mean, we've been dating for six years. I'm not sure I'd know how to ask anybody else. Plus, if I did that, it would kind of give us her answer way ahead of time, wouldn't it?"

"I guess so," Pete said. "So, what then, you gotta do some soul-searching or something like that?"

"Something like that, sure," Henry said. "But I was kind of hoping for a little advice from my friends. I mean, what do you think?"

Pete took a sip of his strawberry milk shake, keeping his eyes locked on Henry's. He sat back and thought for a second.

"What do I think?" Pete repeated. "I mean, I think it sounds screwy, if you want my opinion. But so does dating somebody for six years and not proposing."

Tempted to thank Pete for being blunt, even at the expense of his feelings, Henry forged ahead.

"Thanks," he said. "But I guess I'm more interested in information. Like, how did you know you wanted to marry Catherine?"

"See now, that's a good question," Pete said. "A good question."

And for a minute, as Pete looked around the restaurant as if wondering why his lunch was taking so long, Henry wondered if that was all Pete planned to say.

"I don't think it was one of those lightning-bolt kind of moments, if you know what I mean," Pete said. "I mean, it's not like you're walking in the desert and out of nowhere you hear a voice and you know it's time to pop the question."

"All right," Henry said. "After six years, I kind of didn't think it went like that, but it's nice to hear it from somebody else."

"You know what it was for me?" Pete mused. "It was our kitchen."

"Your kitchen."

"Yeah, it sounds silly, but yeah. We were living together, you know, in that apartment in the city, and we were redoing our kitchen. And I mean, you talk about a pain. This is constant conversation about tile and about wood for the cabinets and where this thing should go and which stove do you like better and all kinds of stuff that I could care less about, you know what I mean?"

"Sure," Henry said.

"But there came a point where I was talking to my brother, and I was talking about this kitchen project, and how Catherine was dragging me off to pick out wallpaper or something like that. And my brother says something like, 'Man, what a pain,' or something, and I told him, 'You know, it's really kind of fun.' And that's when I figured I knew."

"I don't get it," Henry said.

"I mean, we're redoing our kitchen, and I could care less," Pete said. "But I was doing something with her, and so it felt great. Sure, you look at it from the outside and you'd say, what a brutal way to spend a Saturday afternoon, picking out tile for your kitchen floor. But I never looked at it that way. It was me and her, doing the kitchen, our kitchen, together, and that was cool."

This made some sense to Henry, who had recently had the bathrooms in his own house redone. He remembered Layla picking out the tile and the patterns and even the hand towels that would hang on the racks. He remembered how badly his feet hurt after another Saturday at Home Depot. But he didn't remember ever feeling like he was fed up. Maybe that was a good sign.

"I think I understand," he said to Pete.

"Yeah, that and the fact that she let me keep my posters up," Pete said.

"Your posters? You mean your swimsuit model posters? You still have those up in your house?"

"Yeah," Pete said. "She didn't like it, but I told her it was a deal breaker. That and the dog."

"The dog."

"Yep. She hates dogs. May even be allergic. But I told her, no dog, no dice. And she says she's figured out how to live with it."

Henry was beginning to understand things even better now, as the waitress put two plates in front of Pete. One of the plates had a hot dog on it. The other had chicken fingers. Henry looked down at his Baja chicken tortilla wrap and wondered what it must be like to go through life as a thirty-year-old kid.

"You should have heard the conversation we had when she asked if I wanted to have kids," Pete said, biting into the hot dog. "Whoo-hoo!"

"You don't want to have kids?" Henry asked.

"You kidding me? You know how much responsibility that is? You know what that does to your sex life? Your social life? Your life in general? Not for me, my friend. Not for me."

"And Catherine is fine with that too?"

"Sure she is," Pete said, wiping a spot of ketchup off his chin. "She's a great girl. Really great."

"Pete," Henry said. "Did it ever occur to you . . ."

"What?" Pete asked, his mouth full of hot dog.

And Henry thought for a second about the value of finishing his thought.

"Never mind," he said, and Pete shrugged before dunking a chicken finger into a dish of mustard.

"Whatever," he said.

* * *

It hadn't been a waste of time, Henry told himself. Pete's insight about the kitchen had actually been pretty good. In a vacuum, it passed for good advice—something to think about as Layla's ultimatum dug its claws deeper into his brain. It sounded surprisingly mature, actually, coming from a man who colored the place mat every day at lunch. But that was the problem. How seriously could he take Pete?

He wondered this on the short drive from Friendly's to the golf course—not the course where Layla was playing, no. Usually on a Saturday he might try to meet up with her, play the back nine if she didn't have a full foursome, or at least bang it around on the driving range for an hour or so before meeting her for a drink after she was done. But today that didn't seem right. Henry didn't know if he wanted to play a round of golf, just hang out at the range, or sit in his car in the parking lot. All he knew for sure was that he didn't want to see Layla, not right away, not after what happened this morning. He didn't want to deal with the awkwardness that would come with not being able to talk about the morning in front of her friends. And come to think of it, he didn't want to deal with the way her friends always made him feel—as if he were some kind of deadbeat because he hadn't gone to law school and didn't put on a tie and sit in an office all day.

No, he'd see Layla soon enough, and they'd talk. She'd promised they could talk, and he planned to take her up on it. But right now he just didn't know how to begin the conversation.

So instead of heading to the club where they played every Saturday, Henry drove in the other direction, to the public course at which he knew almost nobody. He played here occasionally, when the club was closed or when he wanted to play alone. Henry spent a lot of time alone—it was when he did his best thinking. He'd always treasured time to himself, placed a great deal of value on the thinking he did solo, and there had never been a more important time for that than now.

Of course, this being a Saturday, and one of the first truly summery days of the year, the public course was packed. Henry arrived at 12:45 and asked if he could get on as a single, figuring he'd have about a three hour wait. But he got lucky. The starter told him the next group going off was supposed to be a foursome but that only three had shown up. Since he was the only single waiting, he went right off.

His playing partners were an interesting group, as they so often are when the public course throws four strangers together and tells them to have fun and hit it straight. One was a very small, older Hispanic man named José who carried his own bag but didn't seem to mind since there were only five clubs in it. He had a bushy white moustache and white hair cut very close to his scalp, and when he swung the club, he came to a complete stop at the top of his backswing and actually rotated his left foot a quarter turn before bringing the club back down to hit the ball. Henry had never seen anything like it, and he was stunned the first time José took a swing and the ball went right down the fairway. Not far, but straight. Every time, straight.

The other two did appear to know each other, and Henry found out later that they'd actually played in the same foursome earlier in the week. So, while their relationship wasn't lengthy, they were united by the fact of a prior acquaintance.

The first, whose name was John, was a big, burly type who looked as if he could hit the ball a mile. He was about Henry's age, outfitted with all of the latest oversized clubs and the big fancy bag and head covers. He wore a green Brooks Brothers polo shirt and a black goatee. His handshake felt like a clamp, and he had that too-loud voice that just didn't belong on a golf course, though who was going to tell him?

The other one's name also was John, though he was not quite the specimen the other John was. This John was older, with tousled whiffs of white hair scattered about the top of his head. His face was darkly tanned and cluttered with deep pockmarks, and the sweat already had begun to soak through his shirt at the armpits and around his loosely hanging man-breasts. His handshake felt like a washcloth.

After José poked his first tee shot about 140 yards down the middle of the fairway, Big John flipped a tee that landed with the point facing Henry. That meant he was next, and without any warm-up he lined his first shot down the right side of the hole and into a fairway sand trap. Not a good start.

After pockmarked John had hooked his tee shot into the woods on the left, Big John stood up and bellowed, "Plenty of fairway out there for the Big Dog." Henry offered a chuckle, in part because it was the polite thing to do but mainly because Big John frightened him. He watched as the man uncoiled a surprisingly smooth and steady swing and belted the ball down the middle of the fairway, well past poor little José's ball.

Henry had no idea if he would have much conversation with these men. José had a thick accent, but his English appeared to be fairly good. And Big John seemed like the kind of man who would monopolize any discussion and keep it focused on golf. But Henry surprised himself as they walked away from the first tee and Big John slapped him on the back and asked, "So, Henry. You married?"

"John," Henry responded. "That's a real good question."

Three

Layla wasn't surprised that he hadn't joined her for the back nine, or even for a drink. She'd expected as much after this morning, and had set her own mind to be patient with Henry over the next week. After all, she did want to marry him. Why else would she have hung around for six years? And with Susan in her ear all day talking about how she was going to drive him away, she had to keep reminding herself about this, and about how important it was to create a comfortable environment in which Henry could make his decision. That was the reason for the French toast, though she was sure he would think she'd used it to trick him.

She wasn't surprised he hadn't shown at the golf course, but she was a little surprised that he wasn't home when she got there. For a second she panicked, wondering if the ultimatum itself had driven him away on its very first day. She hollered his name once from the front door, while it was still open, once more after she dropped her keys on the kitchen counter, once more at the bottom of the stairs before she went up to look for him.

But there was no outward sign of a man who had departed for good. Everything was in place in his closet. No luggage appeared to have been packed. His toothbrush was in its regular place, in the green cup on the shelf above the sink, right next to hers. She looked in the mirror and saw that she had a piece of lettuce stuck to one of her front teeth. Great, she thought, and her hair still in the stupid ponytail from the golf course. One good thing about him not being there—at least she had time to get herself cleaned up before he got home.

Funny. All these years later, and she was still trying to impress him. Most girls, they're with a guy for six years, they don't have to worry about that kind of thing anymore. Most of them are married by now, maybe even have a couple of kids. Sometimes she wondered if that was Henry's plan—to hold off marrying her so she wouldn't let herself go. And if it was, as she looked in the mirror right now, she had to admit it wasn't a bad plan.

As Layla undressed for her shower, she noticed what was wrong. The stubborn little love handles that all those crunches couldn't knock out. Her shoulders, which she'd always hated, always thought were too broad. But all in all, her body looked a lot like it had when she was twenty, and it was hard to complain about that. Layla was especially proud of her legs, since they were the products of five hard miles a day, six days a week, without fail. She'd been running those miles since college, with the hope that they'd help her fight off age. So far, so good.

Realizing she was staring at her own naked body in the bathroom mirror with the door open behind her and the window shade open across the room, Layla shook herself out of her trance and started the shower, where she always did her best thinking.

She loved the life she and Henry had together. She really

did. But she was dealing with a body clock here, and she had to know. Last week, when Gloria finally got through laying out worst-case scenarios over burgers, she finally decided it was time. Gloria's points were all about timetables and the fact that Layla's were running short.

"Think about it," Gloria had said, while Susan sat by and rolled her eyes. "You're going to be thirty. Say tomorrow he shows up and decides it's over. Whatever reason: another woman, midlife crisis, whatever."

"Wow," Layla said.

"Hey, we're talking realism here," Gloria shot back. "It doesn't do you any good to let you fantasize about living this perfect life forever. These things could happen. These things do happen, every single day, to women much like yourself."

"You mean working women?"

"I mean clueless women." Gloria was now looking sideways at Susan, who grabbed her pocketbook and stormed off to the bathroom.

"That might not have been nice," Layla said.

"She's made her position clear," Gloria replied, her brown eyes flashing determination and toughness as she hammered her fork into her lunch salad. "Here's what I'm saying: say he dumps you tomorrow, whatever reason. You're now looking at a solid three years before you can have kids."

And that had brought it home. Layla had been unable to respond to that, especially once Gloria went right on, ticking off the schedule:

> *Six months, minimum, to get over a six-year relationship and be in the right frame of mind to find a decent guy. And that, they both agreed, would be moving pretty fast.*

Eight months, give or take, to get to the point where you
knew it was the right guy, and to get him to the point
where he even started thinking along those lines. And
that's assuming it was the right guy. If it wasn't, you
were looking at eight wasted months and square one
again.

A year to plan the wedding, assuming he'd proposed at
the eight-month mark.

Nine months, minimum, to have a child, assuming she
talked him into starting a family right away and got
pregnant basically on her honeymoon.

"That comes to thirty-five months, Layla, and that's with
everything breaking perfectly," Gloria had said, chewing
a large chunk of tomato. "I mean, perfectly. And that's if
it happened tomorrow. You wait another year or two, and
then he dumps you? You're backing it up that much more.
You need to know soon."

Layla knew that Gloria had been right. Harsh, but right.
That's what she got, she guessed, for hanging out with other lawyers. Brutally straightforward analysis.

When Layla got home that night, she knew something
had to be done to force Henry into a decision. It might
be painful, especially if Susan's worst fears were right and
the ultimatum drove Henry away for good, but she had to
do it. She didn't know how many times over the previous
six years she'd contemplated something like this but never
determined what form it should take. Now, with Jack and
Gina's wedding coming up, was her perfect chance.

But tonight, what she'd expected was to come home and
find him here, having spent the day mulling the morning
and ready to talk things over. Briefly, she'd fantasized about

coming home to roses and candles and soft music, finding Henry on one knee, offering up a diamond ring. But she rushed that fantasy right out of her mind, knowing it was nearly impossible and deciding that even if it were to happen, she'd rather be surprised than disappointed. Instead, she'd been plotting answers to questions she figured he might have, and ended up disappointed that he wasn't there to ask them.

They'd also made no plans for dinner, which was unusual for a Saturday night. As Layla finished blow-drying her hair, she thought about calling his cell phone, but decided to wait a while. All part of the don't-push-him plan. Wrapped in her bathrobe, she flopped onto the corner of the sofa and pointed the remote control at the television. It was just after five o'clock, and she figured he'd probably gone over to River Dunes to play by himself. She'd give him another hour, at least.

Henry was trying to make a ten-foot par putt on the sixteenth hole at River Dunes. The putt was straight and uphill, which would have made it pretty easy had Big John not just waved the flagstick over his head in an effort to distract him. The whooshing sound in his ears shocked Henry before he realized Big John had just pulled an old high school golf trick on him, and the entire foursome collapsed on the green in drunken laughter. José was in tears.

"I'm sorry," Big John blurted between belly laughs. "Did that distract you?"

"Son of a bitch," Henry said. "Now I'm glad I stepped on your ball in that bunker on twelve."

And more laughter.

They'd each had at least a six-pack since the start of their round. The group in front of them had played its way out of sight, and the group behind was undoubtedly calling the course marshals to tell them the drunks in front of them were playing too slow and screwing around with rakes and flagsticks. But Henry, Big John, John, and José couldn't have been more ignorant of the events transpiring around them. Big John had managed to fake serious a few holes earlier, when a ranger drove by and politely asked him if the group could speed things up. But as soon as the ranger drove out of sight, the break in the laughter ended and José was crying again.

Henry couldn't remember the last time he'd had so much fun on the golf course. Maybe the day before Pete's wedding, when they all played golf, smoked cigars, and guzzled so much beer that they were useless at the rehearsal dinner. Pete had made a speech that barely mentioned Catherine, except in the context of various things he and his friends had done in college to pull pranks on her and her friends. Catherine might have got mad that night, if she ever got mad at Pete. But she didn't, and Pete, Henry, and the rest of the gang got to roll around laughing and pretending they were all still in college.

This felt a little like that day, being out here on the course with José and the Johns. Except on that day, he hadn't been worried about himself and Layla.

On this day, he'd surprised himself with his answer to Big John's first-tee question about marriage. By the time they made it to the first green, he'd spilled all of the details, along with the appropriate background information, about Layla and the French toast and the deadline she'd issued only hours before. Contrary to first impressions, Big John had listened intently, without interrupting, to the entire story. The only two things he'd said between the tee shots and the final putts on the first hole were, "So, Henry. You married?" and, "You want the flag in or out?"

But when they finished up on the first hole, Big John whacked Henry on the back again, looked him right in the eye and said, "My friend, if it's marriage you want to talk about, you've come to the right place. I'm what you call an aficionado."

Wondering aloud what a "marriage aficionado" could be, Henry was interrupted by Big John's reverberating shout at an oncoming golf cart. This particular golf cart had a green awning and a large cooler on the back, and its driver was a young blond girl in short khaki shorts.

"Over here!" Big John had shouted, causing golfers on three different holes to look up in confused anger as he waved his massive arms. "Over here!"

Terrified, but convinced she had a sale, the girl in the shorts drove her cart over to the second tee, where Henry, José, and the Johns were waiting to hit their next shots.

"We're going to need some beer for this conversation," Big John said.

He handed the beer-cart girl two twenty dollar bills and immediately began filling the cooler on the back of José and Sweaty John's cart with cans of Miller Lite. Henry lost count, but Big John got no change, which meant either he'd ordered way too much beer or was a really big tipper.

"Both!" Big John bellowed when Henry asked the question out loud, and he flipped one of the ice-cold cans in his direction. Henry caught it, and surprised himself again when he popped open the tab and started drinking it.

"Attaboy!" Big John laughed, and Henry cringed as he anticipated another backslap. José and Sweaty John sat in their cart, looking like two guys watching a drive-in horror movie.

But by the sixteenth, the rest of the foursome had forgotten any objections they might have had about Big John's second-tee beer binge. Four hours of drinking, laughing, and making lousy efforts at golf swings had made theirs the loosest group on the course. It also helped that by then Big John had run out of wives to talk about.

He'd spent the second hole, a long par five, talking about his first wife, Linda, who had produced his two children. "Looking back, I have to say she was still the best one," he said, too wistfully for a guy on his first beer. "That might have been my biggest mistake, leaving her."

The third hole, a little par three over water, was devoted to Ginger, who was first Big John's secretary and then his second wife. Apparently, Linda had caught him cheating with Ginger and shocked him by having the emotional strength to leave him and take the kids with her. Once that happened, Big John believed he should marry Ginger, since she'd already cost him so much. Their marriage lasted only two months, and the best thing Big John could say about it was that he hadn't let her get as much of his money as she'd been seeking in the divorce.

"She thought she was pulling one over on me," he said. "But it's all about who has the best lawyer. And I got a good one."

From the sounds of things, Henry thought, he's kept the guy in business.

Big John spent the fourth and fifth holes talking about his third wife, Leilani, whom he'd met on a Hawaiian vacation (who goes to Hawaii by himself, as a single guy?) and swept off to Vegas to marry after spending two weeks in her bed. They'd stayed married for two years, somehow. Big John believed it had something to do with his traveling so much for work at that time and her carrying on affairs with at least three of their neighbors during the second year of their wedded bliss.

"I couldn't keep up with her," he said. "I mean, you know, sexually."

By this time, everybody had a good buzz on, and this was greeted with guffaws even from the two in the cart. Big John laughed, too, but he wasn't kidding.

"Seriously," he said. "One day she comes to me and she

says, 'I can't be with just one man.' And I say, 'How long ago
did you decide this?' And she tells me about all the other
guys. Seriously, she was a sweet girl, she just liked sex too
much. I think she moved back to Hawaii."

The amazing thing about Big John was that, as drunk as he
got, and as many stories as he told about his dizzying marital past, his swing never wavered. As the rest of the group
started to miss more and more fairways and giggle more and
more through their short putts, Big John kept drinking, talking, laughing, and hitting great shot after great shot.

He spent the sixth hole talking about his fourth wife, a
young woman named Alexis, who was a cell-phone-tot-
ing, business-suit-wearing "career gal" who never seemed
to have as much time for him as he had for her. Big John's
retrospective conclusion was that Alexis wanted him only
for sex, and that she used him to take out the frustrations
of the workday. They got married because she'd had a panic attack about turning thirty and not being married yet
(which rang a bell for Henry), and because Big John obviously had no compunction about getting married. But after
a year she'd been transferred to London, and they decided,
somewhat matter-of-factly, that a divorce would make the
most sense.

"We were sick of each other," Big John said, flipping an
empty beer can into the metal trash can beside the seventh
tee.

And then, after the group hit its tee shots on seven, Big
John brought out the guffaws again when he said, "And
then my fifth wife . . ."

"Jesus Christ!" Sweaty John squeaked. "How many are
there?"

"Well, five," Big John said, as if that were perfectly normal.

"Fifth wife . . ." José was saying, wiping beer out of his
moustache. "Five times, married. Unbelievable."

And Big John went on to talk about his fifth wife, Carla,

who was in her forties, like he was, and had a teenage son, like he did. They'd met at their sons' baseball game, got to talking, gone on a few dates, gotten drunk, flown to Vegas (where, Henry thought, Big John probably should have a chapel named for him) and got married. On the flight home, they decided it had probably been a bad idea but that they would give it a shot, see how it worked out. They liked each other's kids, and they'd had fun spending all of this time together, so why not?

"One more lesson," Big John said. "You don't marry somebody for their kids."

This was getting way out of Henry's league. He was a guy who'd made it from grad school into his thirties with one gorgeous girlfriend who'd never once pressured him about getting married until this morning. Now he was listening to a man who got married for sport. He appreciated Big John's effort to help, but he had no idea how these stories were actually going to help him. He said nothing of significance for the rest of the front nine, which Big John, who appeared to be sizing up the beer-cart girl as a possible wife number six, basically spent drinking, joking, and playing golf. They stopped for lunch after the ninth hole, and as they sat on the bench eating their burgers and waiting for the group in front of them to tee off on the tenth hole, Henry thought it was time for a question.

"So John," he said. "I don't get it. Should I not get married? Or should I get married over and over again?"

Laughter from the cart, where José appeared to have shot a piece of burger out of his nose.

Big John explained that he didn't mind the institution, just that he hadn't been able to get one of his marriages right.

"By all means, if you've got a good woman, do what it takes to keep her," he said. "Beats running around all your life looking for her."

Again, solid-sounding advice from a questionable source, Henry thought. This guy was older than he was, appeared to have married almost every woman he'd ever seen, and at this very moment was drunk as hell. They'd received wary looks from the golf course personnel as they placed their lunch orders, and Henry wasn't surprised that they were monitored more closely on the back nine. But it was hard to care. After Big John's tenth-tee philosophical musings, they'd left the topic of marriage and deadlines and Layla behind and just banged the ball around the course.

By the sixteenth, when Big John whizzed the flag over Henry's head, he'd determined that he wouldn't be spending this day over-thinking Layla's ultimatum, and that maybe that was a good thing.

It was quarter to seven when Layla heard Henry fumbling with the keys at the front door and she rushed down the stairs to open it for him. She spent a few seconds trying to decide whether to be angry or relieved and settled on angry, since she'd spent the past half hour trying to call him. She'd called his cell phone, but his cell phone was in his golf bag, in the trunk of his car, where he couldn't have heard it even if he hadn't been driving home drunk with the radio turned all the way up.

"Hi, honey," Henry slurred as Layla flung open the door in front of him. "I'm home."

She looked at him for a full second before turning around in a huff (she did a very good huff) and storming back up the stairs.

"Are you mad?" he asked, still in the doorway at the bottom of the stairwell.

She didn't answer.

"I think that's a yes," he muttered to himself. Then, louder, "Can I come in?"

Still no answer. And no laugh, despite the attempt at

drunken humor. She was mad and didn't want to give any other impression.

"I'm sorry," he said, his glassy eyes trying to meet her downcast ones after he mounted the stairs. "I could have called . . . should have called, I mean. I mean, I'm sorry."

And she finally looked at him again, and she said, "I guess we're not going out to dinner, then."

And he actually laughed as he fell onto the sofa, burrowing into one of the pillows and flipping off his golf shoes. He'd driven home in his golf shoes.

"Dinner," he said.

It was the last thing he said all night. Layla waited until the first distinguishable snore before she went to see what was in the fridge for her to heat up in the microwave.

PART II

Sunday

Four

"What's that noise?" Susan was asking on the other end of the phone.

"That's Henry, snoring," Layla said. "Hold on. I'll take the phone downstairs."

Not that she was worried about waking Henry. She could have landed a 747 in their bedroom right now and probably not woken him. He hadn't stirred (or stopped snoring) when she'd kicked him, or when the phone had rung. Hadn't been bothered by the light that had been on since eight A.M., when she woke up and decided that if she couldn't sleep, she might as well read. That light had been on for two hours now, and she was grateful when the phone rang, because it was way past time for her to get out of bed anyway. Waiting for him to wake up was going to be a losing proposition.

"Sounds like somebody's doing work on your house," Susan said. "Like, with a jackhammer."

"Nope," Layla said, wrapping herself in her robe and heading down the stairs. "That's my boy. He snores when he's drunk."

"Yeah, so tell me about that," Susan said. "He came home drunk?"

So Layla told Susan the whole story, about how she'd come home and worried that she might have scared Henry into leaving her, and how she worried when it got later and later in the day and he still hadn't come home—or even called. She told her friend about opening the door and seeing him there, rocking unsteadily with his golf bag over his right shoulder, and how she'd been relieved but also so mad that she didn't want to let him know how relieved she'd been.

"I can't remember the last time he got that drunk," Layla said. "He doesn't really drink much, usually."

"You think you freaked him out?" Susan asked.

"I guess I must have. But I guess that was kind of the point."

She was in the kitchen now, and she had to laugh.

"What's so funny?" Susan asked.

"I guess somebody got hungry in the middle of the night," Layla said.

There were four different plates on the kitchen table, each bearing evidence of a failed attempt at a midnight snack. One had on it a single strawberry Pop-Tart, which had grown too gooey in the microwave, where it didn't belong, and had only one bite missing from one of its frosted corners.

Where on earth did he find a Pop-Tart?

Another plate had a half-eaten slice of pepperoni pizza and one pizza crust. That was the snack that appeared to have worked out the best. The third plate had a partially frozen boneless chicken breast that hadn't defrosted enough to qualify as food, and the fourth and most comical had an unopened cardboard carton of Chinese food sitting in the middle of it. That one, apparently, had never even made it to the microwave. That must have been when Henry gave up.

Layla estimated that the surrender had come shortly before one A.M., the time Henry had made his way up the stairs. His attempt to be quiet had been pitiful, especially the part where he slipped on the stairs, hit his elbow on the wall and cursed loudly enough to wake the neighbors. Determined not to help him, she stayed in bed, and rolled over so her back was to the door. As an apparent gesture of courtesy, Henry had not turned on the light in the bedroom or bathroom, but this made for even more noise as he fumbled his way through the medicine cabinet looking for Advil. Five different medicine bottles landed in the sink, each making its own separate crashing or rattling noise. Once the Advils were down, he brushed his teeth and banged his way back through the darkness and into bed.

He had managed to get his pants and, thankfully, his golf shoes, off before flopping into bed next to her, but that was it. Henry slept in his boxer shorts, golf shirt, and the pullover windbreaker in which he'd played his eighteen holes. It wasn't until he'd been in bed for five minutes—and started snoring again—that Layla rolled over to face him. When she did, she noticed that he didn't have any blankets covering him, so she actually got out of bed, walked around to his side and tucked him in as he slept and snored. And he'd never, ever know, would he?

"You tucked him in?" Susan said. "That's so sweet. See? You do love him."

"I never said I didn't love him," Layla said with a sigh. "I know I love him, and I don't think I want to think about living without him. It's just . . ."

And she sighed and stopped talking.

"This is all Gloria's fault," Susan said, a bit more nastily than usual. "I told her not to push you, and now look what she did."

"Oh, it's not Gloria's fault," Layla said. "I would have come to this point sooner or later without Gloria. If anything, it was a good idea to do it sooner. I don't know how I would handle being on my own again, but I know something has to change. This can't keep going on the way it is."

She was looking at pictures now, in one of the photo albums she kept stashed under the coffee table. She was flipping through pages of pictures of her and Henry in the Bahamas, from three years before. He looked cute in the one she'd taken with the underwater camera, with the snorkeling gear on and his hair sticking up in the water. But every time she lapsed into such thoughts, she kept coming back to how mad she really was.

"So, what do you want to do today?" Susan asked. "It's raining."

"Well, I was kind of hoping my boyfriend would wake up in a mood to talk about our relationship, but I can kind of see that's not happening anytime soon. So I don't know. Maybe we should do something. You got any ideas?"

"Not really," Susan said. "Hey, maybe we should take you out and get you drunk, huh? Fight fire with beer?"

"Funny," Layla said. "Let me call Gloria and see what she's up to."

"Okay," Susan said. "Call me back. If I don't pick up, I'm in the shower."

Still on the sofa, Layla flipped through the photo album. Tucked in the back were a couple of letters Henry had written her when he'd been away on book signings. Letters and postcards. She flipped through them, stopping at one he'd sent from Boston. On the front of the card was a photo of Faneuil Hall. On the back was his sloppy handwriting, in which he'd written a forty-five-word love letter that had made her melt. She read it again, along with the first two paragraphs of one of his letters. They always made her a little bit jealous, his letters, because she wished she could write the way he did. Legal writing was so boring. Henry's writing was . . . well, it was like Henry—gorgeous in its spaciousness, broad and vast enough to hold his full, flowing range of emotions. Henry's writing was fun and spontaneous, just like he was. It was easygoing and surprisingly touching, just like he was. It could make you feel like you were inside a hug. One of Henry's hugs.

But really, seriously, she had to keep reminding herself, she was mad at him. So she shut the album and got up from the sofa. She thought about cleaning up the kitchen, but decided to leave it for Henry. Sure, that meant there was no guarantee it would get cleaned up, but she was trying to make a point. And besides, it wouldn't hurt him to start wondering a little bit about what it would be like if she weren't always around to clean up after him.

"That's right," Gloria was saying a few minutes later on the other end of the phone. "Shake the guy up. That's what this is about. You're jolting him, kicking him, rolling this relationship over so you can find out what it really is. A week from now you'll either know that what you have with Henry is the real deal, or that it wasn't. For God's sake, Lay, it's not like you need to give him more time."

Gloria was her lifeline on this. It was Gloria's cold analysis that Layla was determined would help guide her to next Saturday. Susan was the good friend who told you that you were great and that everything was going to be okay, and Layla was pretty sure she'd need plenty of that in the coming days. But Gloria was the one who told it like it was—the friend who told you that, yes, those jeans did make you look fat, and that you should try on a different pair.

The fact that Gloria made so much *sense* when she was assessing her relationship with Henry was what drew Layla back to her for counsel. She knew she needed to be level-headed about this, or else she'd lose control of it entirely.

"I think I need to get out of the house today," Layla finally admitted, after catching her friend up on the events of the previous night.

"Absolutely," Gloria said. "We need to get you drunk, to get back at him."

"That's what Susan said. You guys are finally agreeing on something."

"Oh no," Gloria said. "Maybe I need to reconsider my position."

"I don't think getting drunk would be a good idea," Layla said. "But I do think I should definitely not be here when he wakes up."

"Sure! Play hard to get. Go shower and get out of the house. It's almost noon, for God's sake."

"All right. Where're we going?"

"Tuxedo's," Gloria said.

"The sports bar?"

"Yeah, the sports bar. The Knick game is on."

"The Knick game?" Layla repeated, incredulous.

"It's the playoffs!" Gloria practically screeched. "It's a big game!"

"Who are you? Do I know you?"

"Besides," Gloria went on, "there will be a lot of hot guys there. Maybe you could—"

"Oh, come on now," Layla interrupted.

"Sorry. Getting way ahead of ourselves."

"I mean, I could be engaged in a week."

"Yes. Yes, I guess you could," Gloria said, retreating now. "I'm sorry."

"Okay."

"But we're still going to go out and watch the Knick game. And the hot guys."

"Gloria . . ."

"What? Susan and I aren't married. Or engaged. Or . . . whatever you are."

"Thanks."

"No problem. I'll meet you there at twelve-thirty. You call Susan. I don't want to deal."

Having called Susan, showered without washing her hair, brushed her teeth, and changed into jeans and a white T-shirt without even coming close to waking her boyfriend, Layla pondered the idea of leaving the house without telling him where she was going. Again, it would make sense, from an eye-for-an-eye standpoint, based on the night before. But she watched him sleeping, the tiniest little puddle of drool forming on his pillow, and she decided she'd be better off waking him.

She sat down on the side of the bed.

Nothing.

She gently shook his shoulder.

Nothing. Still snoring.

"Henry," she said in a normal tone of voice. Then, louder, "Henry."

He rolled toward her, onto his back. Finally, a sign of life.

"Henry," once more, just to be sure.

And now his head was up off the pillow, his left eye open, his right still shut. He looked at her as if he were waking from a coma on an alien spacecraft and nothing looked familiar. He said nothing.

"I'm going out now," she said. "It's twelve-fifteen."

"It's . . ." he said. "Huh?"

"Go back to sleep if you want. I just didn't want you to wake up and worry when I wasn't here."

"What's . . ." he said. "What time is it?"

"Twelve-fifteen," she said, and got up off the bed and started to walk out of the room.

"Wait, wait, wait, wait," he said, sitting up now, both eyes open. "Where're you going?"

"I'm going out. I think Gloria wants to watch a basketball game at a bar."

"You're going to a bar?" Henry asked, scratching his right arm.

"Sure," she said. "Why? Is that a problem?"

"No, no, no, no," he said, still looking around as if he'd woken in a different house. "I'm sorry. I'm just . . ."

"Right," she said. Oooh, she was determined to act tough. "Well, you have all day to get over being 'just.' As long as you don't forget we're having dinner at my parents' house tonight."

Oh, wow, Henry thought. That's right. Dinner at her parents'. That was no good at all. Not the way he felt right now, not with what had happened yesterday. And by the way. . .

"What happened yesterday?" he asked.

"What do you mean?" Layla asked in return.

"Did you tell me I had to propose by the time Gina throws her bouquet on Saturday? Or was that just a bad dream?"

"Sorry, babe," she said, feeling now like she had the upper hand again. "No dream. That's the deal."

"That's what I thought," Henry said. "Well, can we talk about it?"

"Sure. Much as you want. I was here all last night, and I've been here all morning. But right now I'm going out with my friends."

"Uh . . . okay," he said. "When will you be back?"

"No idea. In time to go to dinner, though. So be ready."

That seemed like a real stretch at this point.

"Okay. Have a good day," he said. "Love you."

The last part came out almost like a question. Layla didn't turn around.

"Love you, too," she said.

And the next thing Henry heard was the sound of the front door closing, followed by the starting of Layla's car.

He sat on the edge of the bed, trying to reconstruct it all. The morning. The golf. The beer. The Many Wives of Big John. Did he just come home and pass out? Did they talk when he got home? He didn't remember. He was confused. He was ashamed. He was filthy.

He needed some help.

He called his brother.

Five ●

Jake's apartment was not nice.

Divorce had been particularly unkind to Henry's brother, who now lived in a poorly lit studio in which the kitchen was way too close to the bed, and the carpeting, such as it was, had so many stains that it was impossible to tell the original color. Burgundy? Brown? Yellow? No chance to figure it out.

It was the first time Henry had seen the rat hole that had been functioning as Jake's home for the past month and a half, and he'd had no idea it was so bad.

"Jake," Henry said, after the initial shock and speechlessness wore off. "This isn't good."

"Tell me about it, little brother," Jake said, kicking away two empty beer cans on the floor in front of the front door. "Welcome to life after Tanya."

Henry was not dumb, so it didn't take long for him to figure out that this may have been the wrong place for him to come seeking marital advice. In fact, he resolved in his mind that he wouldn't even bring up the situation with Layla. It was clear he hadn't been paying nearly enough attention to his brother over the past few months, because it was news to him that Jake's life had fallen so completely apart.

"Jesus," Henry said. "Is this what it looked like when you moved in? Or did you make this mess?"

"The beer cans are basically me," Jake said. "The rest is pretty much the way I found it. I asked the super if I could get new carpeting. Not sure if he's stopped laughing yet about that one."

"Jake, if you needed money . . ." Henry said.

"Oh, shut up," Jake said, looking at his very loud refrigerator now, leaving his brother to wonder which one of them he was talking to. "I'm all right. I don't need money."

Henry didn't say anything for a little while, fearful that he'd already done enough damage to his big brother's pride. Jake was busy collecting beer cans and dumping out ashtrays. His face looked too thin, his legs like sticks. He hadn't had his hair cut in far too long, and his beard was even growing in, splotchy and sloppy. It looked as if he hadn't left the apartment, showered, or spent a sober minute since the divorce went final. He didn't even have a phone, which is why calling him once Layla left the house had been unsuccessful. He'd decided he might as well drop in on Jake instead, though he wasn't prepared for what he would find.

"Well, all right," Jake said, finally breaking the silence. "I guess I'll let you buy me lunch."

As they drove up Route 17 to the State Line Diner, there wasn't much conversation.

"Did she just basically take everything?" Henry asked, trying more to get information than to spark a long talk.

Jake snorted. "Not basically," he said.

They sat in silence again for the few remaining minutes

it took to get to the diner. But once they sat down, Jake seemed to feel like talking.

"It's not all bad, really," he said. "I mean, at least now I can do what I want most days. I do miss the kids, but there's no way I'd ever let them see that place I'm living in right now. Once I get back on my feet, I think I'll go back in and talk about custody again."

Jake was two years older than Henry was, and he'd made enough mistakes to fill an instruction manual: "How not to live your adult life—a guide for baby brothers." He'd got married at twenty-three, before he finished law school, and dropped out a month before his wife found out she was pregnant with twins. He'd taken a job as a paralegal at one of the most disreputable law firms in New Jersey. When he quit that job, he found another at an even worse firm, got fired from that one, and finally settled into a job answering phones and filing papers for a personal injury/divorce firm that didn't even have enough money to buy a sleazy local cable ad.

But of all the mistakes Henry's big brother had made, the worst had been his choice of spouse.

Tanya was tall and gorgeous, a star college basketball player at North Carolina with long, perfectly straight blond hair that hung halfway down her back. Jake had fallen in love with her long before she'd even noticed him. Once she did, the third or fourth morning he waited outside her dorm, she'd had no interest. Initially, she viewed Jake as a stalker, which was kind of what he was. But over time, she got to know him as a devoted servant who would do anything for her. Jake went through his final two years of college believing that if he stayed close to Tanya and did everything she asked him to do, she would fall in love with him.

By the time graduation rolled around, Tanya had come to realize that Jake was not only a useful person in her life, but that she could stand to be around him, after all. He was going to law school, which meant that he was likely to make some money, and there were worse things than having a lawyer husband who would do anything for you. So when he proposed to her the night before graduation, she said she'd think about it.

They lived together for the entire year after graduation, Jake occasionally bringing up the proposal and the ring she was wearing, in spite of never having officially accepted it. Every time he broached the subject, she either ignored him (as if she hadn't heard) or shot him down, saying something along the lines of "Don't push me" or "These things take time."

The poor bastard never gave up, though, and he must have worn her down. Because before long she said yes and they got married. Tanya wanted to have a family. To her, the kids were the important thing. The husband was the means to the end.

What she didn't figure out until too late, though, was that in all other aspects of his life, Jake lacked the resolve and the strength of will that he'd shown in pursuing her. Hence, the abrupt cessation of law school in the early days of her pregnancy, and the disintegration of the life she had foreseen as Wife of Bigshot Lawyer. She began arguing for a divorce the very week the twins were born. He wouldn't hear of it—always managed to talk her back into staying. By the time the kids turned six, Tanya was sleeping with three of the men in the law firm where Jake was now the receptionist, and she flaunted it. She wanted him to know she was giving his bosses what she wouldn't give him. It took her nearly eleven years of humiliation, degradation, and constant, outright verbal abuse to break him down, and when it happened, he was such a badly beaten man that he'd had no chance in the divorce. The lawyers he worked for were a lot more interested in helping Tanya than in helping him, and they put her in touch with a divorce lawyer who skinned Jake alive.

And so it was that Henry sat across from his brother at a North Jersey diner, trying to make small talk while the weightiest issue of his own life was undoubtedly the touchiest topic in Jake's.

"How's the book?" Jake asked.

"Not bad," Henry said. "Coming along. I'm taking the weekend off."

"Can't be coming along that great, then, can it?"

And Jake was right. When Henry was really into his writing, he never took days off—not even weekends.

"It's all right," Henry said. "Some come easy, some are more work than others."

"How's Layla?" Jake asked.

"She's fine," Henry said. "You know, Jake. If you'd rather talk about what's going on with you . . ."

"Ah, stop," Jake said. "You saw the place. You think I want to talk about it?"

Henry shrugged.

"Hey, I appreciate it," Jake said. "I really do. But I'll call you when I need to talk. Well, when I need to talk and when I get a phone. For right now, I'm just sorting it all out, man."

He was going through breadsticks as if they were baked oxygen, and he was constantly looking around to see if the soup he'd ordered was on its way.

"All right," Henry said.

"So really, how're things with Layla?"

"Well . . . you really want to know?"

"What's that mean?"

"It means," Henry said, "that I might be bringing up a sore subject."

"Little brother, you go right ahead. I don't care how sore

the subject is. I'll talk about anybody's life right now besides mine."

"Well," Henry said, "she told me yesterday she wants to get married."

For six full seconds Jake stared at Henry. He stared long enough for the waiter to put the tomato soup down in front of him and walk away. And then he started laughing, and he laughed long enough for the soup to get cold, and pounded the table hard enough to spill some of it.

Henry sat by, smiling nervously, looking around at other tables to make sure people weren't staring, which they were.

Finally Jake calmed down and looked up at Henry.

"Man," he said. "You are screwed."

"Thanks," Henry said. "See, I thought I might have come to the wrong guy."

"Oh, it's not about that," Jake said. "Not about the wrong guy, not at all. I know I married a world-class bitch, and I know there are good women out there. I know I screwed up my own marriage, and I know you're not as big a screwup as me."

"But?"

"But!" Jake practically shouted, pounding the table again, for emphasis. "But! I have a very practical, very emotionless, very non-divorce, non-Tanya-influenced take on the lovely institution of marriage. And I do think you should hear it before you go any further."

Henry sighed. "And what is that?" he asked.

"Marriage," Jake said, with a triumphant slurp of his soup, "costs too damn much."

"I thought this wasn't about the divorce," Henry said.

His head was hurting now, some sort of a delayed hangover. He hadn't felt right all day, or at least in the hour and a half since he'd woken up, but his head hadn't been pounding, either. Now he really needed that greasy mushroom

Swiss burger he'd ordered. The surefire hangover cure of all time.

"No," Jake said. "This isn't about the divorce. Everybody knows divorce costs money. Everybody knows divorce can ruin you. What I'm telling you, which you don't know since you've managed to live your entire blessed life to this point without having to get married, is how much it costs just to be married. Just to have a simple, happy family life."

"All right," Henry said, silently admonishing himself to find somebody impartial sometime soon. "Let me have it."

"It starts with the ring," Jake said. "Have you ever even looked at engagement rings, just to see what they cost?"

"No," Henry said. "I really didn't think this would ever happen."

"Well, do me a favor," Jake said. "On your break tomorrow, go check out a few jewelry stores. Go to the mall, some discount places, whatever. Just price the things, and see if you can get your bottom lip up off the floor before you leave the store. And remember, there's no deal without one of these things, and it's got to be a really, really nice one."

And Henry said that he would go shop for rings tomorrow, and indeed he planned to. Seemed like a good idea. Go someplace where marriage was treated as a happy thing, just for variety's sake.

For the rest of the lunch, Jake went on rattling off figures on what it cost to get married, to have kids, to share a bank account. Henry's head started to hurt worse, and the burger wasn't helping.

"And the worst part is, every fight you ever have will be about money," Jake said. "I don't care how successful a lawyer she is or how many books you sell, as long as there are bills, there are going to be those uncomfortable nights when you're doing the checkbook, and she's asking you how it looks, and you don't want to say because you want her to believe you've got it all under control but you really don't. And there's no hiding this stuff. You're sharing the same money, it all comes out in the wash. If you're short, she's short, you're both short, and she's going to know. And that's when the fights start."

"But your fights weren't about money," Henry said, trying to fend off the blows.

Jake was unmoved, digging in now to a dish of rice pudding. Henry had never seen anybody eat so much so quickly.

"I told you before, man, it's not about me. You go talk to anybody. Anybody who's married. Ask them if they fight about money. You'll find two types of answers. Either they say yes or they're lying."

Henry was determined not to let this be a drag on him, but so far it was. A little over twenty-four hours since Layla had told him he had a week to decide if he wanted to get married, and the only people with whom he'd talked about marriage had made it sound like a joke or a total disaster—or both. He had to find somebody who was happily married, or he'd spend his week growing more and more convinced that he had to let Layla go. And he really didn't want to let Layla go.

He paid the check and drove Jake back to his apartment, first offering several alternatives (his own house, the movies, the driving range) for places to go. But Jake wanted to mope, and he wanted to do it alone, in his dank new rat hole, with his beer, and far be it from Henry to mess with that.

He dropped off his brother and drove home thinking about his unfinished book. He always felt weird, kind of unsettled, whenever he was blocked. The thing with Layla hadn't helped. In fact, it had made it worse. If he couldn't finish his next book, he didn't know where his next check was coming from. And when you don't know where your next check is coming from, it's hard to see yourself as the responsible husband type.

He drove past Tuxedo's sports bar. For a second he considered stopping in for a beer and watching a game. But then he decided he'd had enough beer the day before, that he could watch the game at home and doze on the couch, which seemed like a better idea than the bar. It would be a zoo in there anyway.

Six

"It's a zoo in here," Layla was shouting back at Susan from the bar, where she was trying to order a second round of beers.

Layla was not generally the type who had a hard time getting the bartender's attention, so the fact that she had any wait at all meant that Tuxedo's was unusually mobbed on this Sunday afternoon. The Knicks were on, which didn't help anything, and so were the Yankees, who always drew a crowd. After the first beer, she told Gloria that she felt like going home, but Gloria convinced her to stay for one more, and she'd agreed.

Once back at the table, Layla did start to feel more comfortable. She wasn't really into the Knicks game, since she enjoyed college basketball much more than she did the pros. As far as she was concerned, this just didn't hold a candle to Duke–North Carolina.

Plus, they were talking about serious stuff.

"Let me ask you this, Lay, and I'm serious," Gloria said.

"Okay," Layla said, sipping her beer as if to strengthen herself for whatever Gloria was about to say.

"Have you thought about why you want to get married?"

Layla paused. Susan started laughing.

"What?" Gloria asked.

"Aren't you the one trying to talk her into this whole thing?" Susan asked.

"Oh, that's not right," Gloria said. "That's not right, Sooze."

"It's okay," Layla said quietly. "I think I understand the question."

"Thank you," Gloria said, still looking at Susan.

Susan humphed and slouched back on her stool.

"I've thought about that same thing myself. A lot," Layla said. "I mean, why get married? We have a good thing going, right?"

"Sure looks that way," Susan said to the floor.

"You know, I never really thought about it at all, until about a year and a half ago, when my mom got sick," Layla said. "That got me thinking."

Gloria and Susan were silent, but they were both looking at Layla now. Layla kept talking.

"The way my dad was with her. The way he sat with her, took care of her. The way he always made sure he was there when she woke up, whether she was napping at home or in the hospital bed . . . I mean, that's it, isn't it?"

"That's what?" Gloria asked, fully aware that she was leading her witness.

"That's it," Layla said. "That's the whole point of finding somebody and sharing the rest of your life with him. So you can be there for each other when it all turns to shit. I mean, right down at the bottom of everything, isn't that what it's all about?"

Gloria smiled. She had taken on Layla as a pet project, correctly convinced that Layla would need help maintaining her conviction throughout this very difficult week. And even Susan, who had been opposed to the plan from the beginning because she feared it would ruin Layla's life, had developed a rubbernecker's fascination with what was going to happen. The mere fact that a day had ticked off the calendar since the issuing of the ultimatum was enough to get Susan more excited than she'd been the day before. Susan was now, without a doubt, into it.

"So, have you talked at all yet?" Susan asked hopefully, trying to lighten the mood a little bit.

"Susan!" Layla said. "Are you two ganging up on me now?"

Susan shrunk back into her seat, but she was still smiling. A little embarrassed, perhaps, at her show of enthusiasm, but still entranced.

Susan was the youngest of their group, still in her midtwenties and still convinced that the perfect man and the perfect marriage were out there. She was very attractive, a stunning redhead with twinkling green eyes and the body of a college freshman, but her love life wasn't what you would have expected, and the reasons for that were the unrealistic expectations with which she approached every date she had. She was always looking for the guy she wanted to settle down with. She believed she would know right away whether a guy was the One. Susan didn't have many second dates.

Then there was Gloria. Sometimes, Layla liked to call Gloria "Witchy Woman," because she reminded her of the Eagles song. "Raven hair, ruby lips. Sparks fly from her fingertips." Gloria was always ready for a fight. Her love life could best be described as "aggressive." Gloria was something of a bully, seeking out men she could manipulate rather than men who would challenge her. She'd been married once, for about five months, but dumped the guy because he told her he wanted to have kids. Layla never could tell if Gloria was covering up insecurities or if she just liked being in the dominant role. But with her striking black hair and dark Mediterranean skin, she had no trouble finding candidates.

Layla was the stunner of the group, a trio that drew a lot of long looks in a yuppie singles bar on a Sunday afternoon during the NBA playoffs. At that very moment, in fact, a tall, trim guy with wavy black hair and dimples was smiling their way. Gloria, predictably, was the first one to spot him. But he wasn't looking at Gloria.

"Lay," Gloria said. "I think somebody likes you."

Layla followed Gloria's eyes and saw the guy. He looked very tall, and very handsome, and she wondered what was going on. Having dated the same man for six years, she wasn't even used to looking at guys in bars. Sure, she knew they looked at her, but she never gave it much thought. This guy, though, was sparking something. Some kind of feeling. What was it?

Oh, that's right.

Familiarity.

"I know that guy," she said to her friends, without looking at either one of them.

"You do?" wide-eyed Susan asked, already fitting the guy with a tux in her mind, contemplating whether he'd be the type to change diapers.

"I do," Layla said, starting to smile. "I've seen him in court. He's a lawyer. His name is . . . oh, crap. I don't know his name."

"Well," Gloria said. "Looks like we're going to have a chance to ask him ourselves."

As Layla and her friends watched, the smile and the dimples moved closer. The guy was coming toward their table, and when he got there, he looked right at her and pointed. He was about to guess her name.

"I know this," he said. "Sally?"

"Layla," she said.

"Oh, man, that's right," he said, snapping his fingers, looking away for a second. "I knew it was a Clapton song. Should've remembered that. How do you forget that?"

"My parents' favorite song," she said.

"I'm Ben," he said.

Sure. Ben. That was his name. All coming back to her now. Ben. The lawyer guy. She shook his hand, said nice to meet you or something like that. Still not sure how to act, wondering why she didn't feel more guilty for introducing herself.

"I'm Gloria," Gloria said. "And this is Susan."

And that got Layla out of her trance.

"I'm so sorry," she said. "That was so rude of me. Gloria, Susan, this is Ben. He's an attorney."

Ben said it was nice to meet everybody, and he asked if he could buy a round for the table. Layla, who'd said she'd stop at two, surprised herself by being the first to say yes. She couldn't exactly leave now, since she was the one the guy knew, and the reason he'd felt comfortable walking over here to talk to three attractive women, even if he had thought her name was Sally. It was pretty unusual for somebody to forget her name.

She was determined not to go home drunk, and to give Henry every chance to talk things out. But she also wanted to have some fun, and play a little hard-to-get, as Gloria had suggested. If he could go out and play golf and get drunk, why couldn't she enjoy an afternoon out with her friends?

By the time she ran through all of this in her mind, though, Gloria and Ben were back at the bar, ordering the drinks. Susan was sitting next to her, smiling. Layla started to say something, and Susan actually grabbed her wrist.

"You're not going anywhere," she said.

And Layla smiled again. "Oh, don't worry," she said. "This just got interesting."

* * *

Two hours later the Knicks had lost, the Yankees had won, the crowd in Tuxedo's was thinning out, and Ben was still at the table with them. Apparently, he'd come on his own, to watch the games, but felt he had to come over and say hello once he'd recognized somebody from work.

And he was a very charming guy. Not easy for a guy to sit down in a bar with three women and chat for two hours. It helped that these particular women were into the games and could talk about them, but Ben kept them pretty captivated on his own, with his own stories.

Before he became an attorney, just a year or two before, he'd been a sportswriter for one of the newspapers in New York City. In that capacity, he'd seen a lot of these games up close, met a lot of the athletes who played them, and had enough behind-the-scenes stories to keep Layla and her friends laughing throughout the afternoon. He had an easy way about him, lapsing into the stories without sounding like he was playing "Can you top this?" and he was very interested in the stories the girls were telling. Susan, for instance, had dated one of the baseball players that Ben had covered, and they were basically swapping stories about the guy, who sounded to Layla like a real loser. Gloria had a story about a football player who hit on her at a bar and the rude way in which she immediately rejected him.

Layla kept pretty quiet, nursing her third beer and rejecting offers of a fourth. She laughed along with the stories and asked a question or two, but she was out of practice, and there was this little pang of guilt gnawing away inside of her like a jalapeño pepper gone wrong, like heartburn that flared up for a second and passed, just occasionally.

Then Ben got up to leave. "Ladies," he said, pushing his chair back from the table. "I must be going. This was a pleasure."

He shook each of their hands. Susan giggled. Old tough

Gloria mooned. And Layla looked at the floor when he said, "I hope to see you around." She said nothing as the other two waved their good-byes, and she had no desire to look at either one of them once he was gone.

"Oh. My. God," Susan said. "Ohmygod."

"Yeah, he was a cute one," Gloria said. "Man, look at that ass."

"Oh my God," Susan kept saying, mouth open.

"Too bad," Gloria said.

"What do you mean, too bad?" Layla asked, fearing she knew the answer.

"Oh, Lay, come on," Gloria said. "He was sooo into you."

Yeah, she thought. She was afraid of that.

"Nooooo," she said, trying oh so hard to fake being mortified. "You think so? I didn't get that."

But Gloria was cackling.

"Come on," she said between breaths. "You can *not* be serious. That guy wanted you so bad, he might as well have had a T-shirt with your face on it."

Layla looked at Susan for help, but she was smiling and nodding vigorously. No help.

"Sorry, Lay," Susan said. "She's right. I think everybody in the bar could tell."

Even Susan, Layla thought. Sweet, innocent Susan. There was nowhere for her to turn. She could only try to punch her way out of this one.

"Well, it doesn't matter, obviously," she said. "I mean, you know, I haven't been on a date in six years, and I'm not about to start now. I could be engaged in a week."

"You could be single in a week, too," Susan said, and Layla's head snapped up to look at her.

Susan's right hand shot to her mouth as soon as the words were out. Gloria gasped. Even she hadn't had the guts to say that when the opportunity presented itself that very morning.

"Oh, I'm so sorry, Layla," Susan said. "I didn't mean—"

"No, no, no," Layla said, waving her hand. "It's okay."

"I'm so sorry," Susan kept saying as Layla got up and started to get her things together to head to her car. "So sorry."

"Really," Layla said, trying in vain to compose herself. "Really, it's fine. Listen, I have to go anyway. I'll catch you guys tomorrow."

"All right," Gloria said. "Drive safe."

"So sorry," Susan said, looking up and looking truly pitiful.

"It's really okay, Sooze," Layla said.

And as she walked out, that's what she was thinking. It's really okay.

After all, Susan was right.

Seven

"So, what's it, like, a John Irving book? Like Owen Meany, Garp, something like that?"

"Something like that," Henry said, desperate to change the subject. He hated talking about his current book, mainly because he was so terribly blocked that he had no idea what it was about or where it was going. He gave sketchy details when asked, and he probably would have agreed with any characterization Layla's father offered in response.

"So, what's it, like, a coloring book? Like *See Spot Run, Goodnight Moon*, something like that?" her father could have said.

"Something like that," he would have replied, desperate to change the subject.

Fortunately, the subject changed with breathless frequency in the hemp-dominated home of Mr. and Mrs. James Starling. The first time Henry visited the tiny three-room house, he had been, justifiably, wary. He'd lived basically his entire life in New Jersey without realizing it contained a dwelling such as the one that housed the parents of the woman he loved, and he guessed that most of his fellow New Jerseyans would have been as surprised about it as he was.

The basic premise was that there was nothing in the house that could not be grown in the ground. That meant a complete absence of air conditioners, ceiling fans, or any devices that might serve to keep the place cool in the summer. It also meant a lack of a central heating system, though that wasn't as big a problem. There was a small clay fireplace and an ample supply of hemp blankets, so the winter chill stayed away. James and Cindy Starling cooked their meals in the fireplace, dumped their garbage in the backyard compost heap, and relieved themselves in the simple, squat outhouse in the backyard. The outhouse was a place Henry had never visited, since he'd been warned of its existence prior to his first visit and, at Layla's advice, always made sure he went before he left his own home.

The absence of running water meant that the Starlings bathed themselves in the stream that ran through the back portion of their property (they said the stream was the reason they'd bought the land and built the house there). The absence of a refrigerator meant that the only food they served was cooked right before they served it. James Starling brewed his own beer and kept it in clay jars on ice in a makeshift cooler. It was not good, but Henry always accepted the one he was offered when he stepped through the lockless door. It would have been impolite, after all, to refuse, especially since Layla's dad seemed so proud of his concoctions.

"This one's got a little carrot flavor to it," he'd told Henry that Sunday night when Henry had staggered in hung over from the drunken golf and the ultimatum of the day before.

"Hmm," Henry had said, taking the clay jar in his two

hands (damn things were heavy) and having no clue what else to say. "Interesting."

Much to Henry's horror, James Starling's description was accurate, and so he sipped his carrot beer carefully. Henry never had more than one. His excuse was always that he had to drive home, but it had more to do with the beer's taste and his determination never to see the inside of that outhouse.

"We've been doing a lot more growing out back this year," Layla's father said. "We cut back a lot of the overgrown trees and our garden got about three times bigger."

James Starling was pointing toward a backyard that seemed completely covered in overgrown scrub bushes. Henry had no idea if there was any grass in the Starlings' backyard, because of the outhouse and the stream that ran through it and the way the creeping shrubs and trees appeared to have created a thatched canopy likely not to be found anywhere else outside the Amazon. Layla's father was pointing out there, but he wasn't looking, and he didn't seem to care if Henry was either. It was as if he'd been told the thing about the pruning and the garden expansion but had never bothered to check it out—as if he were just repeating it because it sounded good. Henry gave a cursory look, still smarting from the first sip of carrot beer.

"So, you're growing carrots now?"

"Always grew carrots," James said.

Ah. Henry thought. Just never had the idea of making beer out of them. Wonder why?

It hadn't always been this way, Layla had once told Henry. Her parents had been hippies in the sixties and seventies, but turned into hard-core yuppies in the eighties. When Layla was a teenager, her father and mother actually both worked on Wall Street and made piles and piles of money in a world that, to her understanding, bore a perfect resemblance to that portrayed by Michael Douglas and Charlie

Sheen in the movie. They wore power suits, drove black BMWs, kept a place in the city for late work nights, and raised their children in a mini-mansion in Upper Saddle River. The home in which Layla grew up was roughly fifteen times the size of the one in which her parents now lived, and her childhood memories were good ones. Her parents worked hard, but they managed to make it home for dinner almost every night, and they were involved in their daughters' lives. If Layla or her sister had a field hockey game or a piano recital, at least one of their parents always made it. She had no idea, looking back, how this was possible, but they pulled it off, and the result was that everybody around them believed they had the perfect family life.

Then the kids went off to college and the parents sold everything. Dumped everything, basically. They made enough money off the sale of their worldly possessions to put each of their children through college and graduate school and to set them up with whatever they needed in terms of transportation and lodging, then gave the rest away to various charities and decided to return to their hippie roots. When asked for a reason, they made vague references to having done what was right for the kids and now wanting to return to what they really were—a couple of tie-dyed children of Woodstock who had no use for material goods except to make sure their children were happy and cared for.

In some ways Layla found it better now. When she was growing up, she always had to explain how she got her name. Now, people who knew her parents had no problem figuring it out.

Besides, she'd always believed she drew the long straw on the name thing anyway. At least her name came from a well-known Eric Clapton song, not some obscure Tony Orlando and Dawn number that nobody remembered thirty-some years later.

"We spoke with Candida this morning," Layla's mother

was telling her in the portion of the main room that func-
tioned as the kitchen.

"Oh yeah?" Layla asked, helping her mother wash lettuce
leaves in the pails of water that they'd brought in from the
stream.

"For a while, actually. You know she got that eight hundred number."

Layla looked at Henry and smiled. He scowled back, but
only because he'd just taken another sip of the Bugs Bunny
beer.

The eight hundred number was a running joke. The Starlings had no telephone, so when they wanted to make a call,
they had to either walk or to drive their gas-electric hybrid
Toyota to the 7-Eleven a mile and a half away. They almost
always ended up walking, since the Toyota was almost always out of gas. Henry couldn't count the number of Sunday afternoons that he and Layla had spent driving out to
wherever her parents had abandoned their car, filling it with
enough gas to get it to the station, driving it to the station to
fill it up, then driving it back to their house, where James or
Cindy always said, "Thanks. We just couldn't see the point
of buying another tank. We hardly use the thing."

Anyway, the only way the Starlings had of keeping in
touch with their daughters was through semi-regular pay
phone calls, and these inevitably got interrupted when they
were too late putting more change into the phone. Candida's announcement last Thanksgiving that she'd secured
a toll-free number was greeted with much enthusiasm by
Cindy and James. And since it had happened, Cindy had
been gently hinting to Layla that she might want to get one
too. So far, Layla had resisted, though her reasons for doing
so were growing weaker all the time and she believed she
would eventually give in.

Oddly, Henry didn't mind. Any of it. He did not see the
Starlings as freeloaders, believing they'd forever immunized

themselves against such labels by forsaking their true selves in an effort to make enough money to raise two children. He enjoyed spending time with both of them, though he generally preferred that it be at his own home or a restaurant somewhere (again, mainly because of the outhouse). He found James especially stimulating, since James was about the best read person he'd ever met.

Since retiring from his Wall Street life, James had done little besides read books and smoke marijuana, and the pile of paperbacks that spilled out of his bedroom closet, along the floor, out the hallway, and into the living area was a source of fascination for Henry. He never forgot the time he found a beat-up copy of his own first novel in the pile. He'd been so proud that James had read it, he never even asked him what he thought. Sometimes, he wondered why James had never brought it up. Layla always insisted her father hadn't hated the book, but she also changed the subject quickly when it came up.

It made Henry wonder, and it was one more reason he didn't like talking about his writing with Layla's father. In spite of circumstances, he craved the man's approval. He never would have to worry about impressing James Starling by being rich and successful, because that stuff didn't matter to James Starling. But sometimes, when he was writing, he'd catch himself wondering what Layla's father might think.

Henry had been begging Layla for years for her permission to ask her parents if he could write a book about their lives, but she'd refused without equivocation. Candida didn't like the idea either. Henry thought it would be a good story, starting with them in their old hippie days, taking them through the responsible-parent years, and then focusing on the return to hippiedom—an ultimately touching tale of two people who stayed with each other through major life changes. A wife who loved her husband for richer or for poorer, in lucid times and in dopey. A husband who always made his wife feel secure, years ago with money, more recently when he stayed by her hospital bedside as she recovered from a serious illness.

But Henry still had to wonder if it would even be possible to write such a book. He believed they would agree to it, since they were very agreeable people, but he thought the book would be impossible to research, since neither seemed to have an ability to stay on the same topic for more than about ten minutes at a time.

Probably had something to do with all the weed they were smoking.

"Bowl?" James offered, and Henry thought about it. He caught a sharp look from Layla out of the corner of his eye, and he remembered their deal—that they would never accept marijuana from her parents (they'd never agreed on whether the same rule applied to his own parents, he was fond of pointing out). But the way the last couple of days had gone, and the way his beer tasted, Henry had to admit the idea was intriguing.

"No thanks," he said, and, as always, that ended the discussion.

James Starling drew a long breath from the bowl as his wife and daughter husked corn a few feet away and Henry eyed the teetering stack of books in the corner by the hammock.

"So, James, what are you reading these days?" he asked.

"Irving, again. The whole catalog," James said. "That's why I asked. Yours reminded me of something of his. *Hotel New Hampshire*, something. I can't peg it."

Ick. Back on the topic of his book again. His own fault, Henry realized, but what were the odds? The last three times he had asked that question, the answers had been, in order "Voltaire," "Grisham's latest," and "That DiMaggio book that came out a few years ago." James Starling literally read everything he could find. Once, when Henry and Layla came for a visit, they'd found him in the hammock, reading a Frommer's travel guide to Belgium.

"Planning a trip, Dad?" Layla had asked.

"Nope," was the entire answer.

On this particular Sunday night, the one that found Layla's father in the middle of a reread of the works of John Irving, Henry felt, for the first time, uncomfortable in this house. It had nothing to do with the Starlings, their eccentricities or the specter of the outhouse looming beyond the open, screenless kitchen window. Rather, it was about the blank pages on which his next book was supposed to be, about the bombshell Layla had dropped the day before in their own home, and the fact that they hadn't discussed it since.

Layla had arrived home that afternoon from Tuxedo's and was late. She changed quickly and hopped in the car with Henry, who, to her shock, had been ready to go when she arrived. Henry, still reeling from the sight of his brother's apartment, had little to say on the ride over. Also, he had no idea how to approach the conversation they were supposed to be having. Layla, still reeling from her encounter with Ben in the bar, also had little to say on the ride over, and was determined that he be the one to begin the conversation they were supposed to have. The drive was awkward, with the only conversation a gratuitous exchange about directions to her parents' place. In fact Henry knew the way and Layla knew he knew the way. It was just nice to break up the silence.

It got easier when they arrived, because her parents were oblivious to the issue that hung over both of them. Her parents' entire lifestyle could be described as oblivious, of course, but in this case they were unlikely to sense any tension. Henry was of the belief that they felt the same way about their daughter's relationship as he did. He believed they were cool with the idea that he and Layla were hanging out, making each other happy and harboring no concrete plans for the future.

Of course, until the day before, Henry realized, he had believed the same thing about Layla.

He wasn't worried about Layla running off and discussing the situation with her mother behind his back, since the two of them were architecturally prohibited from being in a different room while preparing dinner. In fact, Henry saw this parental visit as a break from the stress he'd been feeling ever since that first fateful bite of French toast. Here, the two of them could pretend nothing had happened—that they were just over for a Sunday dinner, like they'd been so many times before. He could talk books with her father, she could talk about her older sister with her mother, they both could get a buzz off the fumes from what her parents were smoking. Heck, he might even have a chance to have sex tonight, if things got relaxed enough and the drive home was pleasant.

But he knew he was getting ahead of himself with that last part. Sex was a big-time long shot with the ultimatum still unaddressed and he with no idea how he planned to address it. And besides, there was something strange about the way Layla's mother kept bringing the conversation back to Candida. Layla noticed it too, the third time it happened.

"So, Candida and Derek have their ultrasound tomorrow," Cindy said.

Sounded funny, a woman who didn't have a phone, a lock on her door, or running water, talking about an ultrasound.

"Are they going to find out this time?" Layla asked, eyeing her mother warily.

"They are," Cindy said. "With Alex, I think they ended

up sorry they didn't find out. I think it'll be fun this way, knowing ahead of time."

Alex. Layla's nephew. Henry remembered that saga, Candida and her husband deciding not to use modern technology to learn the sex of their child, then picking the name with a month to go and deciding they'd use it either way. It gave Henry the creeps, the way the kid got named with no respect to gender—as if he could be raised either as a boy or a girl. If he ever had kids, he knew he would definitely want to know ahead of time.

Wait a minute, he thought. If I ever have kids? What's this?

These were not thoughts he was used to having. Even when Derek and Candida went through it, Henry looked on as a detached observer, dealing with it in the abstract, never even wondering if it might someday apply to him. And now, all of a sudden, he was thinking thoughts that began with "If I ever have kids." Was it even possible that Layla's ultimatum had forced such a thought into his mind?

He didn't have time to think much more about it, though, because before long it was clear that it was on somebody else's mind too. Henry was in the middle of a difficult sip of carrot beer when Cindy Starling spoke to her younger daughter again.

"You know, it would be nice if we had two daughters working on giving us grandchildren," she said, apparently to the ear of corn she was holding.

Henry swallowed hard, the beer slipping down his throat like a spiked brussels sprout. He looked right at Layla, who looked back at him in horror. He was startled. A little angry too, but startled was what came across to the rest of the room.

"Ha!" James Starling said, letting out a sharp chuckle. "No pressure there, eh?"

* * *

Dinner passed in an uncomfortable quiet that even the Starlings appeared to notice. Cindy apologized to Layla almost right after the grandchildren comment, and it seemed clear as the night went on that she was aware she'd brought up a sore subject. She tried to make up for it with an unprecedented second offer of marijuana, but Layla and Henry turned it down immediately, and simultaneously, while giving each other angry looks. They hugged and kissed her parents good-bye and climbed into their car to begin a contentious ten minute drive home.

"I can't believe you're mad at my mother," Layla began.

"Mad at your mother? You must be out of your mind if you think I'm mad at your mother."

"Okay, then what are you mad at?"

Henry was seething. The past thirty-six hours had been the first in which he could ever remember feeling uncomfortable talking to Layla, and now they were in a fight. He wasn't even sure if he was *allowed* to be in a fight with her right now, considering what was going on between them, but he was mad. And since she'd asked. . .

"Come on, Lay," he said. "You don't think I know what went on there?"

"What?"

"You put her up to it!"

"Oh, wow," Layla said, trying to make eye contact as he stared ahead at the road. "Wow."

"What? What wow?"

"You're more screwed up than I thought," she said.

Later, she would regret that part of the conversation, since it had never been her intention to convince Henry that he was "screwed up." But the tension of the previous two days was bubbling to a boil, and neither was thinking very hard about what they were saying.

"Screwed up?" Henry bellowed, taking his eyes off the road long enough to flash her a look. "Screwed up? That's what I get? You and your mother gang up on me and you're telling me I'm the one who's screwed up?"

"How could you think that's what happened?" Layla asked.

"Because, Lay, in six years, that's the first time I've ever heard either one of your parents express any kind of yearning for grandchildren. It's the first time I've ever heard either one of your parents wish for something they didn't have, and it happens to be grandchildren, and it happens to come the day after you spring this deadline on me about proposing to you? So I'm supposed to think, what, that it's a coincidence?"

Silence. Nothing at all from the passenger seat. Layla was steaming. In the driver's seat, Henry was determined that she would be the one to speak next. Neither spoke until he pulled the car into the parking lot in front of their apartment. They sat in the car for a minute after he parked it, not speaking. Finally, he caved.

"I don't have any more to say," he said.

"Okay," she said, and kept sitting there.

Finally, after another full minute of silence, Henry turned off the car and opened his door. Layla did the same, and followed him inside the apartment. Neither spoke again the rest of the night. Layla went upstairs to read. Henry flopped onto the sofa and began flipping through channels. He listened as she moved around upstairs, but his gaze never left the TV screen. He flipped between *SportsCenter* and TNT, which was showing *The Shawshank Redemption* for the eleventh time that weekend. He changed the channel at commercials, or just when he got bored. Eventually, with the remote control still in his hand, he fell asleep.

* * *

The next morning, for the first time in the four years Henry and Layla had lived together, Henry woke up on the sofa, Layla in the bed.

"Damn him," she said to herself when she realized he hadn't come to bed.

"Damn it," he said to himself when he realized the historical significance of his night on the couch. "I've got to start figuring this out."

PART III

Monday

Eight

The weird thing was, he wasn't even hung over. He'd had maybe half of one carrot beer at Layla's parents' house and gone to bed angry. Hadn't even taken the edge off.

So it was hard for him to figure out what the guy in the gray suit and the very high starched white collar was talking about. He could have sworn the guy had just asked him if he knew about the horsies.

"Did you say horsies?" Henry asked.

"I apologize, sir, if I was not speaking clearly," said the guy in the gray suit, speaking as clearly as anybody Henry had ever heard in his life. "I asked if you knew about the *four seas.*"

"The four seas?"

"Yes, sir. The four seas. Cut, color, carat, and clarity."

Henry remained confused. *Cut. Color. Oh . . .*

"The four C's," Henry said. "I get it."

"Yes, sir," gray suit said, with what Henry believed was remarkable patience. "The four C's are the guide to selecting the stone. Do you have a few moments to spend with us today?"

Henry had the whole morning. His mission had been to find out what he should be expected to spend on a diamond engagement ring, should he decide to buy one after all. But after three minutes here, at the Tiffany's at the Riverside Square Mall, it was clear that there was going to be more to it than just walking in and asking, "Yeah, how much for that one there?"

"Sure," Henry said. "I have a few minutes."

Gray suit guy led him off to the side, where he offered Henry an extremely comfortable chair and pulled a small box out of a drawer. He handed Henry a glossy black pamphlet whose cover advertised it as "Your Guide to the Perfect Stone" and whose inside appeared to discuss the aforementioned "four C's." But Henry didn't have a chance to peruse the pamphlet, because the guy in the gray suit was fiddling with all kinds of little tools. He had a diamond in a small pair of tweezers, and he handed it, delicately, to Henry. He then handed Henry a little black plastic gadget that contained a small magnifying glass.

"Take a look at that one," gray suit said, and Henry squinted through the glass at the diamond. He had no idea what he was looking at.

"That's a round stone," gray suit said. "It's also a premium cut, which means it's cut to the optimal depth and table width. You'll notice that the light comes through brilliantly, right at the top. In fact, if you cupped that stone in your hands, you'd notice that it even would shine in the dark. Any light at all is going to come through that kind of stone. It's a nearly flawless stone, very few inclusions."

"Inclusions?" Henry asked.

"Yes, they show up as markings, or some people would say smudges, on the interior of the diamond. If you look very closely, you might be able to see a few spots, though on a stone like that, I'm not sure they'd be readily obvious."

Henry was dying to ask what a diamond like this cost, but he worried about sounding too tacky, especially since he was at Tiffany's. Plus, he had a hunch he was only at the beginning of the process.

While Henry was sitting in an extremely comfortable chair, listening to classical music and checking out precious stones with a little monocular magnifying glass, the woman for whom the diamond may or may not have been intended was having a much different morning.

Layla's twenty-five-minute commute had taken just fifteen minutes. The problem was, it hadn't reached its destination. The wall of steam rising up from the hood of her spiffy red Acura got so bad on Route 17 that she had to pull over because she couldn't see, and she was thinking that she looked rather unspiffy as she stood by it on the side of the road in her black skirt and white blouse and weighed the pros and cons of flagging down a passing car for help.

She decided, finally, to call AAA, where the snotty woman who picked up the phone assured her that someone would be out within a half hour to take care of her. She called work to tell them she would be late, which wasn't a big deal because she was just going to kill the morning in the office doing paperwork until her afternoon court appearance anyway. And she climbed back in the car to sit and wait for the tow truck.

When the tow truck arrived, it came complete with a driver who made Layla wonder if she'd stumbled onto the set of a bad adult movie, or a soap opera. He was young-looking, with long, flowing black hair and a butt that looked so good in its jeans that she caught herself wondering when was the last time she was checking out some guy's butt. When he saw her get out of the car, he smiled, and her knees buckled. He had dimples. Layla was a sucker for dimples.

The next several minutes went by in a haze. The hunky AAA guy (whose name was Jon, with no "h," according to the red script on the left breast of his gray work shirt) went through the motions of checking out the Acura. He popped the hood, fiddled with some things, and even got behind the wheel and tried to turn the key to see if he could start the car. But Layla was no idiot, and she knew he was putting on a show. The problem with the car was not whether it would start. The problem was the steam still rising from the engine, and Layla was pretty sure, long before Jon arrived on the scene, that she wasn't taking her red Acura to work today. But she didn't mind. He was fun to watch.

Eventually, Jon indicated that the car would, indeed, have to be towed. When she remembered it all later, Layla wasn't even sure if she'd answered or merely smiled in assent. Jon had disarmed her, and she was pretty certain she'd spent the short time of their acquaintance with a goofy grin glued to her face.

The best part was when the tow truck dropped her and the car off at the Acura dealership. Jon hustled out of the driver's seat and around to where she was opening her door and actually took her hand to help her down to the ground. He was still smiling, his few brief, unsuccessful attempts at making conversation during the trip having failed to daunt him. And just before she was about to thank him for his help, he shocked her by saying, "You know, I don't usually do this."

It was here that Layla looked up from her shoes and made eye contact with the tow truck driver, knowing what he was about to say but still not believing it.

"Would you like to have dinner with me sometime?" Jon asked.

Layla's smile grew bigger and she worked hard to contain a laugh. Wouldn't be fair to the kid to laugh. He seemed serious. With her morning having gone from miserable to hysterical in a span of about twenty minutes, she had all kinds of things going through her mind. But one thing of which she was certain was that she was not about to take Jon up on his offer. Jon had a place in her life, but that place would be an illicit spot in her memory, to be taken out when she was feeling fat, or ugly, or just generally down about herself. Layla knew all of this in an instant, but that instant probably felt much longer to Jon, who stared down into her smiling face waiting for an answer.

"Wow," Layla said. "That's sweet."

And she watched the hope fade from poor Jon's face. He said nothing. She went on.

"That's really very sweet, I mean it," Layla said. "That's not just something we say, you know, to make guys feel better."

"So," Jon said. "This is a no?"

"It's a no," Layla said. "I'm sorry, but I'm involved with someone right now."

"Involved?" Jon asked. "That's a funny way to put it. Makes it sound complicated."

And here, she had to laugh. A short, somewhat frustrated laugh, and she looked back down at her shoes.

"Complicated," she said. "Yeah."

"Oh well," Jon said, already moving toward the back of the truck, where he'd begin unloading the car. "It was worth a shot."

"Trust me," Layla said. "I appreciate it."

"Oh yeah?" Jon said. "You don't get asked out a lot?"

"No," she said. "I can't remember the last time, actually."

"Huh," Jon said, looking back at her as the back of the truck was lowered toward the ground. "That's hard to believe."

And Layla thought, What a great day this is already.

* * *

Henry had had enough. He was sitting at a table in the jewelry store, looking at the clock up high on the bone-colored wall and wondering how it was possible that only thirty minutes had passed. The salesman was, incomprehensibly, coming back with a fresh tray of diamonds. Henry didn't have the heart to tell him he'd been unable to distinguish between the last four stones. This is this guy's job, he thought. Who am I to make him feel stupid about it?

But he was the one who felt stupid; there was no doubt about it. He was wearing olive green cargo shorts, a gray Long Beach Island T-shirt, and brown sandals. Everybody who worked in the store was dressed as if they worked in a bank. And most of the customers—women, exclusively, some with very fancy-looking strollers with very well-dressed babies in them—were dressed as if for work. Henry felt heavily out of place, and was convinced that everybody who walked into the store was staring at him. He looked up at the clock again, now convinced it was broken or ticking backward, and found himself hoping that Rob would be early for lunch.

After the salesman put the latest tray down on the table, sat down opposite him and began talking about the stones, Henry decided it was time to interrupt. He'd been patient enough. And so far he hadn't found out the one thing he'd come here looking to find out.

"I don't want to sound, you know, tacky or anything . . ." he began.

"Please, sir. If you have a question, don't be afraid to ask."

"Well, I was wondering . . . You know, I'm kind of at the beginning of this thing, just starting to look around and learn about things . . . And you've been a huge help, don't get me wrong . . ."

Silence. The guy was waiting for him to finish his question. Henry wondered how long he could wait. He was staring back at him with this robotic grin, waiting for the end of the question just as if the salesman were Google, waiting for him to finish typing in his query. Henry wondered if he could get up, go to the bathroom, do some shopping around the corner and come back, and the guy would be sitting in the same exact spot, with the same exact look on his face, waiting for his punch line.

Henry resisted the temptation to test his theory.

"I was just wondering how much something like this would cost."

There. He'd said it. Now the conversation was where he had wanted it when he walked in the door.

Almost.

"Something like what, sir?" the salesman said. "I don't get your meaning."

"Well, a ring," Henry said, waving his hands uncontrollably in the direction of the diamonds on the glass tabletop. "An engagement ring, with one of these stones in it. How much are we talking about here?"

"Well, sir, obviously it depends a lot on the quality of the stone, and then you would have to select a band, and—"

"Look, I don't mean to be rude," Henry said. "So please tell me if I am. But I just want to have some idea what I'm going to be looking at spending."

"I understand."

"So let's say, this one," Henry said, pointing to a stone that the salesman had described as a 1.2-carat. "What would this one cost as part of a typical engagement ring?"

"I think I understand," the salesman said. "Let's say you put it in a white gold band, with baguettes on either side . . . Of course a lot would depend on what kind of stones you selected for the sides . . ."

"Just a guess, then. An estimate. I'm not going to hold you to it."

"I'd say something like this could cost you anywhere from eight to eleven thousand dollars."

Henry stared at the main counter, where a blond house-wife with a double stroller was leaning over the glass and looking at key rings. He saw the glint from the diamond on her left hand. It looked massive, and incredibly shiny. Looked a lot nicer than what he was looking at, at least to his untrained eye. And he found himself wondering what her husband did for a living.

He looked over at the back wall, where a very tall, slender woman in a black business suit was looking at china patterns. She had a monster diamond on her left hand too. The light coming off it was blinding.

He looked two tables over, where a saleswoman was showing gold necklaces to an older woman with dyed red hair. The saleswoman had a diamond ring on her left hand. Looked nice.

And, as he processed what the guy in the gray suit had just told him, he did some simple math.

For the price of those three engagement rings—the ones on the two customers and the saleswoman—he probably could buy Layla a pretty nice car.

"Sir?" gray suit was saying.

Apparently, it had been a while since Henry had said anything. The man in the gray suit—no robot, as it turns out—was waiting for a reaction to his preposterous last statement.

"Sir?" he said again.

"I'm sorry," Henry said. "I just got distracted. I thought she looked like somebody I knew."

Gray suit looked in the direction of the saleswoman and the old red-haired lady as Henry looked back at the diamond between the tweezers. Jake had been right. He could not believe the numbers the guy in the gray suit had thrown at him. And those were just an estimate—a forced one—on a basic ring that hadn't even been designed yet. Henry knew, from earlier parts of the conversation, that a platinum band could cost more, that the side stones came in different shapes and sizes, that the damn thing would have to be insured . . .

"Something you want to tell me, buddy?" Rob's voice was saying behind him.

Henry looked back up at the clock. Noon on the dot. What a break. Rob was on time.

"Hey!" Henry said, hopping up out of the chair and shaking his friend's hand. Rob was dressed for the store, in a crisp, dark suit and a prominent pink tie with a huge knot protruding from the top of his pink-striped shirt. He looked as if he could be selling diamond engagement rings, rather than picking stocks, but Henry was fairly sure he wouldn't make that trade. "You're right on time!"

The guy in the gray suit was still sitting behind the table, holding the diamond with the tweezers. Henry turned back to him.

"Thanks," he said. "You've been a really big help. I'm going to lunch now with my friend, but I'll definitely be back here."

In fact he felt anything but definite about that.

"Of course, sir," gray suit said, with a classy touch of the disapproval that salespeople are trained to offer whenever someone leaves a store without buying anything. "Let me give you my card."

Henry took the business card but didn't look at it. He stuffed it into his pocket, shook the guy's hand, and headed for the door with Rob. He couldn't get out of there fast enough. On the way out he held the door for Rob and for a plastic-surgeried blonde with huge sunglasses and gold trim on her white suit. She did not say thank you. Henry did not care.

Layla was finally at work, having picked up a loaner car at the dealership and received an ironclad guarantee from the mechanic that her car would be ready "soon." Upon arriving, she'd rushed past the secretaries, shut the door to her office and grabbed the phone. She had to call Gloria. Gloria had to know about her morning.

Less than a minute into their conversation, Gloria was cackling on the other end of the phone.

"The tow truck guy asked you out?" she was asking for the ninth time. "The tow truck guy asked you out?"

Layla was trying not to laugh, whispering into the phone as she stared out through the slats of the open blinds to see if anyone was staring back into the office at her. She knew she looked crazy this morning, but hey, it was a crazy morning. Wasn't her fault. Anyway, she was enjoying this.

She looked at the stack of pink phone messages on her desk, sorted through them quickly, found none from Henry, shoved them to the side. She reclined in her desk chair, no longer worried about whatever reaction there might be in the office. She'd had a stressful couple of days and a stressful morning, and with nothing to do until court, she decided it was okay to kick back and have a little fun about the whole thing.

Gloria was not available for lunch, which was fine, Layla decided. She could take lunch at her desk and catch up on her paperwork. The problem was, she couldn't concentrate. She couldn't remember the last time she'd been asked out. She wondered what was different, all of a sudden, that was making her wonder about good-looking Ben from the sports bar, or check out the rear end of a tow truck driver. She struggled to remember whether she was doing these same things last week, or last year. She didn't think so.

Restless, she left the office and headed for the bathroom, where there was a mirror. There were two people in the bathroom when she got there, so she made a show of washing her hands until they left. Then she stepped back and looked at herself again. She couldn't see any difference. In fact, if anything, she looked kind of frazzled. Sitting by the side of the road in the summer in your broken-down car isn't good for your hair, and hers was definitely not looking as good as it had when she'd left the house. She spent a few minutes trying to fix it and wondered if she had a comb or a brush in her desk. She worked on a small stain on the left side of her blouse, and smiled when she figured she'd picked it up in the passenger seat of the tow truck. She was smiling at herself in the mirror when two more women walked in, and she blushed, looked down at the floor, and hurried out without greeting them.

Something felt different. She just couldn't figure out what it was.

Henry and Rob walked down the hall to Houston's restaurant for lunch. Henry always got a kick out of meeting his friends for a business lunch, since he was always dressed so casually and they were almost always buttoned up into their suits. Almost everybody else in the restaurant was dressed for work. He was too. His work was just, well, a lot different from everybody else's. He smiled at the hostess who walked them to their table.

"She's checking out my legs," he whispered to Rob.

"You wish," Rob shot back.

There was no malice in the exchange, just pure fun, and the friends understood that. Rob wasn't into checking out restaurant hostesses any more than he was, and that was precisely the reason Henry had wanted to have lunch with him today. After listening to Pete's description of marriage on his own terms, Big John's litany of ex-wives, and witnessing the sad results of his brother's marital sob story, Henry needed to speak to someone who viewed marriage as a good thing. He thought of Rob right away.

Rob had been married for nine years to Valerie, the girl he'd met and begun dating as a freshman in college. They had three children—six-year-old Frank and three-year-old twins, Joey and Emily. Rob was a devoted husband and father who liked his job because it didn't require him to work beyond its nine-to-five constraints and allowed him to be home every single night for dinner. It allowed him weekends off, which was nice now that Frank was starting soccer. Rob's job allowed him to be what he'd really wanted to be, ever since Henry had known him—a family man. Henry wanted to talk to him about his family, and he wanted Rob to make him feel good about it.

"So," Rob said, folding his cloth napkin into his lap. "You want to tell me what that was all about?"

"First," Henry said, "we'll order drinks. I'm having a beer."

"Must be nice," Rob said.

"Well, I figure I'm so blocked anyway, it can't hurt. Something's got to jar something loose sooner or later. Faulkner wrote with a glass of whiskey next to his typewriter."

"Yeah, I remember you telling me something about that. About three hundred times, in college."

The waiter came, and Henry did order a beer. Rob, who was heading back to work for the afternoon, ordered a Diet Coke. The drinks came, and Henry began explaining the past few days. They stopped to order their burgers, and Henry kept explaining. Rob sat in silence, transfixed by the story, seeming to believe none of it.

When Henry finished, Rob stared at him for a few more seconds, as if making sure Henry wasn't about to deliver some big punch line, tell him the whole thing was a joke.

"Wow," Rob said, sipping his soda. "That's heavy."

"So listen," Henry said, still rolling after a swig from his tall pilsner glass. "I wanted to ask you something."

"You asking me to be in your wedding?" Rob said, smiling.

"No, wiseass," Henry said. "I'm still trying to figure out if I want to have one or not."

"I was kidding."

"I know. Anyway, I wanted to ask you . . . How did you know you wanted to marry Valerie?"

Rob sat back and looked Henry in the eye.

"I knew it the first time I met her," he said.

Which baffled Henry, since he remembered being a freshman in college and being certain about nothing whatsoever.

"Come on," he said.

"I'm serious," Rob told him. "It sounds goofy, you know, the whole 'Love at first sight' thing, but I'm serious. The first time I saw Valerie, I knew I wanted to have a family with her. I can't explain it."

"But then, what? You dated all through college. You broke up about six times that I remember. You had fights. You couldn't have been sure that whole time. Could you?"

Rob smiled again.

"I don't know," he said. "It's kind of hard to explain. Yeah, we dated all through college and we had our tough times and whatever. But for me, it always came back to that feeling I had the first time I saw her. And nothing we went through ever changed that feeling. Every time we had a fight or broke up or anything, it might take a while, but I always got that same feeling back again. And so did she."

Henry had ordered a second beer, which raised Rob's eyebrows, and was sipping it at the end of this soliloquy.

"Did you ever wonder . . ." Henry began.

"What?" Rob asked when Henry stalled.

"Well, did you ever wonder if you could pull it off?"

"What do you mean?"

"You know," Henry said. "If you'd be good enough. I mean, being a husband and father, that's big stuff. You've got to be sure you can handle it, don't you? Make enough money to support everybody, be a good dad, keep your kids from being screwed up . . ."

"Geez," Rob said. "You've got a lot of issues to deal with in just one week, don't you?"

"Tell me about it," Henry said, and sipped his beer again.

"You need to finish your book," Rob said.

And Henry decided to turn the conversation back to where he'd wanted it in the first place.

"So," he said. "Is it like the picture you had in your head, way back then?"

"It's better, man," Rob said, slicing a huge wedge of iceberg lettuce with his steak knife. "Every day, with the kids and her, it's better than I thought it would be. Henry, you get to a point where you look at your family and you think to yourself, 'This is it. This is what I was put on this earth to do.' And it feels pretty good."

Henry looked at his friend for a minute but said nothing. They ate the rest of their lunch together, talking, some about the same heavy issues, some about the Mets, some about what little Frank had been up to on the soccer field. On the way out, after Rob won the fight over the check, Henry decided there was one more thing he needed to know.

"Hey, Rob," he said, "if you don't mind my asking. What did you spend on Valerie's engagement ring?"

Layla could have sworn the guy in the second row was staring at her as she presented her case, but she was trying hard to put those kinds of things out of her mind. She was at work now, after all, and it was time to be serious. Funny thing was, she'd never had any kind of problem being serious in court before. Today, the whole morning, had just thrown her off, and she wondered, as the judge jarred her again by asking if she was all right, if she should have called in sick.

"I'm fine, Your Honor," she said. "Sorry."

And she went on with the case. At the end, she felt bad,

because she knew her mind hadn't been on the case the whole time. And she hoped that the judge wouldn't punish her sixteen-year-old clients for their lawyer's flightiness. She really did believe that, while the kids probably shouldn't have been skateboarding in the parking lot, the grocery store owner was way out of line when he fired that shotgun over their heads. And she really did believe they'd suffered some degree of emotional distress as a result. (Though what degree, she could not be certain, since it seemed to her that the life of a sixteen-year-old is one of perpetual emotional distress.)

Out in the hall now, Layla was wondering if she had any reason to go back to the office, or if she should take a rare opportunity to go home early. She'd stopped to sit on a bench in the hallway because it felt like she had a pebble in her right shoe, and she was unbuckling the strap when she saw a pair of black wingtips stop in front of her. She looked up and into the face of Ben, the friendly lawyer she and her girlfriends had met in the sports bar the day before.

"Well," he said, smiling. "This is a surprise."

"Wow," Layla said, shaking out the shoe and hearing the pebble tick the marble floor and roll away. "You're not kidding. You stalking me?"

"Yes," he said, smiling bigger now. "I am stalking you. I've been following you ever since the bar. I can't believe you cut that old lady off in traffic on 287 this morning."

Layla was grinning now too, her shoe back on, and she stood up to face the handsome stranger who'd now made two separate random appearances in her life in two days.

"She had it coming," Layla said. "She had her blinker on for seven miles and didn't change lanes."

She was smoothing out her blouse with her hands, paying particular attention to the place where the spot had been on her left side. She wondered if her hair was looking better. She wondered if anybody besides her could still see that stain on her blouse. She wondered why she cared so much what this guy thought.

"Hey, listen," Ben said. "I have to run to court right now, but I wanted to ask you something, and I didn't feel like asking in front of your friends."

"Okay," Layla said, looking him in the eye.

"Do you want to go out to dinner with me sometime?" he asked.

Layla couldn't figure out what to do. She looked around the hallway, for some kind of hidden camera, trying to figure out if this was some elaborate scheme Henry had put on to get her back. She'd been asked out twice now, in the same day, running her total for the past five years to something like two.

Ben saw her looking around.

"Is there something wrong?" he asked.

"No, no, no, no," Layla said, jolted back to the present again. "No. I just—"

"Hey, it's okay if you don't want to," Ben said. "I was just taking a shot."

"No, it's not that," she said. "It's just . . . I don't know. I have some things going on and—"

"Hey, it's no problem," he said. "I can take it."

But then she stopped and she looked at him. He had only one dimple, on the right side of his mouth. His face looked kind and sweet and safe. He hadn't taken his eyes off her since the start of the conversation. And deep within her mind, faintly, she could hear Susan's words from the day before.

You could be single in a week.

"You know what?" Layla said, straightening up now. "Give me your phone number."

"Excuse me?"

"Give me your phone number. You got a business card, whatever. Let me have it. I'm busy this week, but I'll give you a call early next week. How's that sound?"

"Sounds great," said Ben, finally thrown off, as he fished into his briefcase for a card.

"Great," she said, taking the card and looking at it for a second before slipping it into her own case. "And who knows? Maybe I'll see you around."

"Sure," he said. "I'm getting good at this stalking thing."

Nine

Henry had no idea why Layla's father would be at the Riverside Square Mall, a place whose purpose was to provide humans with the opportunity to purchase material goods, but there he was.

James Starling cut an unusual figure as he ambled through the mall's wide marble hallways, gazing up at the signs above the stores as if he were a caveman who'd recently been thawed out and turned loose in twenty-first-century New Jersey. He wore a dingy-looking gray hemp sweater with a green tie-dyed pattern on the front. His shorts had so many holes in them that it looked as if he'd stolen them off of someone who'd been shot in the thighs with a machine gun. And the ratty old flip-flops on his feet were so small and insignificant that Henry found himself looking a third time just to make sure James had anything on his feet at all.

Henry didn't want to speculate as to his potential father-in-law's mental state and how drug-addled it might or might not be. He wasn't even sure he wanted to let Layla's father know he was there. It would have been pretty easy not to say anything, since James already had walked past the bench where he was sitting, looked directly at him, and not noticed it was the man who'd been dating his daughter for six years. But Henry ultimately decided it would be better, for political reasons if no others, to see if the dazed old hippie needed some help.

"James," he said.

No reaction. James merely stared in wonder at the window of J. Crew.

"James," Henry said again, without raising his voice. He knew it was a matter of patience.

Now, James stopped and turned his head, but he turned it in the wrong direction. He'd obviously heard his name but had no idea were it had come from.

Henry stood up and walked over to the man, who looked into his eyes for five full seconds before registering any kind of recognition. Whoa, Henry thought. Big morning in the Starling house.

"Hank!" James Starling blurted. "What are you doing here?"

A couple of things went through Henry's mind. First, he lived near here and came here somewhat often. Second, he might have been asking the same question of James Starling, whom he'd never seen here. But the biggest thing on Henry's mind was the one he decided to inquire about.

"Hank?" Henry asked, puzzled. "You've never called me Hank. Nobody calls me Hank."

"Yeah, I know," James said. "Just wanted to try it out. You don't like it?"

"It's fine," Henry said. "Whatever works for you, man."

Henry had a bit of a buzz on from his lunchtime beers, and had been sitting on the bench contemplating the price of rings at Tiffany's and the rosy picture of marriage and family life his friend had painted for him over Houston's burgers. He was actually in a pretty good frame of mind for dealing with James Starling, and it occurred to him that he should ask the man to join him at the bar.

Assuming, of course, that James Starling had nothing better to do on this Monday afternoon.

Which, based on Henry's experience, was a good assumption.

"What are you doing here?" Henry asked.

"Ah, it's a long story," James said, apparently unwilling to tell it. "But it's good to see you. What a nice surprise."

James Starling's eyes were twinkling and his yellow smile was genuine. He liked Henry, and no matter how stoned he got, he was never shy about showing it. During the few times over the past two days when Henry pondered the idea of life without Layla, he realized he'd miss her parents too.

"Are you . . . shopping, or something?" Henry asked, still curious but now convinced no answer was forthcoming.

"I'm not really sure. How about you? What are you up to? You want to do something?"

And Henry, who had nothing else to do, suggested the bar at Houston's, and there they went.

"I always liked baseball," James Starling was saying a half hour later, changing the subject for at least the eleventh time since they'd sat down at the bar and started watching the Yankees' afternoon game against the Twins. "I like the contemplative aspect of it. There's so much time for reflection, so much time to assess what you've done, where you are, and how you can get where you want to go. I think football lacks that a little bit. Too much speed and violence."

Henry liked baseball too, but he'd never thought of it that way. It was clear that Layla's father had spent more time than usual expanding his mind on this day. As he watched

Mike Mussina dip low and get ready to throw another pitch to Torii Hunter, James Starling sipped his Killian's Irish Red and waxed philosophical.

"Every pitch is like a chess move," James said, rolling now. "The pitcher's trying to guess what he can throw to try and trick the hitter. The hitter's trying to guess what the pitcher's going to do. And it's all wrapped up in each guy's whole personal history. Each player's whole life has led to that one pitch, and everything they do in that split second will be based on something that's come before. What's he thrown me in the past? What kinds of pitches has this guy swung at when I've faced him before? It's a battle between confidence and self-doubt, and sometimes the winner is just the guy who got luckier."

Wondering when he'd decided to sit down and have beers with A. Bartlett Giamatti, Henry thought it might be time, once again, to change the subject.

"James," he said. "Can I ask you something?"

"Sure," James said, without taking his eyes off the TV screen.

"Do you remember how you knew when you wanted to marry Cindy? I mean, like, was there one moment where you knew this was it?"

Henry wasn't worried about Layla's father jumping to conclusions, because that was not something James did. He also was not worried about any part of this conversation getting back to Layla, because (1) James might well not remember any of it, and (2) if he did remember it, he had enough sense to know that Henry would have expected it to be kept confidential. Within a given moment, James Starling could be very wise and self-aware. It was when the time frame expanded that he started to drift.

In answer to Henry's very deep question, with all of its implications about the future of his daughter, James sat quietly and sipped his beer again. He still hadn't turned his head to look at Henry, and Henry wasn't one hundred percent sure the question had registered. So he prodded again.

"James?"

"I heard you, Hank," James Starling said, and turned to greet Henry with a smile and a wink before turning back to face the TV. "I heard you. Just give me a minute."

Henry had to smile. Layla's father was pondering his question and the best way to answer it. Henry had managed to penetrate the haze of James Starling's Monday and connect with the man in a place deeply personal. He waited for the response, assuming it was going to be a good one.

When it came (during the next commercial break), it came slowly. Layla's father began with a story about his high school days, and how he was kind of a geeky kid who didn't have too many friends. He talked about how well he'd done in his math and science classes, and he told at least three stories that led nowhere and didn't even have Cindy Starling in them. But Henry was determined to let the monologue flow wherever James wanted it to flow. He knew the man was getting somewhere, and it didn't do any good to try and force him out of his pace.

Finally, the stories reached the point where Cindy came into the picture. A dazzler at the junior prom, she'd fought with her date and ended up on a bench out in front of the school. James, late for the prom and dateless, found her there and tripped over his own feet as he offered an awkward greeting on the way into the gym. He fell and slammed his head on the concrete arm of the bench, and the next thing he knew he was in a hospital bed, staring up at his parents, a doctor, and this girl he really didn't even know.

Cindy had loaded James and his bleeding head into her car, driven him to the hospital, and called his parents to tell them where he was. She'd forsaken her prom and a chance to make up with her boyfriend in order to help James, and now she was sitting by his hospital bedside in her blood-stained yellow prom dress even though she'd already fulfilled her responsibilities in the matter and then some.

"Wow," Henry said, sensing a break in the story. "And that's when you knew?"

"No, actually," James said, wagging his finger at the bartender and pointing to his and Henry's glasses in an unspoken request for more beer. "Actually, after that night, I didn't really speak to her again for a number of years."

"Really?"

"Yeah," James said. "It was the end of the school year, and I had to miss the last week of classes while I recovered. The next year, she was in private school and I never saw her. We went to different colleges, and it wasn't until about five years after that prom that we met again, at a friend's party during Thanksgiving weekend during our senior years of college."

James went on to tell of that party, and how the two had hit it off as if it were the day after his fall and they were talking about whether he was all right. There was never any mention of how they'd fallen out of touch, mainly because they'd never been all that close in the first place. But they hit it off, and when they settled in New York City after college, they began dating.

One night, outside a little Mexican restaurant on the Upper West Side, James Starling was trying to flag down a cab to take him and Cindy home. He stepped into the street and right into a deep puddle, twisting his knee and falling onto the pavement, where a passing car ran over his left arm.

The next thing he remembered, he was in a hospital bed, staring up at a doctor and at Cindy, who'd once again rushed him to the hospital. This time, at least, it made some sense, since they'd been dating for a while and were actually out together when the accident happened.

"But it was that night, lying in that hospital bed, on all of those painkillers, that I realized I needed to keep her in my life," James said. "I think a lot of guys, they look for some-body they can take care of—you know, like having a family is about responsibility and providing for your wife and kids and kind of being the one who takes care of everything?"

"Sure," Henry said, mesmerized.

"But for me, I just realized that's not what I needed in my life," James said. "I needed somebody who could take care of *me*. And here was this beautiful, lovely woman, with whom I had so much in common, with whom I liked spending time. And not only that, but she was somebody who already knew what a clumsy wreck I was and not only didn't mind but actually *enjoyed* taking care of me. I'd have had to be an idiot to not jump all over that."

And he swigged his Killian's, and he looked at the TV screen and said, "Home run." And on the very next pitch, Derek Jeter hit a home run.

Henry, dumbfounded, took a minute before speaking.

"Jesus Christ, James," he finally said. "That's one of the best stories I've ever heard about two people meeting."

"Yeah, and now we live together in squalor and smoke weed. And she doesn't mind that either."

Henry offered a short little laugh and stared up at the colorful liqueur bottles on the shelf behind the bar. Layla's father had floored him with his story, and he had no idea what to do with it. Fortunately, he didn't have to wait long to know what to do next.

"Anyway," James Starling said. "You have a car here?"

Henry, startled once again by the abrupt change of sub-ject and the strangeness of the question, took a second.

"Sure," he finally said.

"Great," James said. "I need gas. Think you can drive me up to the Mobil?"

"Sure," Henry said. He wasn't about to let this guy out of his sight.

* * *

James Starling had come to the Riverside Square Mall because his car had run out of gas in the parking lot. This was not a huge surprise, because his car ran out of gas all the time, at various places all over New Jersey. And Henry was more than accustomed to picking up Layla's father or mother and driving them to the nearest gas station to get out of the fix. But what amazed Henry on this day was the lack of urgency James Starling had displayed when they met in the hallway. Layla's father had no problem hanging out, having a laid-back discussion, or grabbing a few beers at the bar with him, even though his car was disabled in the parking lot, presumably still on the way to wherever he'd been headed when the gas ran out.

As they drove to the gas station, Henry pondered James's story, wondering how it was possible that he'd never heard it before, impressed by the ease and freedom with which James had shared it with him now and trying to organize it in relation to the others he'd heard from various other friends about the origins of their own marriages and relationships. Henry had no idea what he was going to do with all of the information he was amassing, but he was sure of one thing—Layla's father had the best story so far. The shame of it was, he wouldn't be able to talk about it with Layla that night. He had no intention of letting her know that he was out looking at engagement rings and soliciting marital advice from friends and potential in-laws.

In fact, he figured it might be best to make sure that position was clear to James Starling.

"Well, thanks," James said, leaning into the driver's-side window of Henry's car, having filled the tank of his own with gas from the red plastic can he always kept in the trunk.

"No problem," Henry said. "I had a great time. And James?"

"Yeah?" James asked, leaning back down.

"Uh, I just wanted to make sure . . ."

"Don't worry, Hank," James Starling said. "I won't tell anybody what we talked about. Far as I'm concerned, we didn't even see each other today."

Sometimes, Henry thought as he sat in his idling car in the mall parking lot, people can really surprise you. James Starling had rarely, if ever, displayed the level of maturity Henry had seen from him on this Monday afternoon, and Henry wondered what cosmic force had been at work to bring them together at a time when he desperately needed it.

Then again, maybe the whole thing was a hallucination. A figment of his addled imagination. A side effect from the carrot beer.

Ten

Layla paused for a second before answering her ringing cell phone. The display read HENRY CELL, which wasn't unusual, since they kept in regular contact most days. But it was already three o'clock in the afternoon and they hadn't spoken to each other all day—hadn't talked since the fight in the car on the way back from her parents' house. And because of everything else that had been going on all day, she hadn't spent much time thinking about Henry or the fact that they hadn't talked.

She thought of all of this as the other customers in the Hallmark store stared at her impatiently, wondering if she would answer the phone on its third ring, then its fourth.

"Sorry," she mumbled, to no one specific, and answered the phone. "Hello?"

"Hey," Henry said on the other end. "What's going on?"

"Not much. Just picking out a card for Jack and Gina."

"Oh, right. Are we giving them a check?" Henry asked.

"I thought that's what we talked about," Layla said, running her finger over the row of wedding cards constructed to hold money.

"Right," Henry said, unsure if Layla was being snippy and was therefore still angry about last night, or if he was being too sensitive. "Anyway, listen. I thought I'd make dinner tonight."

"Oh, that's nice," Layla said, meaning it. "What are you making?"

"I just figured I'd pick up a couple of salmon steaks or something like that from the store, do them with some lemon and broccoli, that kind of thing. Sound okay?"

"Sounds delicious," she said. "Are you home right now?"

"No, I've been out all day," he said.

"Still blocked?"

"Like never before."

"Sorry."

"Yeah, thanks," he said. "I really don't know what I'm going to do."

"You'll figure it out," she said. "You always do."

"Well, anyway, I don't know exactly when I'll be home, but by dinner for sure."

"Okay," Layla said. "I'll probably beat you there. Court got done early, so I'm going home after I'm done here."

She was wondering why he sounded so peppy. He was hoping he didn't sound drunk.

"All right," he said. "I'll see you there."

"Okay," she said, wondering how the conversation would end.

"Love you," he said, surprising her a little.

"Love you too," she said, and they hung up.

And as she slid her cell phone back into her pocketbook, Layla realized that for the past minute she'd been staring at a glass case that contained a porcelain figurine of a bride and a groom.

Stop it, she told herself, and went back to picking out a card for Jack and Gina.

The Barnes & Noble was new—a massive, gleaming, green corporate monolith that made Henry wonder how many small bookstore owners who were going out of business must want to stop and get out of their cars and spit on it each day. And as a fellow lover of books, he sympathized with the plight of such people. But as an author, he'd become sharply aware of the value of sucking up to Barnes & Noble. If they put your book in the front window, or on one of the first tables people see when they walk in, well, it was hard to put a price tag on something like that. Henry had seen the place from his car after he and James Starling parted, and calling Layla to tell her he'd be cooking dinner, he decided to come inside and try to meet the manager. You know. Just in case he ever finished this damn book.

But Henry was distracted—the result of his dizzying emotional morning and all of the beer he'd consumed over lunch with Rob and while watching baseball with Layla's father. And so the first place he found himself was the Starbucks stand in the middle of the store, ordering a caramel Frappuccino. The next place he found himself was in the paperback fiction section, sipping caramel through a straw and checking out his own books to see how many of them were on the shelves. And it was there that he heard his name.

"Henry?" a woman's voice asked.

He blushed. He'd been caught at a bookstore, looking at his own books. How would he explain this? And to whom?

He turned and found the answer to the second question in the person of Catherine Gresham, the lovely, perky wife of Friendly's regular Pete Gresham. She was holding two white glossy paperbacks in her left hand and looking up at him with a half-perplexed, happy-to-see-you smile.

"What are you doing here?" she asked.

People were always asking him that question, and it always amused him. The beauty of his job was that he could be anywhere he wanted, at any time. He kept his own hours, worked from home, and could go weeks without doing a stitch of work as long as he made his deadlines every few months. So the answer to Catherine's question was the same one he gave every time he was asked it.

"Just hangin' out," he said. "What are you doing here?"

It appeared as if she had not yet made the connection—had not noticed that they were standing in front of the shelf that held copies of Henry's five previous novels, and did not realize that she'd caught him looking at his own books. It appeared this way because it was now Catherine who looked embarrassed as she lifted her left arm and waved the paperbacks in his general direction.

"Just . . ." she said, and then tucked the books back under her arm, as if she didn't want anybody to see them. "I don't know. It's good to see you! It's been a long time."

"Yeah," Henry said. "I had lunch with Pete the other day, but—"

"Yeah, he mentioned that," Catherine said, looking down at her light green flip-flops. "He mentioned that."

It was clear to Henry that something was wrong—something was bothering Catherine. But even though he was not fully sober, and was suffering from the worst writer's block of his life, and his girlfriend had just given him a one-week deadline to decide whether he wanted to get married, he figured he should tactfully leave it alone and say nothing. After all, Catherine wasn't really his friend. Pete was. Henry didn't know her all that well—or not as well as he had in college, when everybody was friends with everybody and they went out partying in groups of eight or ten. At this point it really wasn't his business if something about Catherine's life was bugging her.

Which is why it surprised him when she said, "Hey. It's been a while since you and I talked. You want to get a drink?"

Henry, figuring the day might as well continue on its track, said yes, though he worried about what he was getting into.

Henry was pretty sure he'd never been inside the Houston's restaurant at the Riverside Square Mall before this particular Monday. Now, he'd been here three times. The bar was dark—the kind of place that, if you left it in the middle of the day after a few beers, made you squint through a sunshine about which you'd completely forgotten. He no longer spent much time in bars, but he used to, and he remembered from his college days that he never felt quite right drinking in a dark bar and knowing the middle of the day was going on outside.

This time, since Catherine was not as big a baseball fan as James Starling, they got a table. It was three o'clock in the afternoon and the place was empty, though Henry did enjoy the wry looks of recognition he got at the hostess stand and from the waitstaff. I wonder if I'll miss these people, he thought. I wonder if the dinner shift will be as nice.

Catherine's drink had a light red tint to it, and Henry had no idea what it was. His was a beer, since he was determined not to change his pattern at this point in what was unfolding as a cosmically pointed day. Determined to move slowly through this beer—and possibly have only one with Catherine, since he still had to drive home, after all—he'd ordered a glass of ice water to go with it. He was carefully sipping the ice water as Catherine began to talk, and was worried that she was about to start complaining about her marriage or some other problem in her life. But she surprised him, and the conversation quickly became about college days.

"Do you remember the first time you asked Layla out?" Catherine asked.

"Ha!" Henry said. "You don't forget a thing like that."

"I just remember you coming to Pete's room with those other guys and dragging him out there in the middle of the night," she said. "A couple of us followed you guys, to see what you were up to. And then you stood outside her window and sang that Van Morrison song . . ."

"'Warm Love,'" Henry said, trying to help.

"That's right! 'Warm Love.' Can you still do that good a Van Morrison impression?"

"I really don't think so," he said. "It's been so long since I've tried."

"That's a shame," Catherine said.

"But hey," Henry said. "It worked the one time I needed it to work."

"That's true. That's true."

And they went on like that, even ordering another round as they reminisced about the days of borrowing roommates' credit cards to go on dates. Henry brought up the time that he, Layla, and Catherine had to take turns lugging Pete back from the cruise ship that the Homecoming dance had been held on—Pete having combined seasickness with peppermint schnapps and turning into a rag doll before the boat returned to port.

"I think I was the only one whose shoes he didn't puke on!" Catherine said.

Then she reminded Henry of the time that she and her roommate found him and Layla asleep in each other's arms on the sofa in the lounge of the all-girls dorm they lived in junior year.

"We didn't know what to do," she remembered. "You guys were so cute all cuddled up like that, but we didn't want you to get in trouble for being there after hours."

"Yeah, so you woke me up," he said.

"Well, we didn't mean to," Catherine said. "But you were hard to carry."

"I think . . . didn't you slam my head against a doorway?"

"Mmm, I was hoping you wouldn't remember that part," she said.

"Guess you should have slammed it harder."

The subject of Catherine's marriage to Pete came up once, sort of, when Henry asked if Pete still really kept his swimsuit model posters up in the house. Catherine looked down at her drink and said yes, but nothing else. And then she snapped right into another Henry-Layla memory.

"Remember the time, senior year, when you two broke up, and you came over to Pete's place to tell him about it?"

"I remember," Henry said. "He was passed out."

"Right," Catherine said.

"And you made me hot chocolate."

"Right."

"And you stayed up and listened to me."

"Right," she said again. "And all you could talk about was Layla's hair, and Layla's smile . . ."

"Right, right, right," he said, starting to get embarrassed.

"And Layla's legs . . ."

"All right, all right," he said. "Enough."

He was still smiling, but now he was staring into his beer. He was thinking about Layla's hair, and her smile and her legs, and how he'd always loved them, since the first time he saw them all.

"You know what?" Catherine asked, looking down at the tabletop now. "Layla told me once that, when you used to travel a lot, you sent her a postcard from every city you went to."

"That's true," Henry said to his beer. "I never missed one."

"Wow," she said.

And to this, Henry said nothing. He sighed a bit and kept staring into his beer, leading into the first awkward pause of this conversation. Catherine took a few seconds before asking, "Is everything okay?"

Henry snapped out of it.

"Sure," he said. "Fine. You just reminded me, though. I need to get home and cook dinner."

"Of course," she said. "I'm being silly. I need to get home too. Pete will be home soon."

"Hey, but this was . . . this was great, Cath," Henry said.

"Wow," she said. "It sure was. It's been so long since you and I had any time together."

"Probably since college," he said.

"Probably."

"Well, things change, obviously."

And now it was Catherine's turn to say nothing, which was fine, since they were both in the process of standing up out of their chairs, throwing twenty dollar bills on the table and offering each other friendly hugs.

"You take care," he said, and worried that it sounded phony.

"You too," Catherine said. "Thanks again. And we'll see you this weekend, all right?"

"We will?" he asked. "Oh, right. The wedding."

And they parted, and Henry headed for his car. Enough, for one day, with this mall already. It was time for him to go home and think.

He came through the door with two plastic grocery bags in one hand and flowers in the other, and Layla jumped off the sofa. A little too quickly? she wondered. He smiled at her as she leaned upward for a kiss, and he handed her the flowers—yellow roses. He always brought roses.

"For me?" she asked, as was their ritual.

"For who else?" he asked, playing his part.

"Thank you, sweetheart," she said. "They're beautiful."

She'd changed into a light white sweatshirt and black jogging shorts, and in her bare feet she padded into the kitchen to put the flowers in water.

She smelled beer on his breath, which disappointed and confused her, even as she decided not to make an issue of it. Henry was not an alcoholic, not as far as she knew, at least, and she'd known him six years. Even when blocked, he never resorted to drinking. He could spend his days any number of ways, from playing golf to driving for six hours to hanging out at shopping malls (the last one always made her worry that someone would take him for a potential child molester), and he never told her where he was going because he never planned it ahead of time. She always figured it was part of the creative process—that he had to get out of the house and do something random in order to jar loose whatever part of his story was refusing to come out. He'd been pretty successful with it, so, while she didn't understand it fully, she made no stink about it. In a way, she, with her nine-to-five office life, was jealous. Henry's chosen profession offered him tremendous freedom.

But he'd never used that freedom as an excuse to hit the bottle, and so she worried, of course, that he was drinking in reaction to her ultimatum. That made her uneasy, but then she looked at the flowers again and felt better. Deep within her mind a voice was wondering if he'd come home to propose. Way down inside of herself she concocted an image of Henry on one knee, in this very kitchen, possibly even minutes from now, but then she shoved it aside.

Can't afford to fantasize, she told herself. *If it happens, it happens . . .*

Henry, for his part, was acting as if nothing unusual had happened at all in the last few days. He was taking the fish out of the bag, setting up the cutting boards and getting everything ready to go. Layla sat in a chair at the kitchen table, legs crossed, and figured a conversation might not be a bad way to go at this point.

"So," she began. "What'd you do today?"

Henry had been anticipating this question but remained undecided on how to answer it. He didn't want Layla to know he'd been looking at engagement rings, or having lunch with Rob to ask him about the state of his marriage. He wasn't sure he should tell her the story of running into her father (although it might give him an excuse for the beer breath that he could tell she'd already noticed). And he didn't exactly know how to handle the whole Catherine situation, since, while nothing bad had happened, he still had been having drinks in a bar in the middle of the afternoon with an attractive woman who was not his wife. He imagined she would have to find out eventually, but right now he just didn't know what to do.

"I went over to the mall and hung out for a while," he said.

"Henry . . ." she said.

"I know, I know. But I don't think anybody thought I was a stalker."

"More like a homeless guy," she said.

"Nice."

"Which mall?" she asked.

"Riverside."

"What did you do there?"

"Well, research, I guess," Henry said. "There's a mall scene in my book."

This was not, necessarily, a lie. There very well could end up being a mall scene in his book. He was stuck on page nine. The whole damn book could end up taking place at a mall, as far as he knew.

"Was it productive?" she asked.

"Not bad," he said. "I ran into your father."

Sure. Why not?

"Really?" she said, newly interested. "What on earth was he doing there?"

"Guess."

"Out of gas?"

"Bingo."

"Oh, Henry. I'm so sorry."

"Hey, it was no big deal. We had some fun, actually. Hung out at the bar in Houston's, watched the Yankee game for a few minutes."

"Aha," she said. "That's why you smell like beer."

"Yeah," he said. "I just had a couple. Sorry."

"Hey, as long as you're careful."

"I was," he said, and wondered again what would be so wrong about telling her the Catherine part of the story.

"So, my car died," Layla said, apparently content to change the subject.

"Oh, yeah," he said. "I meant to ask you about that. I didn't see it out there."

"Yeah, just crapped out on the way into work."

"You should've called me. I would have come and picked you up."

"It had to go to the dealer anyway," she said. "Triple-A took care of everything, and I got a loaner."

The small talk continued through the preparation and the consumption of dinner. Henry surprised Layla again after dinner by opening the freezer and removing a pint of her favorite ice cream. They sat on the couch with two spoons, taking turns trying to beat each other to the little pockets of cookie dough. She was very competitive. He liked to needle her about it. When the ice cream was over, they smooched, as was their ritual, to taste the sticky chocolate on each other's lips.

But this time the smooching went further. They smooched once, smooched twice. Then there was a full, open-mouth kiss that seemed to last awhile. Then another, that seemed to last longer. Then Layla was lying back on the sofa, Henry on top of her, and they were scrambling to get each other's clothes off.

"Upstairs," she said, her voice muffled by his persistent kissing.

"You got it," he said.

She hopped off the sofa and he chased her upstairs. When they got to the bedroom, she'd already slipped her sweat-shirt up over her head and onto the floor. She hit the bed running and wriggled out of her shorts, giggling as Henry stumbled into the room with his unbelted pants around his ankles.

They made love, twice, and in between he actually asked her something that made her giggle even more.

"Do you remember when I used to get you to cut class so we could do it in your dorm room when your roommate wasn't there?"

"Wow," she said. "What brought this on?"

"Ah, you just looked so good in those shorts," he said.

And they made love again, and Layla felt like she was in heaven—as if some truly special corner had been turned. For the first time since Saturday morning, she really felt like everything was going to be all right.

When she came back from the bathroom, Henry was snoring. She smiled again, a little disappointed, but lay down next to him and turned out the light. She had no trouble getting herself to sleep.

PART IV

Tuesday

Eleven

Layla couldn't wait to get to work.

It wasn't that she was anxious to get out of bed—the bed was fine, and waking up there next to Henry immediately reminded her of all the sweetness and the sexiness of the night before. She woke with a smile on her face and watched Henry sleep for a long few moments before she climbed out of bed and headed out for her run.

It wasn't that she was particularly looking forward to the day of work either. Not much awaited her except more paperwork and a meeting with the partners, in which she was expected to impress six different people who always seemed to be impressed by six different things. Most of her morning would be spent in preparation for the meeting while her head was still spinning from the night before.

No, the reason Layla was so anxious to get to work on this sunny summer morning was that she couldn't wait to call Gloria. As she had the day before, she rushed past those who tried to greet her and shut the door to her office. This time she thought about snapping the blinds shut, but figured it would arouse too much suspicion.

Within two minutes of dialing Gloria, she was wishing she'd called Susan instead.

The conversation began all right. Gloria seemed genuinely excited as Layla told her of the events of the night before—of the surprise phone call in the afternoon, the easy, casual conversation as Henry cooked dinner, the ice cream, the fooling around on the couch, and the sex that reminded her of the sex they'd had back in college.

But then Layla said something that made Gloria say something else, and the whole day changed.

"I swear, Gloria, I thought he was going to do it last night," Layla said. "I thought he was going to propose."

"Yeah?" Gloria asked. "Then why didn't he?"

It was at this point that Layla realized Gloria had been stringing her along—had only been feigning excitement before dropping the bomb on her. It was at this point that Layla, who said nothing as she held the phone receiver in front of her open mouth, realized that her story had played right into Gloria's naysaying hands. It was at this point that she realized she was in for yet another lecture.

"Look," Gloria said, making Layla wonder if that would end up being the first word on Gloria's tombstone. "I don't mean to burst your bubble here, Lay."

"But you kind of did . . ."

"Oh, I know. Look, I understand my role. I'm the friend who's here to tell you the truth. You want to moon about your beautiful, romantic night and how great things are going to be, you go ahead and call Susan."

Reading my mind, Layla thought as Gloria continued her rant.

"But do you want me to tell you the story I just heard?"

"Sure," Layla mumbled, looking out the glass wall of her office. No one was watching her. She desperately wished for someone to come in and interrupt her phone call. She felt as if she'd just eaten bad cheese.

"I just heard you tell me a story about a guy who has no day job, who came home with a beer buzz on, to his girl-friend—the girlfriend he's never felt any pressure to marry," Gloria said.

"Mmm-hmm," Layla said, fumbling with a pen, flipping through her desk calendar, trying to do something to make the time pass until the end of the storm being unleashed on the other end of the phone.

"And this guy, he makes his girlfriend dinner, and he feeds her ice cream, just the way they've done it for years—all the years he's never felt any pressure to marry her. And then he takes her to bed, and they have sex—the same great sex they've had all these years he's never felt any pressure to marry her."

"All right, all right," Layla said. "I get it."

But Gloria acted as if she didn't hear.

"And what's he want to talk about during the sex? College. How great things were in college. Back when he never felt any pressure to do *anything*."

Now, Layla was silent, and no longer fiddling with office supplies. Now, Gloria had her attention.

"So, Lay, you've told me a story of a guy who doesn't seem to think he has to grow up. You've told me a story of a guy who seems to want things to keep going the way they are. You've told me the story of Henry, circa last week, before you made the big speech and gave the big deadline that was supposed to shake him up, and you've set it two days after the speech. And, worst of all, you seemed to expect me to share in the misguided excitement you apparently feel at this latest development. Am I right?"

Silence from Layla's end. She was no longer angry at Gloria, but she was still angry.

"Lay, I'm your friend," Gloria said. "I don't want to hurt

your feelings. But I will if I feel like it's going to keep you from getting seriously hurt in the long run."

"I know," Layla said weakly.

"I'm glad you guys had such a great night. I'm glad you can still be so sweet with each other. But Lay, if Henry isn't trying to work out this problem in his own mind before Saturday, he might be answering your question already."

"My question?" Layla ventured.

"The question of whether you two should really be to-gether."

Silence, again.

"I mean, isn't that the question you're trying to answer here?" Gloria asked.

And Layla remained silent, but she was answering the question to herself. She stared out her office window, which overlooked railroad tracks. A huge, long freight train was rolling by slowly. Traffic was backed up at the intersections where the tracks crossed.

She had been trying hard not to think of the situation in the stark terms that seemed so easy for Gloria and "You could be single" Susan to place on it. She'd put Henry in this difficult situation and forced him to confront the idea of marriage, but she did so assuming he would confront it quickly and easily and come to the conclusion she desired—namely, buying a ring and popping the question.

She did not want to think about what Gloria was asking—about the idea that the two of them, even after six years as a couple, might not be right for each other long-term, and that the deadline might be the thing that revealed that. She had been putting that idea out of her mind, even as she knew it was one possible way for the whole mess to end.

But now, five days before the deadline, here was Gloria, putting the question to her as bluntly as anybody could have, and making her wonder whether her life was about to change a lot more this weekend than she'd anticipated.

"Lay?" Gloria was saying, making Layla wonder how long she'd gone without responding. "You still there?"

"Yeah, yeah, yeah, I'm sorry," Layla said. "Just kind of . . . spacing out . . . thinking. You know."

"Hey, I'm sorry," Gloria said. "I know I sound bitchy. Work is driving me nuts, and there's this guy who won't stop calling me and—"

"No, no, it's okay," Layla said. "It's okay. You're right, anyway, and maybe I needed some bitchiness to bring me back to reality."

"Look," Gloria said. "This could all still turn out okay, all right? I don't mean to be so negative about it. It could still work out fine. Probably will, right?"

"Honestly, I have no idea."

"You free for lunch today? We can talk about this some more, after you've had the morning to figure out how mad you are at me."

"I'm not mad at you," Layla said, and wondered at whom she was mad. Henry? Herself? The guy at the Acura service department who'd called to tell her it could still be a few days?

"Good," Gloria said. "Let's have lunch. How's twelve-thirty?"

"Should work."

"Great. And I'll call Susan. Maybe she can cheer you up."

Layla looked at the two manila folders on her desk that were supposed to prep her for a partners' meeting that started in six minutes and thought, Somebody's got to.

Not two minutes after she'd hung up with Gloria, Layla's phone rang. It was her mother.

"Remember when we used to get together for lunch?" Cindy Starling asked. She had a way of beginning a conversation as if she were already in the middle of it.

"Hi, Mom," Layla said. "How are you?"

"I'm serious, Layla," Cindy went on, sounding determined. "We used to get together for lunch once or twice a week. It was so nice."

"Yes," Layla sighed, thinking she had bigger things on her mind than this. "I remember. It was nice."

"Good," Cindy said. "Well, I think we should start that up again. How's Thursday for you?"

"I'm sure it's fine," Layla said, unable to concentrate. "Just come by the office. I'll be here."

"Wonderful!" Cindy Starling said. "That was a lot easier than I thought it was going to be."

And then, as she was getting ready to say good-bye, something struck Layla. And suddenly her mother had her attention.

"Hey, Mom?" she asked.

"Yes, dear?"

"Do you remember when you were sick, and Dad used to sit next to your hospital bed all night, just in case you woke up?"

"Of course," Cindy said, a touch of mother's wariness creeping into her voice. "Of course I do. Layla, is everything all right?"

"Oh, yeah," Layla said. "I'm sorry. No, I'm not sick. Everything's fine."

"You scared me," Cindy said.

"I'm sorry. I was just . . . I don't know. I've been thinking about things with me and Henry lately, and . . . I don't know."

"You don't know?"

"I just don't know, you know?"

"Are you thinking you finally want to get married, and he doesn't?"

And she thought about telling her mother the whole story, but then decided against it. Not enough time today. Maybe over lunch Thursday. Now, she had to get out of the conversation and end it without leaving her mother too worried.

"I don't know, Mom," Layla said. "I'm sorry. I may just be a little bit down today. Everything's fine. Really."

"You're sure?" Cindy asked, not convinced.

"Positive," Layla said. "Lunch Thursday sounds great. I can't wait. Looking forward to it."

"All right," Cindy said, still not convinced. "But if you want to talk before then . . ."

"Mom," Layla said. "Everything's fine. I'll see you Thursday."

And that, for the moment, was that.

For a second, after she hung up with her mother, Layla thought about calling Henry. She decided against it for several reasons. First, she didn't want to surprise him with a fight, and it was possible she was just agitated enough at this point that a fight would spring up. Second, she didn't want to wake him if he was still sleeping. Third, she only had six minutes to prepare for this partners' meeting, and she had to have something to tell them.

Now, she was sitting at a huge mahogany conference table, listening to her colleagues drone on and on about the cases they were working on. Her turn would come, but it sure was taking its time in coming. She passed the time by shuffling the papers she'd taken out of her briefcase in an effort to look as if this meeting was keeping her from all of the very serious work she was supposed to have been doing for her law firm.

In reality, Layla was focused on a single, small piece of paper she'd removed from her briefcase along with all of her meeting-related paperwork. This piece of paper read, "Ben—201–555–1731," and it had her attention all of a sudden. Initially, her plan had been to ignore this piece of paper completely, and to throw it in the trash next week after Henry had proposed and things were back to normal. Now, though, she had Gloria's you-can't-handle-the-truth speech ringing in her brain, and there were some difficult realities to consider.

First, there was the chance that Henry wouldn't be making his proposal by the end of the week—something she had not envisioned when she decided to go forward with this plan. Now, she had to ask herself whether she was really going to be able to break it off with him if he called her bluff.

Second, there was the question of Ben, who seemed very interested and very nice, who had no idea there was such a person as Henry, and who deserved at least the benefit of a phone call. Should she be single next week, Ben would loom as a very attractive option. Layla thought back to Gloria's timetable speech the week before and realized she wouldn't have much time to wallow in sorrow and misery. Getting back into dating after so long was going to be brutally hard, and here, on this little yellow piece of paper, was an opening she was unlikely to find anywhere else. What if she waited a week to call him, only to find out that he'd gone out over the weekend and met the girl of his dreams in a bar on the Upper West Side?

She tried to shake such thoughts out of her mind, in part because Paula, sitting to her right, had just begun her own presentation—meaning it was her turn next—and in part because she figured she wouldn't be able to spend the rest of the week like this. These thoughts were going to drive her insane, and it wouldn't do to be insane by the end of the week if the week were ultimately going to turn out the way she'd hoped all along.

And it was, wasn't it? There was no way, after six years, that Henry would kiss off the whole thing just because she'd decided she wanted to formalize it. That just didn't make any sense. She thought about what it would mean to her to find out she'd spent six years with a guy and didn't even know him well enough to see something like that coming. She and Henry *were* supposed to be together, and she knew it. He just needed a little nudge.

As Paula went on about her child custody case, Layla looked toward the head of the table, where the partners were arrayed in a semicircle. All six of them were listening very seriously. That was the thing with these people—you couldn't half-ass these meetings, because they listened to every single word and judged you on aspects of your presentation that you couldn't have imagined would be important.

Layla's eyes fell on Jessica Standridge, the only female partner, and the huge diamond ring on her left hand. Jessica Standridge was one of the most evil bitches Layla had ever met in her life. On Layla's first day at the firm, Jessica Standridge—who, presumably, began her career with an understanding of the difficulties facing women in a male-dominated workplace—refused to shake her hand. The first words Jessica Standridge had ever said to her, on that same day, were, "Don't think you're going to get by with just those legs."

It was the kind of thing Layla figured she'd hear, maybe even from one of her bosses, but not from a woman. And it shook her up. It also put her in the position of doing everything she possibly could, every day of work, to try to impress Jessica Standridge. She determined, from that very first day, that she would consider herself a success on the day Jessica Standridge paid her a compliment. She took on extra work if she knew the cases were pet projects of Jessica's. When she had more than one task to complete, she always made sure to finish Jessica's first, and to present it to her in person, so Jessica would know. But the best she ever got was a nod and a grunt, and she could never tell if the grunts were grunts of approval or disdain.

At the moment, though, as two of the male partners grilled Paula about the child-custody case, Layla found herself wondering not how to impress Jessica Standridge, but about the identity of the person who'd bought her that ring. She had never noticed Jessica's engagement ring before, and it occurred to her now that she knew nothing of her personal life. But clearly there was someone who didn't think she was too big a bitch to marry.

Layla amused herself by picturing Jessica Standridge's home life. She imagined a weak, feeble, nebbishy husband completely dominated by the force of Jessica's personality. She wondered if she'd found someone she could bully into marrying her, and in her mind she put Jessica and her husband (who in Layla's imagination bore a sad resemblance to *The Simpsons* character Hans Moleman) into funny typical home scenes. Husband makes dinner, for instance, then waits nervously by the table as Jessica takes her first taste. Jessica grunts and nods, and husband is happy to not be yelled at, but still left to wonder if he's made her happy.

The play that was being acted out in her mind made Layla smile, and she was smiling right at Jessica Standridge. She didn't realize this until her eyes snapped back into focus and found themselves locked with those of Jessica, who was tilting her head to the side in a look of confusion.

"Is something funny, Layla?" she asked, sounding a lot like a third-grade teacher.

Layla felt her face flush. Instinctively, she hid the paper with Ben's phone number under another, larger sheet, the way a third-grader might hide a note that had been passed to her once she realized she'd been caught. She had no idea what to say. If there were thirty people in the room, then it felt like ninety of them were looking at her.

"I'm sorry," she muttered, staring down at the conference table and breaking, for the one hundredth time, her vow to always maintain eye contact with Jessica Standridge when addressing her. "No. It was . . . it was something else."

"Well, then," Jessica said. "Perhaps you'd care to enlighten or amuse us regarding whatever it is you've been up to these days."

And Layla knew she was screwed. She knew, before she even opened her first manila folder and began addressing her first case, that Jessica Standridge was going to make this a very unpleasant meeting for her. Jessica had no idea why she'd been smiling at her through Paula's presentation, but she didn't like it. And so, while the five male partners sat back and watched, Jessica proceeded to interrupt Layla after every second sentence for a question, a clarification, or just to be a pain in the ass.

"Jesus, Lay," Paula whispered as they left the conference room. "What'd you do? Steal her broomstick?"

Under normal circumstances, Layla might have laughed. But circumstances these days were anything but normal, and she was starting to find herself in a bad mood. Things appeared to be falling apart all over her life, and even those that were going well had issues behind them—the tow truck guy was too young, Ben didn't know about Henry, Henry still didn't seem to be taking things seriously enough, her new running shoes were giving her a pain in her left big toe. Nothing was simple or easy, and being raked over the coals by her nemesis in front of the whole firm didn't do anything to make her feel any less out of control.

She peeled away without responding to Paula, who stood in shock at being ignored, and she raced into her office, slamming the door behind her. Through her window, she saw Jessica Standridge turn her head toward the sound of the slamming door, but she couldn't tell whether the look on Jessica's face was one of concern, anger, or satisfaction at just having fed on the decaying carcass of a dead zebra. She fought the temptation to give her boss the finger, assuming that getting fired wouldn't do much to help the quality of her week, and she fell into her desk chair and buried her face in both of her hands.

Her watch told her it was ten minutes before twelve, which meant she had twenty-five minutes before she had to leave to meet Gloria and Susan. She looked at the phone on her desk and began wondering whom to call.

Fingering the yellow paper, she briefly considered calling Ben. She wouldn't set anything up, she'd just call to chat—to see how he was doing, to get a feel for the situation. Who knew? Maybe he'd be cool enough that she could tell him some version of the truth. No, she couldn't tell him she'd just asked her boyfriend of six years to decide by Saturday whether he wanted to marry her. She didn't figure that would make her very attractive to Ben. But maybe she could say something like, "I'm kind of involved with somebody right now, but I'm not sure where it's going." There. That'd be the truth. There was a lot of truth in that sentence, even if it didn't tell the whole story. And heck, if it wasn't going to work out with Henry and it was going to work out with Ben, there'd be plenty of time to tell the whole story.

She considered calling Gloria to ask what she thought she should do, but she didn't think she could handle that phone call right now. Lunch, even with Susan there, was going to be tough enough on her. Gloria's second assault of the day could wait.

Finally, she bit her bottom lip, picked up the phone, and dialed the number on the yellow sheet of paper.

She got his voice mail.

She hung up without leaving a message.

Oh, that was brave, she told herself. Maybe she should have called Gloria after all.

Then again, maybe she should have called Henry. Yes, she felt angry with him at this point, but that anger was based entirely on one phone call with Gloria. It was possible that

Gloria was wrong, and that at this very moment Henry was at a jewelry store, or buying champagne, or doing something that was going to get her life back on the track she wanted it to be on. After six years, didn't she owe him the benefit of the doubt?

Yes, she would call Henry. She picked up the phone and dialed his cell phone number.

She got his voice mail.

She slammed down the phone without leaving a message.

Where the hell is he? she asked herself. *And why is he acting this way? Is he out drinking again?*

Angrier now, she picked up the yellow paper again and dialed Ben's number. She felt emboldened by Henry's refusal to take her call—she knew the number had come up on the caller ID, and she knew, because of the nature of his job, that he was almost certainly in a position to answer it. And yet he hadn't. So screw him.

She listened to Ben's phone ring on the other end, once, twice. She didn't have big plans for the voice mail—just figured she'd tell him she was calling to see what he was up to, leave her work number. The phone rang a third time, and then. . .

"Hello?" It was Ben.

And Layla froze. Now she had no idea what to do.

Twelve ●

Now this, Henry thought, is more like it.

He'd decided to attack his writer's block head-on, and to force himself to sit in front of his computer and type actual words onto the screen, whether they made sense or not. The technique had always worked for him in the past, but the problem this time was actually sitting down to do the work. At home there was the Internet. There was food. There were the neighbors' incessantly yapping dogs, who always sounded as if they were in a fight to the death but never had the decency to actually die. Home wasn't getting it done as a workplace these days, for whatever reason, and so he'd decided to relocate.

He chose the public library, even though he'd never been the kind of guy who worked well in a library. He figured he needed something different, and especially something quiet, and one thing he knew about libraries was that you were supposed to be quiet. He was a little annoyed, on the drive over, when he realized he'd left his cell phone at home, but then he figured they probably didn't allow cell phones in the library anyway, so he decided not to turn around and get it.

When he arrived at the library, it took him a few minutes to realize what he was looking for—mainly because he didn't know what he was looking for. He thought about setting up at one of the small circular tables in the main front section, but noticed that it was close to the children's section, and he figured that was the part of the library that had the best chance to be noisy. So he went up one flight of stairs, turned a corner and saw a small green plastic sign that read SILENT STUDY.

Perfect.

He entered the room, which was tiny and undecorated. Its window looked out onto the parking lot, and the entire room consisted of ten study carrels—five each along opposite walls —each with a large, comfortable wooden chair. It was well lit and quiet—the only other person there was a young black-haired guy reading his computer screen and scribbling on a yellow legal pad.

Henry set up his computer, took out the outline he'd written months earlier, looked at the paragraph for Chapter One, and began to type. He typed and typed and typed, not caring if he was making mistakes or making any sense. He was going back to the technique he'd used to write his first book—just type and type and type until you have the story on the paper, and then go back and fix the parts that are wrong. The technique worked, mainly, because he was a very fast writer, and banging away on the keyboard in the library's silent study was bringing back memories.

After an hour and ten minutes he hit the word-count button, just for kicks. It told him he'd already typed nearly three thousand words.

Outstanding.

And what was even better was that he was into the story

again, all of a sudden. For months he'd been unable to sit himself down in front of the computer and work on this book because he didn't care much about it—didn't care about the characters, the story, the scenery, any of it. He just wasn't into it, and that made it hard to keep working on it.

Now, as he sat and typed and typed and typed, he was getting caught up again. New characters appeared, and he thought about things he could do with them in later chapters. The original characters were having their mood swings, which was something Henry always enjoyed—the part of the process where you start to feel like your characters are organic, acting on their own and making you take the story down roads for which it wasn't originally intended.

By eleven o'clock, two hours after the library had opened and he'd arrived, Henry had written six thousand, two hundred words—nearly two full chapters. He planned to work for another hour, take lunch, and, if he felt like it, come back and spend the afternoon here. It was working, after all, and he only had about five more weeks to get it to the publisher. Spending six or seven hours here for a couple of days in a row might make a lot of sense.

"Excuse me," someone behind him said, rattling Henry, who hadn't heard a sound other than his own typing for more than two hours now.

He turned his head to look at the black-haired guy, who was wearing a plain white T-shirt and ripped shorts. He said nothing. The guy, who looked to be around twenty years old, went on.

"I'm sorry to bug you," the kid said. "But this is supposed to be a silent room."

Henry, baffled, offered only a "So?"

"Well, you're making a lot of noise."

"I am?"

"Your typing. It's making a lot of noise."

Henry began looking around for the hidden camera. Was this kid serious?

"I'm sorry," he said. "The *typing* is bothering you?"

"It's just very noisy, and the sign says 'Silent Study.'"

The kid was serious, Henry realized now. But this wasn't going to work. He'd finally found a place where he could get some serious writing done. He had big plans for this room. This was the room that was going to get his book written for him. He didn't intend to back down, especially because he didn't think he was doing anything wrong.

"Look," he said, "I'm pretty sure we're allowed to type in here. I mean, the room's set up for computer workstations. I'm sure I'm not the first one to come in here and type. You have a computer yourself."

"I'm reading," the kid said.

"I don't know what to tell you," Henry said. "I can't imagine they'd forbid typing in here."

"Well, I came in here because it said it was a *silent* room," the kid said, as if Henry's ability to read the sign was the issue.

"Yeah," Henry said. "Me too."

"Well, I'm studying for a bar exam," the kid said.

So sue me, Henry thought.

Instead, he said, "I don't know what to tell you. I was going to work for another hour and go get lunch, so you have to put up with me for another hour, unless you want to go find somebody to kick me out of here. But I really don't think they're going to kick me out of here for typing."

"It's just that, it says *silent* study," the kid said.

Henry was annoyed now.

"Yeah, and you know what I thought that meant?" he asked. "I thought that meant you weren't allowed to talk."

The kid appeared to get the point, and he heaved a sigh and went back to his legal pad. Henry, angry now, turned back to his computer. But it was no use. His concentration was broken, and the roll he'd been on before the interruption was over. He had no intention of leaving, since he didn't want the kid to think he'd won, so he stayed in front of his computer for the next hour. But the story didn't flow the way it had for the first two hours. So he went back to read and revise what he'd already written—an important task, sure, but not the one for which he'd come. He'd come to type, and pile up words and chapters, and he'd been interrupted.

So he opened a new file on his computer and began typing something different. He made two lists, one titled WHY and the other WHY NOT. For some reason, he began typing under the second heading first.

He typed:

Can I afford the ring?

Can I afford to buy her a house?

Can I afford to support us both if we have kids and she wants to quit work?

Can I afford any of this if I can't write this damn book?

And he sat back for a second and looked at the screen, where the second column was filling up and the first sat empty. And he clicked under the WHY column and typed one item:

Can I afford to lose her?

At exactly noon, Henry rose, packed his computer into his bag, and left the Silent Study, leaving the door open as one final, extremely immature shot at the bar-exam kid, who had to get up and close it himself after a few seconds. Muttering to himself in anger, Henry descended the stairs and heard his name.

"Henry?" a man's voice said.

Henry had never been in this library before, and had no idea how much socialization apparently went on here.

He looked up and into the huge, round, red face of a man

with whom he'd shared eighteen holes of golf and way too much beer just three days earlier.

"John?" he said, incredulous.

"I thought that was you!" Big John bellowed, drawing nasty looks from every corner of the library—looks he didn't appear to notice. "Man, this is some coincidence!"

"It sure is," Henry said, scared of the man, worried about being too closely associated with a person who was speaking so loudly in a library.

"No, I mean really," Big John said. "I was just heading out for a quick nine holes. You up for it?"

Henry thought. He wondered whether there was anything he still had to do. He came up with nothing. He looked around one more time at the annoyed librarians and smiled.

"Sure," he finally said to Big John. "Where're we playing?"

"You know," Henry was saying now, sipping his second beer of the afternoon as they stood, waiting on the fourth tee. "The thing is, I probably would have asked her to marry me, if you want to know the truth. I probably would have got around to it sooner than later. But once she threw this deadline at me, I don't know . . ."

"Gets you to thinking, doesn't it?" Big John asked, with a knowing grin on his face. "Gets you to wondering. If she can control this part of it, does that mean she gets to control everything? Is that what you're in for? You get married, and all of a sudden she feels like she can tell you what to do."

"Kind of . . . I guess," Henry said, staring up at the green, where the foursome in front of them was taking far too long to putt out.

"Makes sense to me," said Big John, into whose marital pontifications a touch of bitterness appeared to have seeped on this sunny summer afternoon. "Nobody likes to have a gal telling them what to do all the time. It's like you say, maybe you were going to ask her anyway. But you sure as hell don't want to be forced into anything."

"Right," Henry said, thinking that Big John was making some sense. "You're absolutely right."

"And if you think it doesn't get worse, believe me, you're wrong," John went on. "Wait till the kids show up. Then, you won't even believe the way you get bossed around. She'll make you feel like you don't do enough around the house. Then, when you offer to take care of the kids, she'll make you feel like an idiot who doesn't know what he's doing."

"Yeah, I guess," Henry said. "But she's not like that."

"That ring changes things, my friend. You'd better believe it. Take it from me. I'm the expert, after all."

Big John let out a boisterous chuckle, set down his beer and took a heavy whack at his ball with a seven-iron. The ball landed in the middle of the green. There was nothing that could throw off this guy's game.

Three holes and two beers later, Henry was playing the eager pupil while Big John was happy to act as teacher.

"What you have to do, my friend, is get control of the situation," Big John said. "She's basically threatened you, and you have to call her bluff."

"Call her bluff?" Henry asked.

"Yeah. She's bluffing. Do you really think she's going to walk out on you if you don't propose to her by Saturday? How long have you two been dating?"

"Six years."

"Six years! And you think she's going to kiss that off just because you don't meet a deadline? If that's the case, then she's looking for a way out anyway."

Henry hadn't thought of that. What if Layla was looking for a way out? What if this was her way of ending things, betting that there was no way he could make up his mind on so serious an issue in less than a week. It was the first time he'd thought about it this way, and it made him feel . . .

Angry?

Upset?

Scared?

He really didn't know. He was drinking beer, playing lousy golf, and listening to a man who made marriage sound like some kind of prison boxing tournament, and somehow Big John was making sense.

"You're right," Henry said boldly. "When she comes home tonight, we're going to have a talk."

"Attaboy," Big John said. "That's better."

"I need to get control of this situation. This has to happen on my terms, or not at all."

"You tell her," Big John said, sinking a forty-foot putt.

"Man," Henry said. "Do you ever miss?"

Thirteen

"So, did you guys talk for a while? What'd he say? What's he like?"

Susan sounded like a bird. Layla was trying to tune her out as she decided between a skimpy little salad or a big fat cheeseburger.

"Yeah," said Gloria, in a tone much flatter and more clearly sarcastic than Susan's. "You got a date?"

Layla decided on the salad, put down her menu, folded her hands on the table in front of her and took a moment to predict what Gloria's reaction would be.

"Yes," she said. "I think we have a date."

"*What?*" Susan screamed, loud enough that people at every table within fifty feet turned to look.

Layla hadn't wondered what Susan's reaction would be. She was focused on Gloria, who was studying her face to determine whether she was serious. Gloria's expression had not changed in the seconds that elapsed since the words came out of Layla's mouth. She and Layla were the only two people in the restaurant who'd shown no reaction to Susan's exclamation.

"You're serious," Gloria said.

"I am," Layla said, sure that the look on Susan's face was priceless, but determined not to check. Gloria was her strength here, and she needed to lean on it.

"Wow," Gloria said, finally breaking eye contact and looking down at the table, where she played at rearranging her silverware. "Wow."

"You're serious?" Susan asked, still operating at an octave more suited to dolphin communication.

"I'm serious," Layla said. "We made a date. He's taking me to dinner Wednesday night."

"You mean next Wednesday," Gloria said.

"That's right. Next Wednesday."

"As in, not tomorrow."

"That's right."

And then there was some silence as Gloria and Layla stared at each other again. And then Susan, showing off one of her best skills, broke the silence.

"Ohhhhh," she said. "I get it."

"What?" Layla asked, still addressing Gloria. "You think I'm a wimp?"

"Oh, God no," Gloria said, softening now for the first time all day. "Lay, no, no, no. Actually, I'm impressed."

"You are?"

"I am," Gloria said. "I really am. This shows you're at least starting to deal with reality."

Okay, that stung a little bit, but she was determined to fight through it. There remained a chance, however slim she might want to convince herself that it was, that she would be single in a week. And if she was, she had a date all set up.

And if she wasn't, she could always call Ben and cancel. Something came up, etc. Getting engaged would qualify as a decent excuse to blow off a date, wouldn't it?

* * *

The conversation with Ben had been difficult at first. Even though she was the one who called, it was clear to Layla from the beginning that he was the comfortable one. She just hoped he couldn't tell how uncomfortable she was.

He'd impressed her with his smoothness and confidence in each of their two meetings, and while surprised to hear from her, he nonetheless projected nothing but cool over the phone.

"I have to say, I wasn't expecting you to call," he said. He had a nice voice. A strong voice.

"Oh no?" she asked. "Why not?"

"Well, you didn't seem so sure. And I think you told me it would be a few days."

"Oh, right," she said. "I did."

"So what's up?" he asked, as if they were longtime friends making plans for the weekend.

"Not much," she said, twirling a strand of her hair as she leaned back in her desk chair. "Not much."

She really didn't know what she wanted to say.

"Okay," he said. "So, you're just calling to . . . what? To say hello?"

"Well, I don't know," she said. "I hadn't bumped into you yet today, so I wanted to make sure everything was all right."

He laughed on the other end of the phone. He had a nice laugh too.

"I'm taking a day off from the stalking," he said.

"Well, I was thinking about what you asked me," she said.

"Oh yeah?"

"Yeah. And I was wondering if you were free next week. Say Tuesday?"

Figuring Sunday was the trip back from Maine, Monday was a day to unpack, cry her eyes out, try and figure out who had to move and whose stuff went where, all that crap.

"Tuesday," he said. "Let me see."

She could hear him moving around, as if to check his calendar.

"Tuesday's no good for me," he said, and her stomach sank a little bit. "How about Wednesday?"

"Wednesday works," she said, and wondered immediately if she'd said it too quickly. "I mean . . . sure. Wednesday's just as good. I'm kind of free all week, at least the nights."

He chuckled again. Clearly, she'd presented herself as a blubbering idiot and he was just humoring her—just following through because it was he who'd proposed the date in the first place, or because he liked her legs. Could be that. A blubbering idiot can probably still get dates if she has nice legs.

"All right," he said. "It's a date."

"Great," she said. "So, we'll just talk again, what? Next week, to see when and where?"

"Sure thing, Layla," he said, using her name for what she believed to be the first time. "I'll call you Monday."

"Sounds great," she said, and they hung up.

Now, as she related this story to her girlfriends over lunch a half hour later, Layla took some artistic license. She was not, in the retelling, a blubbering idiot. She came off instead as practical and calculating—covering herself in the event of a disaster. Making sure she had a tall, dark, and handsome life preserver on hand in case the ship she'd been sailing on for the last six years decided to sink over the weekend. She believed her friends would be impressed.

They were.

"Lay, I have to tell you," Gloria said. "I really didn't think you'd be handling this thing so well."

"Ha!" Layla said. "Thanks a lot."

"No, I mean it. I'm impressed. This shows some guts, some

strength. I mean, most people, they date the same guy for six years, they'd have a hard time jumping right back in like that. And here you are, all ready to go."

That's precisely the way she was thinking about it. Here she was, experiencing the little-girl thrill of meeting a new guy—something she hadn't experienced in more than six years. She found herself worried about what she would say to him, how she looked. She was already thinking about what she would wear Wednesday, if in fact she found herself on a date with Ben. She was still of the belief that it wouldn't happen, but she was allowing herself the fantasy, and now she'd invited her friends to come along with her.

"So, I can't figure this out," Susan said. "Do you still want Henry to propose, or not?"

"Of course I do!" Layla said, surprising herself with the force of her own answer. "I mean, Jesus, Susan. That's the whole point here, to shock him into doing something he should have done a while ago. Right?"

"All right," Susan said. "Sorry. But then, so, what's the deal with this other guy? I mean, are you just stringing him along?"

"I don't know," Layla said, as a small smile began to form and she met her friends' eyes with a slightly wicked look on her face. "He's cute."

Gloria practically roared. She threw down her purple cloth napkin and proclaimed, "That's it! What are you doing the rest of the afternoon?"

"Not much," Layla said. "Just working in the office."

"Well, not anymore, you're not," Gloria proclaimed. "You're clearing your schedule. I'm clearing my schedule. Susan's clearing her schedule."

"I am?" Susan asked meekly.

"You are!" Gloria said, standing up now. "We're going shopping!"

Layla was smiling broadly now, looking up at her friend while the rest of the restaurant was wondering when these lunatics were going to leave.

"Sounds great, Gloria," Layla said. "But shouldn't we wait until we finish lunch?"

"Oh yeah," Gloria said, sitting back down. "I meant after lunch."

And they all laughed together. Shopping did sound like a great way to kill the afternoon.

And shop they did. They went into Ridgewood and shopped the place dry. They shopped for shoes, and Gloria bought four pairs.

(Something was on Gloria's mind, and Layla had a hunch that it had something to do with "this guy" she'd referred to earlier that day, who wouldn't "leave her alone." Generally, she stayed out of Gloria's love life, since it was a frightening minefield that made no logical sense to her or anyone else she knew besides Gloria. But Gloria had taken such pains to be helpful during her personal crisis that she wanted to make sure Gloria knew she could count on a return favor. She must know that, Layla thought. And she would certainly ask for help if it were needed. In the meantime, it seemed the best thing to do was to tell Gloria how great her new shoes looked.)

They also shopped for dresses, since Gloria and Susan (who was now firmly on board) insisted that she would need something new to wear on next week's date, if it did indeed come to pass.

"Something slinky," Susan said, looking vaguely ashamed of herself for saying it.

"Yeah," Gloria said, looking downright evil. "Something to show off those gams. How many miles a week you running now, Lay?"

"Stop it," Layla said, eyeing a short black dress that would, indeed, show off her legs to anyone who cared to look at them.

She tried it on. She tried on others. She tried on designer jeans. Susan bought a pair of new sunglasses. They all went to Starbucks and got mocha/caramel/latte coffee drinks (though Layla ordered hers skim, without the whipped cream, prompting a smile from Gloria, who seemed to be thinking along with her). They sat on a bench watching guys go past, and Susan lamented the large number of "cute" ones who were pushing baby strollers. Gloria and Susan caught Layla looking at a tall, twenty-something guy with longish blond hair.

"Ooh, he looks a little young, Lay, doesn't he?" Susan asked.

"Did they spike your coffee?" Layla shot back, looking away quickly from the long blond hair.

"I don't know," Gloria said. "Nothing wrong with a younger man, I don't think. He could be your Thursday night date. No reason not to play the field."

Layla was enjoying herself. When she stopped to think about things, she made sure she told herself it was all fantasy and that she wasn't going to be dating this time next week. But she was stopping to think less and less as the day went on. The girls were making this fun.

"All right," she said after slurping up the last bit of caramel from the bottom of her plastic cup. "Where to now?"

Gloria pointed, and Layla followed her finger across the street to a hair salon.

"You need a haircut?" Layla asked, puzzled.

"No," Gloria said. "You do."

"Oh, I don't know about this . . ."

"Come on, now, Lay," Gloria said. "When's the last time you changed your hair?"

She had to think. It had been years. She couldn't remember the last time she'd felt she had any reason to change her hair. She liked her hair.

Didn't she?

"Well, I guess it's been a while," she said, standing up now, checking herself out in the window of the police car that was parked in front of them, playing with the back of her hair, wondering what it would look like if she got it done like . . . like who? Diane Lane? Or Meg Ryan. Maybe Meg Ryan—short, with those little flare kind of touches on the sides and the back.

"I think she's up for it," Susan said, chucking her empty plastic Frappuccino cup into the trash can next to the cop car. "Come on, let's go. I could use a trim anyway."

Susan would not get a trim. She'd only been offering support for the idea that Layla go in and get her hair changed. As they waited, Susan seemed to take over the role of egger-on from Gloria, peppering Layla with ideas. They flipped through magazines looking for styles. She talked about how great it would be to get it done now, so it had a week to grow in before the date with Ben.

And maybe because this was Susan getting all excited instead of Gloria preaching, Layla was into it. She picked out a few styles from some magazine pages—all of which would represent a somewhat dramatic shortening that everyone she knew was sure to notice. She thought about some color, but Susan talked her out of it.

"No way," she said. "I love your hair color. If I could get my hair dyed your color, I'd do it."

Which settled that.

Finally, with Susan practically applauding and Gloria offering a thumbs-up from outside the front window, where she was chatting on her cell phone on the sidewalk, Layla got up and headed for the chair.

"So," said the hugely uninterested stylist, dressed as if for a fancy Saturday night party, her own hair so perfect that Layla wondered why she'd bothered with the magazines. "How do you want it?"

"Well . . ." Layla said. "First of all, shorter."

And just like that, the hugely uninterested stylist was transformed into a tittering, excited little girl.

"Ooh," she said. "Are we doing something dramatic?"

Layla figured she was talking about hair. But the way things were going, she could have been talking about anything.

"Sure," Layla said. "Why stop now?"

When it was over, she wasn't so sure. She spent about ten minutes looking in a mirror, tugging on the ends of the back of her hair as if she could pull more out of her head and make it longer. The stylist looked on like a third-grader who wanted to know what her parents thought of her art project.

Layla turned to face Susan and Gloria with a very worried look on her face. They gave her just what she needed.

"Wow, Lay," Gloria said. "You look amazing."

It was a stunning tone of voice—stripped of the preachiness Gloria had been using with her the past week. Instead, Gloria sounded genuinely impressed—as if she looked good enough to catch her off guard. The way Gloria said it meant more, Layla thought, than what she said.

"Wow," Susan said. "Wow."

"You like it?" Layla asked.

"It's you," Susan said. "It's just you. It's perfect."

Layla turned back to the mirror, smiling now. This time she kept touching her new hairdo, but she was teasing it, loving the way it held in place, dreaming of easy mornings that would require so much less time with the blow dryer. Wondering if she could make it look just this way.

There was no way she could make it look just this way.

She turned back around in a fresh panic.

"I'll never get it to look like this myself," she said.

"Oh, please," Gloria said. "It'll be so much easier than you're used to."

Layla thought the stylist appeared to take exception to that, but she kept her permasmile as she handed Layla a receipt. Layla paid her in cash, including the tip. Then she, Gloria, and Susan headed back out into the sun-splashed afternoon.

"Where to now?" Layla asked, feeling cooler and lighter than she had with her old hair. "This is fun."

PART V

Wednesday

Fourteen

"I really do like it, you know," Henry said.

Layla smiled as she switched legs. Just back from her run, she was doing her stretching in the living room while Henry stood sheepishly in the doorway to the kitchen and tried, once again, to explain his role in the awkwardness of the night before.

"You look beautiful," he said.

"Henry, you don't have to keep saying that."

"But it's true. I mean, I really think it looks great. I always loved your hair, and I wouldn't have thought you should change it, but now that you did, I'm really amazed. It's you."

The truth was, he did like it. A lot. He'd liked it from the moment she walked in the door. He thought she looked like a movie star—or even better, really. She looked like Layla, done up for the movies.

His mistake, of course, had been hesitating. He hadn't been expecting Layla to come home with a completely new hairstyle. He'd expected her to come home looking exactly the same as she always did, and he had planned a get-tough conversation with her about their relationship. But she prevented that with her very appearance. He was surprised. His first, very natural reaction was to be surprised, and that surprise showed on his face, and it didn't take a minute for him to realize that he'd made a mistake.

"You don't like it," she'd said.

"No, no," he replied, meaning to contradict her, not to validate.

"No?" she asked, looking hurt.

"No, I mean, yes," he said. "I love it. I think it looks great. I really do."

By then he'd got up off the sofa and moved closer to examine the new haircut more closely. He'd checked her out as if she were a fallen meteorite, peering around the back to see the whole thing for himself while she stood there with a concerned half smile. He'd been genuinely amazed, but the damage was done in the first split second, when he'd gaped and said nothing.

Now, here they were, the next morning, and he was still working on repairing the damage.

"I'm sorry if I hurt your feelings," he said. "I didn't mean to. I was really just surprised, that's all."

"You didn't hurt my feelings," Layla said, crossing her feet in front of her and bending down to touch her toes.

This was a lie. The look he had on his face when she walked in the door had hurt her feelings. Yes, he explained himself adequately, and yes, she understood that he'd been shocked by the dramatic, unplanned, unannounced change in her appearance after six years together. All of that made sense. But she'd been hoping for a specific reaction and didn't get it. And that meant, for that one second, that her feelings had been hurt.

It resulted in a strange night, with him trying to be overly nice, and Layla trying to act as if nothing were wrong. With him slurring forced compliments, and Layla trying to hide her disappointment that he'd come home drunk again. In the light of the morning, with the daily five miles behind her, she felt better about the whole thing. Now, though, she wished Henry would figure out a way to change the subject. She was more worried about what was going to happen after her shower, when it was time for her to try and make her hair look as good as the stylist had.

As Layla stood up from her stretch, she caught Henry staring at her legs, and that made her smile too. With the exception of that first few seconds in the house last night, she had been feeling a surge of confidence ever since lunch with Gloria and Susan. She felt so good, in fact, that she thought nothing of changing the subject herself, and forcing Henry into a discussion about the elephant in the room.

"Hey, so, not to change the subject?" she said.

Henry, eager to change the subject, said, "Yeah?"

"Well," Layla said. "It's Wednesday."

This was true, and Henry nodded to indicate his agreement.

"Well," she went on, "I was just wondering if you'd been thinking at all about what we talked about Saturday."

Henry, who had been thinking about little else, was shocked that Layla would so brazenly direct the conversation this way. He'd been planning to talk with her about some major, future-related issues when she'd come home last night, but the haircut thing threw him off so badly that he hadn't had a chance.

"Of course," he offered, looking at the carpet. "Of course I have."

"Anything you want to talk about?"

"There are a couple of things on my mind, sure," he said.

Relieved to hear this, Layla waited for him to go on.

Henry took his time, wondering how much he wanted to

reveal about the activities of his week so far and the questions he'd been pondering. In a way, he was upset about Layla forcing him into this discussion so roughly. He hated when his agent or his editors would call and check in to see how the book was coming, weeks before the deadline.

"Any updates on the book?"

"Updates?" Henry would ask, annoyed. "The update is, you'll have it by the deadline."

Same thing here. He didn't like being pushed. Had Layla given him a Wednesday deadline, he might have had a decision by now. God help him if he knew what it would have been, but he might have had one. Instead, she'd given him a Saturday deadline, which, by his calculations, gave him three more days to figure the thing out. So he hoped she wasn't looking for clues as to what his decision would be. He didn't think he had any to offer, anyway.

But there were some things on his mind, and he'd been thinking a talk might be in order, so why not?

"Well," he said, looking at the TV, which was not on. "And don't take this the wrong way . . ."

"Okay," she said warily.

"Well, I mean . . . why do you want to get married?"

"Huh?" Layla asked.

"Seriously," Henry said quickly. "I just really want to know what you like about the idea of being married. Why it's important to you. I mean, in six years, we've never talked about this."

Layla thought about this, and it made sense. Henry wasn't arguing against getting married. He was soliciting information. It was the way he approached everything—research for his books, shopping for a car, selecting a new ice cream flavor—and while she hadn't thought about it this way, it made sense that it would be the way he'd approach her ultimatum. She wondered if he'd been out all week talking to people about their marriages.

"Well," she said. "All right. I guess I feel like, as long as we're just dating, hanging out, living together, whatever, we really aren't doing anything different than we did when we were in college. Does that make any sense?"

"I think so?" Henry half said, half asked.

"I mean, the last six years have been great, don't get me wrong. But it's just like a continuation of the relationship we had when we started out."

"Okay," he said.

"And Henry, there are some things I want to do," Layla said. "I've always wanted to have a family, to have kids, to make a life of my own with somebody else. And I feel like we just keep putting off getting started on that."

Henry said nothing. What she said made sense. It would have helped if she'd started saying it a year earlier and given him until this week to make up his mind, but whatever. He understood her point, and it led into the next part of the discussion he wanted to have. He had many new and complicated questions in his mind, and he wanted to run them past her.

"I have to shower and get ready for work," she was saying now, apparently impatient for his response.

"I'll come upstairs," he said. "We can talk some more while you're getting ready."

Layla was thrilled to hear this, and eager for his next question. This was what she'd envisioned on Saturday when she issued the deadline. That they'd spend the week talking things over, having serious discussions about their future together. This was the whole idea, really, and here it was finally.

When she got out of the shower, he was sitting on the edge of the bed, looking at her.

"Can we talk some about kids?" he asked.

"Sure," she said, trying to play it cool. "What do you want to talk about?"

"Just wondering how you see it. Like how many, how soon, stuff like that, you know?"

"Well," she said, "I don't know about how many, really. I guess you always picture it the way you knew it growing up, and it was me and my sister, so I always envision two. But I don't know if that's right or wrong or what."

"Doesn't it scare you?"

"Doesn't what scare me?"

"The idea of having kids."

"Oh, sure," she said. "I think it's probably about the scariest thing you can do. I mean, what if you do something wrong? What if you screw them up for life? What if you do everything right and they still turn out to be bad kids? Or bad people? How do you pay for college? There's a lot of scary stuff with that."

"That's kind of what I was thinking," Henry said, remembering what Big John had said about kids, but declining to share those thoughts. He was pretty sure Big John and Layla wouldn't agree on many of these issues.

"But for me, Henry, I think that's kind of what it's all about," Layla was saying. "Having kids is something I want to do. I want to raise a family, to raise kids and try to help them become decent people. I want to hold a baby in my arms. I want to put Band-Aids on their knees and hug them when they cry and watch them play soccer and baseball. I want to have a family that sits around the dinner table and talks about how the day was. I want to cry when they all go to college. Oh, listen to me. I'm making a speech."

Henry was smiling at her now, because he liked when she made speeches. He loved it when she'd get on a roll and totally forget about how she was supposed to act or what she was supposed to say. He loved that she didn't mind showing him her deepest soul—loved how easily they shared the big things with each other.

"Why are you grinning like that?" she asked.

"No reason," he said. "I like your speeches."

While she dressed and did her hair, they talked some more. They talked about where they'd live, since their current home wasn't big enough for a family. They talked about possible names for the kids—whether Sam was a better name for a boy or a girl, whether it made sense to name a boy Henry Jr.

The whole time they talked, Henry just sat on the edge of the bed, sometimes looking at her, sometimes not. Layla got the feeling that all he was doing was taking mental notes—that nothing dramatic was going to come out of this conversation, that he was just going to file away everything they talked about and consider it later, along with everything else. She was dying to ask him if she was right about her theory that he'd been soliciting advice from friends and acquaintances all week, but she didn't want to get too pushy. Besides, this morning's conversation had made her very happy, very encouraged.

She reminded herself not to call Gloria first thing and tell her about it. Maybe today she'd call Susan instead.

"So what are you doing today?" she asked.

"Going back to the library, I think," he said.

"The library?"

"Oh, I didn't tell you. I decided I'd spend a few hours every day at the library, thinking it might help me work without getting distracted. I got a lot of good work done on the book yesterday."

"Wow," she said, trying to conceal the disappointment she felt at having been wrong about the way he was spending his days. "That's great."

"Yeah, I'm starting to think I might have a shot to finish it in time after all."

"You always do," she said.

"So far, yeah. Then in the afternoon, I'm playing golf."

"Oh yeah?" she asked, confused now, wondering how he had so much time in his days.

"Yeah. Yesterday, I ran into one of the guys I played with Saturday and we went and played nine holes. He said he had an opening at twelve-thirty today, wanted to know if I wanted to play. So I said sure. Figure I'll get about three hours of writing done and then hit the links."

"This is one of the guys you keep getting drunk with?"

"Yes it is," Henry said. "But don't worry. I can't see that happening again today."

"Hey," she said. "Whatever. I'm not your mom."

"Yeah, maybe just two or three this afternoon," he said with a childish grin.

"All right, I'm going to be late if I don't go right now," she said.

"What? No breakfast?" he asked.

"No time," she said.

He looked at her disapprovingly.

"What?" she asked. "I ran out of time. Our talk was too good."

"Whatever," he said, following her downstairs.

"I promise I'll get a bagel or something at work," she said.

"Good," he said.

As he leaned in to kiss her, she saw him slip one of those fruit-and-cereal bars into her pocketbook.

"Love you, dear. Have a nice day," he said, affecting a 1960s TV sitcom falsetto.

"Love you," she said.

God help her, she did love him.

Fifteen

Henry watched as Big John went through his first-tee stretching routine, contorting his huge frame in ways Henry couldn't have imagined it would go. He slid his driver behind his lower back and twisted, six times to the left, six times to the right. He twirled the club over his head for almost a full minute. He touched his toes. He leaned back so far Henry thought he would either topple over or snap in half. He thought he heard something crack, but he wasn't sure. Might have been a squirrel on a branch.

"All right," Big John said. "All set. You all set?"

"Sure," Henry said, fearing the woeful inadequacy of his own warm-up routine. He'd taken three practice swings.

"All right," Big John bellowed. "We didn't keep score yesterday. Who had the low round Saturday?"

This time Henry laughed.

"Who the hell knows?" he asked. "I think by the end I was too drunk to read the scorecard."

"Aha!" John said. "That reminds me."

And he lumbered off in the direction of the clubhouse, leaving Henry to wonder what he was supposed to do. Was he supposed to go with him? Was he supposed to tee off? He looked out at the fairway, which was clear. He hoped nobody else would show up and want to play, because he wouldn't know what to tell them.

After about five minutes Big John came jogging back down the paved cart path from the clubhouse with a six-pack of beer in each hand.

"Oh, man," Henry said. "I don't know if I can do that again."

"Don't worry," Big John said. "We don't have to drink 'em all. We can bring some home. And hey, you never know who you might meet out there."

He flipped a cold, sweaty can to Henry, who, caught up in his new friend's aggressive joviality, cracked it open and took a swig. Tough to beat that taste on a hot day.

By the third hole they were talking about marriage again. Henry had confessed, on the first hole, to wimping out of his plan to get tough with Layla the night before. But he felt he had a good excuse, and Big John agreed.

"Yeah, that'll throw you off every time," Big John said. "The haircut."

On this day, Big John didn't seem as angry about life and the idea of marriage as he had the day before. But he was never short on interesting theories.

"Not everybody should get married," he said.

"You know, that sounds funny coming from you," Henry said.

"But I'm precisely the prime example of why some people shouldn't get married," Big John said.

He paused to put down his beer and take a huge swing with a six-iron at a ball buried deep in the rough. The ball sailed high into the air but didn't go far—a rare miss from

Big John, even on his third beer. He reached down to pick up the can, took a sip and flopped back behind the wheel of the cart. Henry, still nursing that first can, wondered if he would be better off driving the cart.

"I'm precisely the prime example," John repeated. "Most of those women I married, they shouldn't have got married. They weren't up for it. At least not the 'till death do us part' part of it."

"That does seem to be the heavy part," Henry said.

"Sure does," John said. "To me, that's the problem with the institution."

"What is?" Henry asked.

"The whole idea of it being a permanent, lifelong thing."

"Well, isn't that the whole point?"

"That's what they tell you, yeah. But when you think about it, it doesn't make any sense."

Henry hopped out of the cart, slid a five-iron out of his bag, took aim at the green, took one practice swing, and then hit his ball. It was a perfect shot that landed softly and rolled a few feet back toward where the pin was.

"Yeah!" Big John roared. "That calls for another cold one."

When Henry returned to the cart, another cold can of beer was waiting for him, replacing the little bit that was left in his original can, which had turned warm.

"Nice shot!" John said, still a bit too loud. "Nice ball!"

"Thanks," Henry said, reaching for the beer and taking a sip.

"Where were we?" John asked.

"Till death do us part," Henry said.

"Oh yeah. Doesn't make any sense, right? I mean, the whole concept of marriage is like two thousand years old. Back then, the human life expectancy was about what? Thirty?"

Henry was smiling. John kept talking.

"So, you get married at sixteen, seventeen, whatever, you

only have to be married for like fourteen, fifteen years. Am I right?"

"I guess," Henry said, enjoying the new perspective.

"Nowadays, people live into their eighties. You get married at twenty, you have to be married for sixty years! It doesn't even make any sense!"

Henry had never thought of it that way. He wondered if anyone besides Big John ever had.

"You know how they do it in South America?" Big John asked.

"Do what? Marriage?"

"Yeah. Marriage."

"No," Henry said. "I do not."

"In Peru, I think, or maybe it's Chile, when you go in for a marriage license, the judge or the justice of the peace or whoever does the thing, before he gives you the papers, he asks you, 'All right. How long do you want to be married?' And you can tell him two years, six years, ten years, whatever."

"Wow," Henry said. "Is that true?"

"Sure!" Big John said, driving the cart off the path and onto the grass for one scary second. "And I'll bet that's not the only place where they do it like that. Think about it, it makes sense. Marriage as a contract, like any other contract. You get a six-year deal, and at the end of it, you want to re-up, fine. But if it's not working out, you're sick of each other, the kids are moved away, whatever, you can just walk. No guilt, no messy divorce, no alimony, nothing."

In some way, Henry had to admit, John made a little bit of sense. Still, he couldn't escape the feeling that John was the wrong person to be talking about this.

"Let me ask you something," Henry said as John stood over his ball with a pitching wedge.

"Yeah?" John asked, not looking up.

"How many of those contracts would you have actually made it to the end of?"

John now had to step away from his ball, because he started laughing.

"That," he said, "is a good question."

Against his better judgment, Henry had begun helping Big John make a serious dent in the beer supply. They'd played nine holes and were now in the café, sipping fresh beers, eating hot dogs and debating whether to play the back nine. Henry looked up when he heard a familiar voice, and at the counter, ordering a Gatorade and a pack of peanut butter crackers, was his friend Pete Gresham.

This struck Henry as strange, since it was a Wednesday afternoon, and Pete should have been at work—or at least taking a late lunch at Friendly's.

"Pete?" he said, prompting Big John to look up and in the direction of the counter.

Pete turned around.

"Hey, man!" he said, genuinely surprised to see Henry. "What's going on?"

"Not much," Henry said. "Just banging the ball around, you know."

Henry introduced John and Pete, who shook hands. Pete sat down at their table.

"Yeah, I just knocked off work early, figured I'd see if I could get nine holes in," he said. "You guys going or coming?"

"Kind of both," Henry said. "We just played the front, and we're deciding whether to play the back."

"Well, if you decide to play the back, you mind if I tag along?"

They did not mind, and they did decide to play the back nine. Now a threesome, they headed back out toward the tenth tee. Pete stopped to pick up his bag. His woods were adorned with colorful head covers, each one representing a different superhero member of the Justice League.

They looked brand new.

"Pete, I didn't think you played anymore," Henry said.

"I don't get out too much—not as much as I'd like to," Pete said. "But sometimes I feel like it's a good place to do some thinking."

"Oh yeah?" Henry said, wondering when was the last time Big John had been silent for this long.

"Yeah," Pete said. "Catherine's being kind of a pain these days. She's starting to bug me about the posters again."

Now Big John looked inquisitive, and Henry and Pete offered a brief explanation of the posters. The explanation amused Big John and loosened him up, and he offered Pete a heavy slap on the back and a fresh, cold can of beer. Pete shrugged and opened the beer.

"See, Pete, if you want marital advice, John's your man," Henry said. "I've never met anybody with more experience."

By the fourteenth hole Big John had Pete practically doubled over in laughter at his lengthy and fascinating marital history. Henry enjoyed the retelling of the stories of the many wives of Big John, since there were a few details he'd either forgotten or that had been omitted the first time. Five holes into the back nine, Henry and John were pretty much tanked, and Pete had done a fair job of catching up with them. Henry figured he shouldn't be surprised that drunken golf on a Wednesday afternoon was something that appealed to Pete. He seemed to draw particular joy from the many times he sneaked behind trees or bushes to urinate.

Zipping up as he rushed to join them on the fifteenth tee, Pete called out to Henry.

"So," he said. "What's the deal with you and Layla? You getting married or not?"

"This guy don't beat around the bush, does he?" Big John asked.

"Not so much, no," Henry said, lining up his tee shot and trying to focus on a spot in the fairway. "You'd think he could wait until a guy hits his ball, huh?"

"You'll be lucky not to miss that ball anyway," Pete said, reclining on the concrete bench next to the tee box, his feet up on his bag, the Green Lantern head cover adorning the driver he held in his hands and pointed at his friend.

Determined now, Henry bore down and tried his very best to make clean, solid contact with the ball. He topped it. It rolled about sixty yards straight away from the tee box.

"See?" Pete said.

"Hey," Henry said. "At least it was straight this time."

After Pete hit his ball, he broached the subject again.

"Seriously, man," he said. "I've been meaning to ask you. How's it going with that? She still on your case?"

"She's not really on my case," Henry said. "I mean, it's not like she's been pestering me about this nonstop. She just mentioned Saturday morning that she needs an answer in a week. Actually, we've been getting along pretty well this week."

Pete snickered.

"Nice," Henry said. "That's not what I meant."

"Oh no? Not getting any, huh?"

Henry shook his head as he leaned over to hit his second shot. This time he dug the ball out of the rough with a four-iron and sent it sailing well down the fairway.

"Nice shot," Pete said.

"Thanks."

The two friends were alone, because Big John had taken the cart to the distant location to which his uncharacteristically erratic tee shot had sliced—well past the fairway of the next hole over. They wondered if they'd ever see him again, or if this might be the time he finally wrapped his cart around a tree.

"I'd miss him," Henry said, staring out at a spot where Big John might or might not be, beyond the trees.

"How long have you two known each other?" Pete asked.

"Since Saturday," Henry said. "But we're very close."

"Hey, maybe you should marry him instead of Layla."

"Maybe, Pete. Maybe."

They strolled up the fairway to where Pete's ball had settled after an incredibly lucky bounce off of a huge maple tree that sat well to the left of the target area. Henry began talking again about Layla.

"I just can't figure out what I'm supposed to do," he said.

"What do you mean?" Pete asked, rolling his ball over with the top of his club, making sure it had the Batman logo that identified it as one of his.

"Well, it seems like the easy thing to do—propose, get married, all that," Henry said. "I mean, it's been six years, it's been nice, most people get married before they get to this point."

"All true," Pete said, lining up his shot.

Henry waited for him to hit the ball, which he barely did, sending it skidding into a sand trap about twenty-five yards away and to the right.

"Just missed that one," Henry said.

"Yeah. I was right on it," Pete deadpanned.

"It's just . . . I don't know," Henry said. "I can't figure out how it's supposed to feel. I mean, I think about getting married and spending the rest of my life married and settling down and buying a house and having kids and sending them to school, and I'm just not sure I can handle all of that."

"Talking to the wrong guy here, Henry," Pete said.

"Yeah, I know," Henry said. "But you're the only guy here. Big John may be dead."

"Sad," Pete said.

"And then there's the question of whether I can even afford all of that stuff," Henry said.

"What do you mean?"

"Well, in case you hadn't noticed, Pete, I don't exactly have a steady job. I mean, if I can't finish this book, or if I can't come up with an idea for the next one, it's going to be a while before my next paycheck. You think Layla can handle living like that?"

"Well, yeah," Pete said. "I mean, doesn't she make enough for both of you?"

Henry sighed and looked up the fairway.

"I guess I just wonder why things can't be the same as they are," he said. "I mean, what's wrong with what we've got?"

Pete seemed to think about this for a while. Or else he was just scratching an especially nasty mosquito bite on his left elbow for a while. Finally, as they stood there waiting to see if Big John was coming back, Pete spoke.

"I guess that's not really the issue," he said.

"What's that?"

"I guess that's not the question you're dealing with, Henry," Pete said.

"It's not?"

"Not really. I mean, things can stay the way they are. You guys get married, your lives aren't going to change that much. Yeah, maybe you have kids, but that's more like the next natural progression—you know, for some people."

They watched a ball sail onto the green, bounce once, and roll over the back. They assumed it meant Big John was alive, well, and still firing away at the hole from his remote location.

"I'm not sure I see where you're going with this," Henry said.

"Well, you've got to give me a minute," Pete said. "I'm a little drunk."

"All right. Take your time."

"See," Pete said. "The way I look at it, your life is going to stay pretty much the same. You already live together. You don't date other people. It's not like the night before you get married you're going to go out and sniff cocaine off the bare ass of some off-duty stripper while you're hanging out the sun roof of a stolen Mercedes speeding up the highway at a hundred and ten miles an hour."

"Right. What movie was that from again?"

"Harold and Kumar Go to White Castle."

"Jesus, you see some crappy movies," Henry said.

"Come on!" Pete protested. "It's the guy from Doogie Howser, playing himself, hanging out the sun roof of a stolen Mercedes snorting cocaine off the bare ass of an off-duty stripper!"

"All right, all right. Get to the point."

By now they'd arrived at the green, having found a way, in spite of their high levels of intoxication and relative lack of natural ability, to navigate their balls to the putting surface. They stared into the distance, watching Big John bounce the cart down a frighteningly steep hill, swerving around pine trees with shocking agility.

"Well," Pete said, "I guess the decision you have to make is not whether you want things to stay the same, but whether you're ready to decide, right now, at age twenty-eight or whatever you are—"

"Thirty," Henry said.

"Thirty, whatever. You have to figure out if you're ready to decide that you want things to stay the same for the rest of your life. That, my friend, is your decision."

And neither one looked at the other, because they were both watching Big John's cart careen down the hill. Somewhere, while Pete was speaking, it became clear that Big John had lost control of the cart. Now, profanities were streaming from his mouth and the cart appeared to be picking up speed, bouncing higher. Golfers all over the course had turned to watch. For a few breathless seconds all activity in Bergen County seemed to cease except for that involving Big John, the cart, and the terrifying, inevitable power of gravity.

And then, with one last huge bounce, the cart sailed into the air and came down—on its wheels, thankfully—in the middle of the stream that ran in front of the fifteenth green. When it landed, it tipped slowly over, tumbling onto the driver's side as its driver tumbled out. Henry could swear he saw a beer in John's hand, and he figured that couldn't possibly help the big man's case, assuming he'd have to make one.

Silence fell across the course as everyone who'd seen the disaster stared at the toppled cart. Finally, after what seemed a second too long, Big John stood up, dripping with mud and green algae, raised a hand over his head and bellowed, "I'm all right."

Pete and Henry were still staring at the scene. Somewhere on the course, somebody began to applaud. Others laughed. Pete and Henry just stared, until Pete turned around to look at his friend.

"Either that," Pete said. "Or you could turn into that guy."

Henry didn't look at Pete. But he heard him. Loud and clear.

Sixteen

Layla left the house in such a good mood, and within ninety minutes could barely remember what it had felt like.

Her first stop had been the Acura dealership, where once again she was told she would not be getting her car back that day and that the mechanics had no idea when she would. Something about a part they had to order, which she figured was what they always said when they either couldn't figure out what was wrong, had forgotten completely that they were supposed to be working on her car, or were just too lazy to get to it. She'd aired out the guy at the front counter at the service department, and he offered apology after apology that failed to satisfy her.

When she got back into the loaner and headed for work, she began to feel good again. Her plan was to call Susan—not Gloria—and tell her about the morning she'd spent with Henry. She felt great, totally encouraged. The only times all morning she'd even thought about Ben were when she caught a glimpse of her new hair, reflected in a mirror or in the window of the Acura service department lobby. For the first time since Saturday, she believed her plan might actually be working, and that romance and drama might await her in Maine this weekend.

She began to picture how Henry would go about it. Would he get on one knee? Would he do it in private, when it was just the two of them together in the hotel room? Would he ask her to go for a walk on the beach, and do it there?

Her reverie was cut off by the sound of a honking horn, as the car behind her decided she was driving too slowly for the lane. She flashed the driver a middle finger as he raced past her after she moved over, and he laughed, which made her even angrier. She felt a little embarrassed because of what she'd been thinking about. Had Gloria been there—"there," in this case, being her imagination—she would undoubtedly have told her she was getting ahead of herself. And she'd have been right. Things appeared to be going well enough that there was no reason to screw around with them—no reason to do anything that might jinx her desired outcome.

Another horn, and Layla threw up her hands in disgust. Finally, the exit for her office was coming up, and she wouldn't have to put up with these people anymore.

Layla made a cheerier entrance to the office than she had on the previous two days. She greeted the receptionist with a smile and asked how she was doing. She waved at Paula, who was on the phone in her own office. And when she got to her desk, she thought for a second about leaving the door open today.

But then she decided not to, shut the door and dialed Susan's number. Susan picked up on the third ring, and Layla launched immediately into her story about the sweet morning she and Henry had spent together.

Susan listened, saying nothing, and when Layla finished, asked, "So that's it?"

Layla began to worry. "Yeah," she said. "What do you mean?"

"Geez, Lay," Susan said. "I don't know. Sounds to me like he might be scared."

"Oh, I'm sorry," Layla practically shouted, standing up out of her chair, "*Gloria!*"

"Lay—" Susan tried.

"I thought I dialed *Susan!*" Layla barked. "I must have made a mistake!"

And she slammed down the phone and fell back into her chair.

Nice day so far, she thought.

The phone buzzed. She pressed the intercom button.

"Layla?" It was one of the secretaries in the outer office.

"Yeah," she muttered, trying to convey her annoyance at having her angry fit interrupted.

"Jessica wants to see you right away."

Oh yeah. Real, real nice day so far.

Jessica Standridge was dressed impeccably, as she always was. She wore a bone-colored suit and an astounding pair of diamond earrings that made Layla wonder if they were visible from space. She spent the first two minutes that Layla was in her office simply staring at her, as if trying to detect something in Layla's face, or hair, or the new black pumps she'd bought the day before with Gloria and Susan.

Attempting to fend off the awkwardness, Layla focused on the wall behind her boss. Family pictures with the husband and the kids offered heretofore absent proof that Jessica Standridge could, indeed, smile. They were interspersed with Jessica's degrees and diplomas. Princeton undergrad, Yale law school. Jesus. Was there anything about this woman that wasn't intimidating?

"You got your hair cut," Jessica finally said, as if answering a trivia question.

Layla never knew what the correct response was to anything Jessica said.

"I did," she guessed.

Jessica nodded, kept on staring. She was leaning back in a huge black leather chair, her hands folded in front of her face. Jessica was no longer staring at her, but instead was looking over her shoulder, as if an executioner were there, waiting for the go-ahead, and she was pondering it.

"What's going on around here, Layla?" Jessica asked.

This time, Layla was truly stunned. She had no idea what her boss could be talking about. Her facial expression must have shown it.

"What I mean is, is there something wrong?" Jessica pressed.

Layla still didn't know what to say.

"All right," Jessica said. "Either you don't know what I'm talking about or you need me to spell it out before you'll admit anything."

"I . . ." Layla said, but could say no more.

"You've disappeared the last two afternoons, with no explanation . . ."

"Monday, I had court—" Layla began to protest.

Jessica cut her off. "You've come in late every day this week . . ."

"My car—"

" . . . you've been shutting the door to your office, gabbing on the phone with your friends. You show up today with new clothes, new shoes, and a new haircut."

Layla had no idea that Jessica Standridge paid such close attention to her. She was kind of flattered.

"I'll tell you what I'm seeing here," Jessica said. "I'm seeing somebody whose personal life is having an impact on her work."

Layla gaped. "Oh, Jessica, I would never let . . ." she said, and just trailed off.

"All right," Jessica said again. "Let's get it all out on the table. I know you don't like me."

"No, that's not—"

"I know I've been hard on you sometimes," Jessica continued, "and that I haven't let you know any of this before, but I actually think you're one of the most talented people in this firm."

"Thank you," Layla offered, wondering where this was all going.

"The reason I'm hard on you is that I expect big things from you. I think you're as sharp and as talented as any young attorney that's come through here since I've been a partner. I think you're outstanding in court. And your work in here is always impeccable."

Layla smiled. She'd always known it would be worth working extra hard on the assignments that Jessica had given her.

"So, that's your problem right now," Jessica said. "When somebody who never makes mistakes starts turning in shoddy paperwork, it's easy to figure out that she's distracted by something."

At this point Jessica slid a file across her desk at Layla, who picked it up and opened it. There were markings in red pen all over the first page. And the second. She felt like she was back in school and had failed a test.

Jessica kept talking.

"So," she said, getting up out of her chair, walking around Layla and across the room to shut the door to her office. "I'll ask you again. Is there anything going on that you want to talk about?"

And Jessica sat on the edge of her desk, folded her hands in her lap, looked down at Layla and smiled.

And then Layla started talking.

* * *

She didn't know what had come over her. Maybe it was the result of all the compliments Jessica had paid her. Maybe it was the smile. Whatever it was, out of nowhere she began pouring out the whole story of her and Henry. She talked about how they met in college, how they decided to move in together, how they'd dated exclusively for six years, and how, four days earlier, she'd given him a one-week deadline to pop the question or quit the whole thing for good. She mentioned Ben (though not by name, just in case Jessica knew him), and talked about how strange she felt to already have a date set up for next week, in case things didn't work out.

To Layla's surprise, Jessica didn't speak during the entire monologue. She appeared genuinely intrigued, entertained and sympathetic. Only when Layla finished did she realize what she'd done—how raw and exposed she'd just been in front of a woman for whom she'd always put on her most effective masks. She looked at the floor and blushed.

"I'm sorry," she said. "I don't know where that all came from."

Jessica didn't say anything for a few seconds. Neither of them did. Layla didn't look up until she finally heard Jessica's voice.

"So," Jessica said. "He's got three more days to decide, or else you walk?"

"Yup," Layla gulped, momentarily stunned by the stark terms Jessica had just assigned to her plan.

"Wow," Jessica said. "That's a lot gutsier than anything I'd ever do."

Now, Layla looked right into her boss's eyes. Her own were trying hard not to well up with tears. The morning had been an emotional wringer, and now she was about to hear something from Jessica Standridge that she'd always dreamed but never expected she would hear.

"I'm impressed," Jessica said.

The clock was creeping close to eleven A.M. Layla wondered how it was possible that Jessica's phone had not rung at least once since she'd been in the office. She wondered if Jessica had cleared her entire morning just for her. She wondered if Jessica had even more wisdom than she had always ascribed to her and foreseen the entire conversation. She wondered if she'd ever look at her boss the same way again. She figured she wouldn't.

"Let me tell you a story," Jessica said.

"Okay," Layla said, finally composed.

"It's about me and my husband, Arthur. Well, before he was my husband."

Layla couldn't wait for this one. Plus, she was tired of talking. She was all set to listen.

"Way back, a hundred years ago, when Arthur and I were dating, the one thing we never talked about was getting married," Jessica said. "We went out for about two and a half years, and a couple of times we talked in general terms about having kids or families, that kind of thing, but never specifics, and never anything about actually getting married.

"I always figured it was understood—that at some point he'd pop the question and we'd get married and start our family. After about a year of going out, you start to think that way, whether you talk about it or not. Right?"

Layla chuckled her agreement.

"Well, like I said, we'd been dating about two and a half years when, one night, we were out at this bar on the Upper East Side with some friends of his. Some guy he knew from work and his girlfriend. I remember his name. Dan Friedman. I'll never forget Dan Friedman.

"Anyway, at one point on this night, Dan's girlfriend was in the bathroom or something, and Arthur was taking a long time getting the next round of drinks at the bar. And Dan and I were talking, and I asked him about this girl, and how serious it was. And I remember him laughing and saying he never dated anybody seriously, that he was determined to never get married and to live his life as a bachelor in Manhattan. Said he'd never found anything he liked doing as much as he liked that.

"And then, I remember, he looked over at the bar, where Arthur was, and he said—I'll never forget this—'He'll never get married either.'"

"Wow," Layla said.

"I know!" Jessica said. "Can you imagine saying that to somebody's girlfriend?"

"The guy must have been drunk," Layla said.

"Anyway," Jessica went on, "Arthur came back from the bar, and things were kind of awkward. And he and I had a big fight that night. And I never said anything about getting married, because I was always afraid that having that talk would be the thing that drove him away, you know?"

Oh, I know, Layla thought.

"But things were strange for a month after that. I remember, we had a lot of fights and arguments, and I didn't like the way he was acting. I started to get very suspicious, very jealous, wondering how he was spending his time when we weren't together. It was awful, and the whole reason was that I put some faith into what this guy Dan Friedman told me at a bar one night."

"I'm guessing it all worked out," Layla said, smiling and gesturing toward the pictures on the wall.

"You know what happened?" Jessica asked. "A month after that night in the bar, he proposed. I got home from work, and there he was, on one knee, the apartment in candlelight, roses on the table, champagne on ice. Like out of a dream. Turns out, he'd been planning it for months. He'd already gone shopping for the ring before that night in the bar. Dan Friedman had no idea what he was talking about."

"Wow," Layla said.

"So, I'll bet you're wondering what my point was in telling you that story," Jessica said.

Man, Layla thought, maybe she really can read minds.

"I'm not sure, Layla," Jessica said. "Maybe it's that you can't control what he's going to do, especially not while you're in here. While you're in here, I need you to be focused on work. I'm sorry you're having a situation in your personal life, and as you can see, I can sympathize. But I need you, when you're in here, to be in here—not drifting away out there. Okay?"

"I promise," Layla said.

"Good," Jessica said, reverting now to the formality that had always existed between them.

Layla began to leave the room, but Jessica stopped her.

"Do you really love him?" she asked, looking at something on her desk.

"Yeah," Layla said. "I really do."

"Well, then," Jessica said, "God help you. There's really not a lot you can do."

Seventeen

"I can't believe the Dragon Lady has a heart," Gloria was saying, looking out at the crowded bar from her perch atop one of three tall stools surrounding a table increasingly cluttered with Coors Light bottles. "That's some story."

Layla was laughing as she recounted her day to her friends. She was glad Susan had made it, since—in spite of about fifteen apologies and acceptances—she was still upset about the way she'd treated her on the phone that morning. Susan insisted that no more be made of it, and Layla managed to go about ten whole minutes without mentioning it, so maybe there was hope.

"How about him?" Susan asked, her right hand strangling the neck of one of the bottles, her nose pointed in the direction of a dark-haired young guy in a blue-striped T-shirt.

"Yuck," Gloria said. "Goatee. No good."

Layla checked out the guy in the striped shirt.

"He's a kid, for God's sake!" she said.

"Hey," Susan said. "Don't knock it. Sometimes all they need is the right teacher."

It was part of Susan's charm that she could not say something like this with a straight face, or even get all the words out without getting embarrassed and laughing. And the fact that they were on their fourth round of beers and hadn't yet paid for a single one contributed to the silliness. All three of them laughed so hard at Susan's proclamation that they feared they would tumble from the stools. They drew more than one glance from nearby tables and people at the bar.

"Ooh," Gloria said, interrupting the gaiety with a slurred attempt to be serious. "How about them, over there?"

She was nodding—not too discreetly, Layla thought—in the direction of three tall blond guys in long shorts and brown sandals. Layla had to admit, all three of them looked as if they'd just come from a J. Crew catalog shoot. Almost as if they weren't real. Which, for her purposes, was perfect.

"Perfect," she said out loud. "Whose turn is it?"

"It is Gloria's turn," Susan said, pointing a shaky finger at Gloria. "And besides, she needs to make up for the last time."

"Hey!" Gloria said. "It worked out fine, didn't it?"

"The guy asked you if you needed help," Layla said. "He thought there was something wrong with you."

"All right," Gloria said. "One mistake. I'll make up for it. Watch."

Susan and Layla sat back as Gloria began the process of trying to make eye contact with one of the J. Crew triplets. The game required one of them to rope a guy or a group of guys into buying them drinks, and so far it had worked four times (in spite of Gloria's apparently painful-looking facial contortions on her first attempt), and smoothly enough that none of the guys had stuck around for more than about a half hour. They'd decided, somehow, that there was an art to getting these guys to buy them drinks with no promise of anything to follow, and they were congratulating themselves profusely as they guzzled light beers.

Layla was having a blast. The day had recovered brilliantly from its bad start. Jessica Standridge, whose story was either inspirational or discouraging (she couldn't decide), was the unquestioned star of the day. No matter what happened in her personal life over the next few days, she would always feel better and more confident in that office from now on. And that was something, wasn't it?

It was something she'd chosen to help comfort her when she arrived home to find Henry passed out on the sofa, smelling strongly of beer and a golf course. She hadn't been angry, or even surprised. Henry was dealing with writer's block, which always threw him for a loop, on top of the ultimatum, and erratic behavior was to be expected. The booze was the only thing about it that she didn't like, but she figured it was unlikely that he'd developed into a full-blown alcoholic in half a week. She was annoyed, of course, since she'd come home hoping for a continuation of their morning conversation, and she was disappointed that there were no roses, candlelight, champagne, or engagement ring. But rather than wake him up and start a fight, she called Susan to apologize again and to ask if she was up for a night on the town. Susan was very much up for it, and so was Gloria, and now here they were, trying to flag down hot young guys to buy them drinks.

"Jesus, Gloria," Layla said, watching her friend contort her eyebrows into strange and frightening shapes. "Is that supposed to be sexy?"

"Screw you," Gloria said, somehow remaining focused.

Across the room, all three J. Crew guys looked very confused.

* * *

A few minutes later, the triplets having represented the evening's first failure, Gloria was trying to change the subject.

"So, Henry was drunk again?" she asked Layla.

"Yeah," Layla said. "I didn't see this coming. Now watch. He'll propose, and I'll have to say yes, and I'll end up married to an alcoholic, and it'll be all my fault."

"Man, if I had a nickel for every time I heard that story," Susan said, speaking into her beer bottle.

"Susan," Layla said. "I think you've had too much to drink."

"How could you tell?" Susan asked.

"You're not usually this funny."

Layla wasn't sure, but it was possible that beer squirted out of Gloria's nose. And her timing couldn't have been a lot worse, because, right after Gloria's snort, the next sound they heard was a male voice.

"Excuse me," it said, with a slight Latin accent.

All three looked up at once and could have sworn they were looking at the second coming of Antonio Banderas. Not one of them could think of a single thing to say.

He seemed to be addressing all three of them, but he never took his eyes off Layla.

"I was noticing you from the bar," he said. "You seem to be having a very good time."

"Oh, we're just having a girls' night out," Layla said, meeting Antonio's gaze with all the boldness that four beers could bring.

"Girls' night out," he repeated. "Very nice. So my friends and I were wondering if you would mind if we bought you a drink."

"Are your friends as cute as you are?" Susan asked, swaying slightly.

Antonio smiled. He had dimples. Dimples to go with that wavy black hair, that dark skin, that two-day stubble.

"No," he said. "But they're pretty cute."

"Wow," Gloria said, as if watching the end of a fireworks display. "Wow."

Layla believed she was still capable of reasonable conversation. Plus, he was still looking at her, and not the other two. So she took the lead.

"Sure," she said. "Bring 'em over. We're drinking Coors Light."

He smiled again and walked back toward the bar. Susan stared at his rear end as if it had crucial safety instructions on it.

"Well," Layla said. "I think this one goes on my record."

"Yeah," Gloria said. "No kidding."

"It's the legs," Susan said. "Those legs are a sure thing. I told you it was a good idea to have her sit on the outside."

Layla smiled and touched her own hair.

"You guys sure it's not the new haircut?" she asked.

She was having a very good time.

It took a while to dispatch Antonio (whose real name was George, but who would forever be Antonio in their memories) and his friends (who were, as advertised, pretty cute). But dispatch them they did. That was, after all, part of the game. Had the guys stayed for the rest of the night, Layla believed, she would be considered the loser. As it stood, once they left, Gloria was the clear loser, since she was only one-for-two, and the one was questionable at best.

"There go three of the greatest butts in New Jersey," Susan said as the three guys headed off for the pool tables, the gals having made their lack of interest clear.

"Amen," Gloria said.

It was past midnight now, and while none of them said it, the game was clearly over. Everybody had to go to work in the morning, and Layla was determined not to be late on the day after she and Jessica Standridge had—sort of—

bonded. They ordered a round of ice waters and decided to have a couple of them before driving home. Gloria ordered coffee.

"So, Gloria," Layla said, squeezing a lemon into her water before taking a sip. "What's up with you and this guy?"

"Guy?" Gloria asked. "What guy?"

"You said there was some guy who wouldn't leave you alone," Layla said. Her censor had clearly drowned. She didn't mean to make Gloria uncomfortable, but her curiosity suddenly had no check on it.

"Oh," Gloria said. "Yeah."

Layla and Susan shared a look. The last time Layla had checked, Gloria was dating about four different men, none of whom had the power to affect her mood even slightly. Her biggest problem, as far as Layla could tell, was a scheduling one, and her lack of concern for each man's feelings was a helpful tool in navigating those troubles. If one of them called and she was busy with another, she'd just tell the truth. If the guy wanted to walk, then so be it. And they never did. Gloria liked men she could bully.

But this look on Gloria's face was new. This, Layla knew, meant that something was going on that was troubling her friend. And that meant that somebody had penetrated the emotional fence.

"Something you want to talk about?" Layla asked.

And Gloria sighed, making Layla and Susan wonder if she was going to say anything. Right before Layla was about to tell her it was all right not to say anything, Gloria started talking again.

"His name is Andy," she said.

"Oh?" Susan asked, looking again at Layla. They were thinking the same thing. Among the four simultaneous boyfriends, there was no Andy of whom they were aware.

"Yeah," Gloria said to her glass. "And he's married."

"Oh," Layla and Susan said at the same time.

Gloria spent the next half hour recounting her chance meeting with Andy, on a weekend retreat she'd taken with her firm three weeks earlier. She didn't work with him—he'd been staying at the same hotel on other business—but they met one night in the bar and went to bed together. In the morning, while they were still naked, he'd told her he was married, and she stormed out. He followed her around the hotel for the rest of the weekend, trying to explain, and somehow he obtained some of her personal information, either from the hotel or from somebody at her firm. When she returned home, he began calling her, first every day and then two, three times a day.

"He's a stalker," Susan said.

"Yeah," Gloria said, with a touch of sadness that seemed out of place.

"Something else to this?" Layla asked.

"Yeah," Gloria sighed again. "There is."

Layla and Susan waited for the next part of the story, wondered when it would come.

"I think I screwed this one up," Gloria said. "I think I really like him."

And that was not something that ever happened—not to Gloria.

This, Layla thought, is some kind of strange week.

Henry woke when he heard her come in, opening one eye to read the red digital clock on the cable box. It told him it was quarter to one in the morning, and he smiled. He'd finally driven her to drink.

Quickly, though, he got rid of the smile and closed his eye. He didn't want her to know he was awake. Wanted to see what she was like when she didn't think he was paying attention.

"Sure," he heard her whisper. "Couch again."

He couldn't tell if she was upset, but she sure did sound

drunk. He didn't like the idea of her having driven home drunk from a bar, but who was he to talk? He was on track for the single-week drunk-driving record for the state of New Jersey.

"Oh," she said, in mock surprise. "What a nice note you left me, explaining your condition. How sweet of you, honey!"

He smiled again. He hadn't left a note. She was cute when she was annoyed. His head hurt, but he was determined to continue his experiment.

Layla dropped her pocketbook on the table and her keys on the floor, turned off one light and turned on another, accidentally. Then she staggered up the stairs in black heels Henry didn't think he'd ever seen before. He heard her fiddling around upstairs for a few minutes, heard the water run as she brushed her teeth, heard her climb into bed, saw the light go out. He lay there a few minutes, knowing how quickly she fell asleep when sober, figured it wouldn't take a minute tonight. But he wanted to be safe. He watched the clock. At one-fifteen he rose from the couch, went into the kitchen to swallow two Advils, turned off the light she'd inadvertently left on, and headed upstairs in the dark.

When he got to their bedroom, he saw her, looking ghostly in the dark. She was wearing a white tank top and gym shorts, and one of her legs was sticking out from under the sheets. Carefully, he tucked it back under and smoothed the blankets over her. He looked at her there, snoring softly. He looked at her hair, her shoulders, her little nose. He looked at her lips as they fluttered slightly to allow the snores to escape. He smiled to himself.

He loved every single thing about her.

PART VI

Thursday

Eighteen

Before long the words ran together, sounded like gibberish and faded out of the conscious realm, which is the way Henry figured it must have felt for the people who worked here.

"Iced venti no-whip vanilla latte."

"Grande skim mocha."

"Venti soy caramel macchiato."

You never heard anything like this at the library, Henry mused. But today, for reasons not specified by the very disappointing sign on its front door, the library was closed. And so he had set up shop in a Starbucks on Route 17. He'd always seen people sitting there, working on their laptop computers, and he figured nobody would mind if he wanted to spend his morning typing out a couple of chapters while the world around him continued its pursuit of the perfect novelty beverage.

"Tall no-whip mint mocha chip Frappuccino."

"Venti iced coffee."

The barely interested calls of the folks making the stuff mixed in with the whir of the blenders crushing ice for the summertime coffee beverages that had, Henry believed, taken Starbucks to a dazzling next level. They probably would have done just fine serving hot coffee drinks all summer, since people who are hooked on coffee drink it year-round. But by adding the frozen drinks, most of which were basically liquid desserts, they'd brought in a whole new faction of people who might not otherwise be tempted to stop and spend four dollars on a cup of coffee on their way to work or school or to wherever people were on the way at ten in the morning on a Thursday in the middle of June.

His first stop had been the jewelry store—the one where he'd spent his Tuesday afternoon after prying a recommendation out of his embittered brother. Jake had a personal friend who ran a small jewelry shop in Paramus, and Henry had gone there Tuesday to pick out the ring he planned to offer to Layla tonight. The guy had told him to come back Thursday to pick it up, so he was there when the store opened. But the ring, the guy informed him, was not yet ready. Should be ready by the afternoon, definitely by five. A bad, sick feeling had started to take form in Henry's stomach at the thought that the day might not go exactly as planned, but he played it cool and told the guy he'd check back in the afternoon. That's when he decided to spend some time writing, which was how he'd ended up at Starbucks.

But he was distracted here. There was Internet access at Starbucks, which meant he could check his e-mail, surf the Web, and peruse the box scores from the previous night's baseball games—something he'd been doing the past few days since Layla's father had enlightened him about the deeper meaning of the game. He would write for a while—short, fun, successful bursts—but then something would snap him out of it. A kid walked in with his mother. The mother went to the counter to order. The kid stood in front of his table, dribbling a large blue ball on the floor as he waited for his mother to return. He was staring at Henry, who tried not to stare back. The ball was really distracting.

"Grande vanilla bean Frappuccino."

"Grande coffee light Frappuccino and a tall strawberry."

"Iced decaf grande latte."

Henry remembered reading somewhere that there were something like thirty thousand different ways to order a Starbucks coffee. He no longer doubted it.

He looked around the store—spacious and airy, this one, which is why he'd picked it. He didn't want to sit in one of the ones that was dark and closetlike. He didn't want to feel as if he were keeping somebody else from having a table if they wanted it. And in between his writing, he liked to watch people.

The woman who had just walked in, for instance, looked familiar.

For good reason, it turned out.

"Henry?" she asked.

"Gloria," Henry said. "How are you?"

"Fine," Gloria said. She hadn't yet taken her sunglasses off, even though she was now inside. "How are you?"

"Oh, I'm fine," Henry said. "Just getting some writing done. I've been blocked. Figured I'd try a change of scenery."

"Sounds like a good idea," she said.

"So," Henry said, "were you out with Layla last night?"

"Why?" Gloria said, smiling. "What'd she tell you?"

"Oh, nothing," he said. "I was still sleeping when she left this morning. But I figured it must have been some girls' night out or something like that."

"Yeah," Gloria said. "We were just over at Tuxedo's. Had a few drinks. Nothing too major."

Even with the sunglasses as shield, Gloria was trying hard not to look at him while she spoke. Not a suspicious person generally, Henry began to wonder if something was going on that he should be concerned about.

Neither one spoke for a while.

"Tall latte."

"Tall iced latte."

"Grande black-and-white mocha Frappuccino."

Finally, Gloria said, "I'm going to go order," and she did. She looked back at him twice while she waited for her drink, and he hadn't yet gone back to his writing.

"You taking a break?" she asked when she got her drink; he hadn't heard what it was.

"Kind of," he said. "I guess. Waiting for my next inspiration to strike."

"You mind if I sit with you for a minute?" Gloria asked. "I'm meeting somebody here, and I'm kind of nervous about it."

Henry looked up in surprise. He'd never known Gloria to be nervous about anything.

"Sure," he said. "Have a seat."

Gloria sat down, and Henry wondered if she were going to fill him in. It did not appear so.

"You guys driving up in the morning?" she asked.

"Yeah," he said. "Got to get home and pack this afternoon. We're hoping to get on the road by seven or eight, get there in time for a late lunch, maybe."

"Sounds good," Gloria said. "I think we'll be right behind you."

"You and Susan carpooling? Going stag?" Henry asked.

She looked at the floor, an uninteresting collection of brown, beige, and blue squares, and Henry realized he'd said something he probably shouldn't have said.

"I'm sorry," he said.

"That's all right," Gloria insisted, looking back up now, her sunglasses still on. "I'm fine. Just a little hung over, I guess."

Another silent minute passed between them. Henry pretended to look at some notes he kept next to the computer. His ever-changing "outline."

"Tall skim caramel latte."

"Venti iced skim no-whip mocha."

"Grande mocha Frappuccino with vanilla syrup."

"Hey, can I ask you something?" Henry asked.

"Sure," Gloria said, sipping her drink, looking out the window.

"How much does Layla tell you?" he asked. "I mean, about what's going on . . . with us?"

Gloria was looking at him now, and Henry could tell in spite of the sunglasses. She didn't smile. She looked pretty serious, actually.

"She tells us everything, Henry," he said.

"Everything?"

"Yeah. Everything."

"Wow," he said.

"Yeah," Gloria said. "Sorry."

"So, what do you . . . I mean . . . what do you think about, you know, all of this?" Henry asked.

Gloria took another sip. She looked at the side door, through which a medium-tall man with light brown hair and a tan business suit had just walked. She raised her hand to signal to him. He spotted her after a second, looked confused to see her sitting with someone, and stopped in his tracks. She rose from her chair and looked back at Henry.

"I think you're a great guy, Henry," she said. "I really do."

And that was it. She walked away, met the guy who'd come through the door. Gave him a peck on the cheek as he strained to look over her shoulder, still confused, at Henry.

Henry was confused too. The feeling in his stomach was getting worse.

"Definitely by five. You have nothing to worry about."

That's what the jewelry store guy had said to him when

he checked back at two o'clock to see if the ring was ready. Assured that he had nothing to worry about, Henry nevertheless began worrying about everything. He had other errands to run—he wanted to get flowers, maybe a bottle of wine. He wanted to get home to find the CD he intended to have playing when she came home from work. But all of the peripheral stuff was dependent on the ring. If there was no ring, there was no need for flowers, music, or wine. If there was no ring, the whole plan had to be postponed, and the deadline took on greater significance.

Momentarily, he got angry with Layla for the deadline, since it had applied too much pressure to this plan. Without the deadline, if the ring wasn't ready, he could just hold off until next week to spring his surprise. Now, if the ring wasn't ready, he could still pop the question this weekend, but he'd have to do it without a ring. He doubted she'd mind very much, but still. There should be a ring to go with that question. If that's how he pictured it, he had no doubt that was how she pictured it too.

But he recognized his role in the fiasco too. He probably should have asked Layla to marry him a couple of years ago. Probably shouldn't have dawdled to the point where she felt she needed to put an ultimatum on it. Probably. But here he was.

Taking the jewelry store guy at his word, Henry decided to run his other errands. He went to the florist to pick up a dozen long-stemmed red roses. They looked great, and he put the long white box on the backseat of his car and drove carefully the rest of the day. His next stop was the liquor store, which he knew carried at least one bottle of wine from one of the vineyards they'd visited on their trip to Napa Valley a year earlier. He'd seen the bottle there a week or so earlier and was determined that he would get it to celebrate the night's special occasion.

By the time he pulled into the parking lot of the Bottle

King, the knot in his stomach had become crippling. He'd never felt anything like this before. He could barely stand up when he got out of the car, and at least one guy stared at him as he hobbled into the store. Damn, he thought, I hope I don't look drunk.

He found the bottle of wine he was looking for and headed, slowly, to the checkout counter. The guy there looked at him, clearly wondering what was wrong, but Henry offered a weak smile and a twenty dollar bill. As he waited for his change, he heard a woman's voice.

"Henry?"

Henry turned and saw Susan, the other of Layla's close friends. Now, this was strange. It was as if Layla had dispatched Susan and Gloria to tail him around for the day. He was glad he hadn't seen either of them at the flower shop, but now, all of a sudden, he wondered if somebody was on to him.

"Susan," he said flatly, looking around nervously. He was freaked out, wondering if it was possible that something about his presence in the Bottle King could reveal to Susan what he was planning for the night, enabling her to call Layla and spoil his surprise.

"Is that for the weekend?" Susan asked, pointing at the bottle.

And it dawned on Henry that he was in the clear here. Had he seen Susan or Gloria at the jewelry store or at the flower shop, things might have looked suspicious. But here at the liquor store, well, he could have been buying a bottle of wine for any number of reasons. There was nothing about his presence here that said, in any way, "engagement."

He thought he felt the pain in his stomach ease somewhat, so he tried to stand up straight. He was wrong, he found out quickly, and he grimaced as he doubled back over.

"Are you all right?" Susan asked.

"Yeah, fine," Henry said. "Just hurt my . . . foot as I was getting out of the car here. No big deal. Trying to walk it off."

Susan seemed to accept this. The guy behind the counter, looking more skeptical, handed him his bottle of wine in a brown paper bag.

"Big night last night?" he asked Susan, wondering if she might let slip some sort of clue as to what big secret thing might be going on.

"Ah, we had fun," Susan said. "A little too much beer, maybe, but we had fun. Just the girls, you know, hanging out."

Unlike Gloria, Susan looked right at him when discussing the adventures of the previous night. He was not seized with the same kind of worry/panic/concern that had got ahold of him during his conversation with Gloria, probably because Susan wasn't giving off the same ominous, inauspicious impression that she was about to dump some poor guy in a Starbucks. He would have thought that would make his stomach feel better. It did not.

"You guys driving up in the morning?" Susan asked him, smiling a polite, fake smile as she avoided the topic that each of them knew was foremost in his mind.

"Yep," he said. "Hoping to leave around seven or eight, get there in time for a late lunch, or whatever."

"I guess we'll be right behind you," Susan said, giving Henry a case of déjà vu.

"Well, have a good trip," he said, wanting to end the conversation as quickly as possible.

"Okay," she said, still forcing her smile. "We'll see you up there."

And as he left, Henry wondered if he should have asked Susan the same final question he'd asked Gloria. Wondered if Susan would have given a less cryptic answer. Wondered if Susan knew as much as Gloria did. Figured she did.

But then, what was the point, right? The decision was made, right? The flowers and wine were in the car, and he was on his way back to the jewelry store, this time determined to wait until the guy produced a ring. Everything was going smoothly, and everything felt right. Right?

This was the big night—the night Layla would always remember. He pictured her showing off her ring all weekend at the wedding, and it made him smile. He knew he was doing the right thing.

So then, why did his stomach hurt so much?

At three-thirty the ring was ready. The jewelry store guy presented it to Henry in a beautiful little red box that flipped open to reveal a dazzling circular diamond. The stone looked a lot bigger set in the ring, just as the guy at this store (and the guy at Tiffany's) had assured him it would. Henry was more impressed with himself than he'd expected to be, believing that Layla would have reason to be proud of the ring, hoping she'd like it as much as he did.

"She'll love it," the jewelry store guy said, as if reading Henry's mind. "It's a beautiful ring."

Henry believed the guy would have stood there all day, holding the ring for him to see, if he hadn't made the next move, which was for his checkbook.

"All right," he said, pulling out a pen. "What was the final total again?"

The jewelry store guy repeated the number, and Henry raised his eyebrows as he bent over to write the check. He had it, since he'd transferred plenty from his book-advance savings account to his checking account the day before, and he knew it was a deal, since the guy was a good friend of Jake's. But it was still a whopper of a price tag for something that didn't have an engine. He remembered Jake's first warning about the cost (was that only Sunday?), and he smiled at the irony of his brother having led him here. He wished it had worked out better for Jake, and he made a silent promise to see Jake again next week, when they got back from Maine. Maybe they'd even have him over.

He ripped the check out of the checkbook and handed it to the guy, who smiled at him and handed him a bag. Henry took it, and couldn't help himself. He reached into the bag, took out the box and opened it, just to make sure the ring was still there. He would do that six more times between the jewelry store and home. He'd never been more nervous carrying something around in his car. All he could think was to get the damn thing on her finger as quickly as possible. He hoped she wouldn't be late getting home from work.

"Hey, it's me," Layla was saying to him through the phone's voice-mail system. "I'm sorry, but I'm going to be late get-ting home from work."

Damn.

"Jessica's all over me about this one project, and I got in late, and that didn't help things," she went on. "Of course, that was my fault anyway, because of going out with the girls last night, which I'm sorry I didn't tell you about, but you were passed out anyway . . . Anyway, I'm babbling. I don't know what to tell you about dinner. I could be here till eight or nine, if that's what it takes to get this thing done. Jessica's really being a hard-ass. I'm so sorry, but I'll see you when I get home, and I can't wait for tomorrow. It's going to be fun."

Beep.

There was a second message. It was from somebody Henry didn't know.

"Layla, it's Ben."

Ben? Who's Ben?

"Hey, sorry to call you at home, but I lost your work number, and I looked you up in the book. Hope you don't mind. I didn't know you had a roommate. Anyway, we're still on for next Wednesday, but the best I could get in the city was a nine-thirty reservation at Nobu. Hope that's okay. If you've never been, it's worth the wait. Anyway, you can call me back, whenever, to let me know if that's okay or not. I'll talk to you at some point this weekend, I'm sure. Talk to you later."

Beep.

There were no more messages. Which was too bad, Henry thought, because that one he'd just heard required some serious explanation. He played it back, twice, to see if he could divine any clues as to why a man he didn't know would be calling his girlfriend (who was hours away from being his fiancée) about a dinner date at Nobu in six days. He could not. He played it back again, to see if it might be a wrong number, but it wasn't. This Ben character said Layla's name right at the beginning of the message. Nobody else had that name.

Henry stood still in the kitchen for a long time, staring at the magnets on the refrigerator. There was one, of a palm tree, from their trip to Maui, that had his attention for a long time. He had no idea how long he stared at it, or what snapped him out of it, but suddenly he was looking at the roses on the kitchen table and pondering his plan.

He decided it needed some tweaking.

He gathered up the roses and carried them into the basement. He placed them carefully in the tool closet—one of the few places in the house that he could be sure Layla would never enter—and he shut the door, just in case.

He came back upstairs, saw the wine, and took it on a trip down to the tool closet too. Either or both of them might make a return appearance at some point tonight, but he was no longer so sure. Strangely, the feeling in his stomach had changed. It was no longer the stabbing, practically debilitating pain it had been all day. Instead, it was a slightly sick feeling, like the kind you get when you know there's bad news coming and you just want to get it over with.

Henry looked at the clock, which told him it was five-thirty, and knew he had a while to wait. He decided to order a pizza, since he figured making something himself would make too much of a dish-related mess on the night before vacation. While he waited for the pizza, he sat down at the computer with the intention of doing some more writing. But again he was distracted.

He flopped down on the couch to watch *SportsCenter*, then an old episode of *The Simpsons*, and he actually dozed off a little before he heard a loud knock at the door. Yes. The pizza.

He paid the pizza delivery guy, who looked even younger than the kid he'd seen interviewing for a job at Starbucks earlier in the day, and grabbed a paper plate from the cabinet and a can of soda from the fridge. He ate five slices, which was two more than he usually ate, and wondered why the feeling in his stomach hadn't affected his appetite all day. By then the Yankee game was on, and he sat back to watch it, thinking again about James Starling's almost mystical assessment of the rhythms of the game.

The Yankees had a 4–3 lead in the fourth inning when Henry heard Layla's key in the door. It was unlocked, and by turning the key, she accidentally locked it. So, after jiggling the knob, she had to turn the key again. He heard her swear outside the door. He made no move to get up.

Finally, she opened the door and huffed her way into the house. Her arms were overloaded with file folders and three-ring binders, which she loudly dumped on the floor in the middle of the living room. Henry offered no reaction. He looked at her, then looked back at the game.

"This is for the weekend, if you can believe it," Layla said.

"And there's another box in the car. It'll be a miracle if I make it to the wedding."

Henry looked at the pile on the floor and whistled.

"When you get a chance, could you help me with that box in the car?" she asked.

"Sure," he said, and lifted himself off the couch. "I'll get it."

He went out to the car, which was still the loaner she'd had from the Acura dealership since Monday. He lifted the box, which wasn't too heavy, out of her trunk, put it on the ground and closed the trunk. Layla appeared in the doorway, wearing a pair of light blue heels that Henry swore he'd never seen before.

"You know, it might make more sense to just load that into your car," she said. "I'm not going to get to that box tonight."

And without a word Henry walked the box over to his car, which they were planning to drive to Maine. From the doorway, Layla popped the trunk with the key chain, and Henry loaded the box into the trunk. He shut it and went back inside the house.

"I'm sorry," she said. "It was a crazy day."

"Sure," he said. "No problem. I just had pizza. You can have the leftovers, although I pigged out."

"Wow," she said, lifting the top of the cardboard pizza box and looking inside. "Somebody was hungry."

"Yeah, I guess," Henry said, looking at the screen, where Mike Mussina was bending down to his toes, standing up straight and exhaling as he looked in at the batter. Runners were on second and third with one out.

"Are we packed?" Layla asked.

"Not yet," Henry said. "Got to get on that."

"All right," she said. "It shouldn't be too hard."

The batter hit a fly ball to right field, where Sheffield caught it for the second out, but the runner from third tagged up and scored to tie the game. The Yankees appealed, saying the runner had left third base too early. The umpire denied their appeal. The game was still tied.

Henry looked at Layla, who was sitting in one of the chairs at the kitchen table, massaging her right foot, which was crossed over her left knee.

"Lay?" he asked.

"Yeah?"

"Who's Ben?"

Nineteen

While the question Henry would ask her at the dinner table later that night would be the clear low point of Layla's day, it hadn't exactly been a stellar day to begin with.

Unused to being hung over at all, let alone on a workday, she'd had the worst possible time getting out of bed. The shower hadn't fixed anything, and no matter how many times she'd brushed her teeth, she couldn't escape the disgusting taste in her mouth or the fear that she would walk into work smelling like a high-speed collision between a brewery and a cigarette factory. She tried to wolf down breakfast (Henry's Sugar Corn Pops, for some reason, sounded good to her), but it didn't work out. The first taste of milk on her tongue made her gag, and she dumped the whole thing into the garbage before racing out the door.

With no time to stop at the Acura dealership to see if any progress had been made on her car, Layla went straight to work, where she was still on time for the first time all week. There was a meeting that morning, and while she hadn't missed any of it, she had precious little time to prepare. And what was worse, Jessica Standridge was standing in front of the receptionist's desk when she walked through the door. After one long look at Layla, Jessica looked up at the clock over Layla's head, then went back to addressing the terrified receptionist. She said nothing to Layla. Not even a fake "Good morning."

Layla walked into her office and froze. The pile of paper and file folders on her desk was so high she couldn't see out the window behind her chair. Figuring there must be some mistake, or, more likely, some elaborate series of mistakes, she moved carefully toward the desk, as if fearing one wrong move would topple the pile or make it double in size.

She jumped when the buzzer on her intercom went off, and she heard a frightened, small voice say, "Layla?"

"Yeah," she said.

"Jessica wants to see you in her office right away. Sorry."

The "sorry" was new, Layla mused, but perhaps appropriate.

"Thanks," she finally said.

She dumped her briefcase and pocketbook on her chair and walked as confidently as she could across the main room and into Jessica Standridge's office. Jessica's back was turned to her when she walked in. She did not turn around.

"Close the door," she said.

And Layla knew this wasn't going to be good.

Jessica explained that the attorney assigned to one of the firm's top cases had turned in his resignation that morning, without notice, and she was expecting Layla to be able to take over the case midstream. She told Layla that the reason she'd picked her was because the case would require someone who could make a strong impression on a jury, and she believed Layla to be that person.

"You know I'm going on vacation tomorrow, right?" Layla asked.

"Yes, I saw that on the calendar," Jessica said. "I'm afraid you're going to have to make it a working vacation. This can't wait. You can have one of the girls in the outer office box up some files for you."

Layla couldn't believe what she was hearing. Jessica knew what the weekend meant for her personally, and still she was dumping this on her at the last minute. Finally, she asked, "Is that it?" and got up to leave.

"Yes, that's it," Jessica said, staring at her desk. "Layla, this is a case that should be yours. I can't cut you any slack just because I know what's going on in your personal life."

Layla said nothing, nodded and made for the door. As she opened it she heard Jessica's voice behind her.

"How's Henry?"

She stopped, unsure of how to respond.

"Fine," she said without looking back.

"Tell him to figure this thing out soon, will you? I have a law firm to run."

A joke? Layla had no idea what was going on. She turned to look Jessica in the face. She hoped her injured expression would convey her opinion that none of this had been funny.

"Okay," she said, and walked out.

She spent the morning trying to make the pile on her desk look smaller. She glared meanly at the secretary who walked in at ten-thirty with a new file.

"Is that for Standridge?" she asked.

"Yes," the secretary said. "She said she forgot it before. Said she was sorry."

"Jessica said she was sorry?" Layla asked.

The secretary smiled, looking down at the floor.

"Put it on the pile," Layla said with a wave of her hand.

She worked on the files for three solid hours following her meeting with Jessica, and at twelve-thirty she was surprised to look up and find her mother in the doorway to her office.

"How long have you been standing there?" Layla asked.

"That's a fine greeting," Cindy Starling said. "How about, 'Hi, Mom, good to see you?' Something like that? No, I get, 'How long have you been there?'"

"I'm sorry," Layla said, smiling pathetically and walking around her desk to greet her mother. "It's been a crazy morning. I didn't even know what time it was."

"Well, we said twelve-thirty, right? I think I'm actually on time."

Crap, Layla thought. Lunch. She was supposed to have lunch with her mother.

While stunned that her mother was actually on time, she was also upset. There was no way she would be able to sneak out for lunch. Jessica had spent almost the whole morning in the outer office. She was out there right now. It was as if she were spying, waiting for one wrong move.

Of course, even if she had remembered the lunch date, she knew there'd been no way she could have contacted her mother and told her it was off. Her mother had no phone. No computer. Nothing. The only way she could cancel a lunch date with her mother was to wait for Cindy Starling to show up at her office and tell her, then and there, that there was no way.

"Mom, I'm sorry," Layla said. "I can't leave the office. I had all this work come up."

Her mother looked very sad. Actually stuck out her lower lip, as if she were a four-year-old who hadn't got what she wanted.

"I really wanted to talk to you," she said.

"I'm sorry," Layla said. "We'll have to do it next week."

"No," Cindy Starling said.

"No?"

"No," Layla's mother said again. "We're going to have lunch today. Together. Here, in this office."

Layla had nothing to say. Had no choice but to wait for her mother to explain herself. But instead of doing that, her mother simply turned on her heel and left, walking out of the office without saying another word. Layla stood there, staring at the place where Cindy Starling had been, before finally shrugging and returning to her desk and her work.

Twenty minutes later Cindy Starling was back in the office, holding a large white paper bag. She'd obtained sandwiches and salads from a nearby health food store and had brought them, along with two bottles of iced green tea, into Layla's office.

"We'll have lunch here," she said. "While you work."

Layla smiled at her mother. "All right," she said. "As long as you don't mind if I work."

"Nope. I'll just keep right on talking. You don't even have to listen to me."

Truth was, there was plenty of busy, adding-machine type of work she could do without concentrating too hard. Just punching numbers into the computer and letting the spreadsheets work them out. She'd been saving this part of the work because she hated it, but this was the perfect time to do it. She opened her laptop as her mother put a sandwich in front of her. It looked very heavy on sprouts and avocado.

"What is it?" Layla asked, hoping she didn't look too disgusted.

"It's sprouts and avocado," Cindy Starling said.

Sure. Why did I ask?

They ate together, as Layla's mother had wanted, and Layla did actually pull herself away from work enough to focus on the conversation. At one point she noticed Jessica Standridge looking in at her through the window. She couldn't tell whether Jessica was upset at her or not, but she decided not to care. Everybody had to eat, didn't they? Even Jessica, though she'd never seen evidence that she actually did.

Layla's mother was going on and on about the project James Starling had evidently taken up on the house. He was determined to build a back room, adding on to the living room and protruding into the backyard. Layla had many questions, including how many years Cindy expected this project to take, given James Starling's propensity to get stoned and take large chunks of the week off, but she smiled through the stories and asked the more appropriate, innocuous questions. Her mother seemed very happy, and she didn't want to wreck it.

"So," Cindy Starling said, signaling a change of subject. "How are things with you and Henry?"

And Layla stopped chewing and looked up. Had her mother found something out? Had she taken a clue from the phone call earlier in the week?

Cindy Starling noticed the look on her daughter's face and she stopped chewing. She hadn't actually expected any kind of serious answer, just a simple "Fine." But it was clear she'd uncovered something.

"Oh dear," she said. "Is something wrong?"

As she had with Jessica Standridge the day before, Layla told her mother everything. As she spoke, she had the strange feeling that she'd been through this before. Her mother looked nothing like Jessica. She possessed none of the natural intimidation. She dressed like a hippie and gave the impression of being a much smaller person, physically, than Jessica was. But as Layla sat there talking, she wondered why she hadn't had this conversation with her mother before she'd had it with her boss. She guessed this was another instance in which it would have helped if her mother had a phone.

When they got to the part about Ben, Cindy Starling laughed.

"You already have a date set up for next week?" she asked. "You're planning an awfully quick rebound."

"It's a date I hope to cancel," Layla said. "I figured, the guy asked, who am I to say no? I could be single next week."

"That's an awfully practical way to look at it," Cindy Starling said.

"I try."

Layla went on, talking about the week, the sweet talk she and Henry had had the morning before. She talked about finding him passed out on the sofa, again. She talked about her night out with the girls.

"A new haircut, a night out with the girls," Cindy said. "Sounds like somebody getting over a breakup."

"I know, I know," Layla said. "Right now, it's all just a game. But I've really been having fun."

"That's nice, Layla. You should have fun. But be careful. You get used to playing the single girl, you might not want to be a married woman all of a sudden."

And Layla took a bite of her sandwich, stuffed a stray sprout into her mouth with her index finger and pondered this. She'd thought about it, of course, and decided it couldn't hurt. If the week made her want to be single, and Henry didn't come through, then she was that much more prepared for the worst-case scenario. If the week made her want to be single and Henry did come through, she was sure the feeling of being proposed to would wipe out everything else. And if the week didn't make her want to be single, and Henry didn't come through, well, she'd be devastated, which she was going to be anyway. So at least there was a cute guy willing to take her out to dinner. Couldn't hurt, right?

"I don't know, Mom," she finally said. "I still think it was the right thing to do."

"That's important, hon. You have to do what you think is right."

"Do you remember? Did you have to sweat it out with Dad?"

Cindy laughed. "Not really, no," she said. "I went years without thinking of your father after we first met."

Layla knew the story, about her father's various hospital visits and her mother staying by his side, even before they were an item. She liked the stories, and she wouldn't have minded hearing another, but she wasn't going to. Her own fault too, since she'd asked a different question.

"But in the end, I had to ask him," Cindy Starling said.

This was a wrinkle with which Layla was unfamiliar.

"What?" she asked her mother, wiping a stray piece of avocado from her lower lip with a paper napkin.

"That's right," Cindy said, staring out the window behind her daughter. "It was typical. He had this grand plan where he was going to take me out and ask me. Had dinner all set up, and he was going to have them bring me the ring in a dessert or something cheesy like that."

"I've never heard this story before," Layla said. "How is that possible?"

"I don't think it's the part he likes to tell," Cindy said. "He doesn't get embarrassed easily, but I don't think this is the part of the story that makes him the proudest."

"Wow," Layla said. "This is good. Go on."

"Well, you know your father. We got to the restaurant, and they didn't have our reservation, and he was all upset, because not only were they supposed to have our reservation, but they were supposed to have the ring. And it turned out to be a totally different restaurant, on the same block, but he'd forgotten. And he made a scene, and they dragged him out of there, and we never did get to the right restaurant that night. We sat and ate hot dogs from a street vendor while your father pledged to sue the restaurant. I had no idea why he was so upset. Of course, I had no idea that he thought a diamond engagement ring was in their kitchen and they wouldn't let him have it."

Layla was laughing now.

"I can't believe I never heard this," she said.

"Well, to make a long story short," Cindy said, "he was so worked up, and he was standing up on these concrete steps, and I knew his history, so I was worried he'd fall and hurt himself if he got any more excited than he already was. So I grabbed him by his hands and pulled him down to face me. And just to calm him down, I swear, I asked him, 'James, will you marry me?' And he stopped, all of a sudden. And he stared at me. And I'll never forget what he said."

"What did he say?" Layla asked, leaning forward in her chair.

"He said—and I remember it word for word—he said, 'Darling, I'd be crazy not to.'"

Layla had tears in her eyes all of a sudden. Her mother was still looking out the window. After a silent few seconds Cindy Starling stood up, wiped some crumbs from the lap of her jeans and said to her daughter, "Well, you need to get back to work, I assume. But this was nice."

Layla, stunned, stared at her mother.

"You all right?" Cindy Starling asked.

"Yeah," Layla said. "Sorry. I was just . . . it's a nice story. I can't believe I never heard it before."

"Well, maybe I was saving it for the right time."

"Thanks, Mom," Layla said, and got up to give her mother a hug. "How about you? You all right? Got enough gas to get home?"

"Ha ha," Cindy said. "Got half a tank. But thanks for looking out for me."

"No problem, Mom. Thanks for lunch."

"It was my pleasure, dear," Cindy Starling said, and started to walk away, then stopped. "Can I say something, without being too motherly?"

"Sure," Layla said, smiling.

"Henry's good for you," Cindy said. "He keeps you from being too serious all the time. Without him, you might never play."

Layla looked down at her desk, waited a few seconds to make sure she wasn't about to cry, and finally said, "I know."

"Good luck, honey," Cindy said, and walked through the outer office and into the elevator.

Layla spent the rest of the day on her paperwork, with only two interruptions. The first came at three o'clock, when Gloria called.

"Hey, I saw your boy at Starbucks," was the way Gloria began the conversation.

"Really," Layla said.

"Looked like he was writing."

Layla laughed. She'd love to write her own book about the ways in which Henry handled writer's block. She figured it would be a best seller. Everybody'd had writer's block—even people who weren't professional writers. The thought of Henry hunched over his laptop in the middle of Starbucks, hopped up on caffeine from all of the coffee he'd had to get through a day there, made her smile.

"Did it look like he was getting anywhere?" she asked. "I know he's been blocked."

"I couldn't tell. I didn't read over his shoulder or anything."

"What were you doing there? Was it the one on 17? Kind of out of your way, isn't it?"

"Yeah," Gloria said. "I was . . . I was meeting Andy."

"You were not!"

"I was," Gloria said. "I know. I just had to end it."

"I'm sorry," Layla said.

"Ah, it's for the best," Gloria said, pretending to be fine.

They talked for a while, Layla in the willing but unfamiliar position of sounding board to a Gloria she didn't know. This Gloria was raw, exposed, and unsure of herself. Layla felt as if she were back in high school, talking to one of her friends about whether the new boy liked her. She tried to listen a lot and say little, but Gloria wasn't overly forthcoming. She had to drag some information out of her.

"I'm sorry to dump this on you at work," Gloria said. "Are you real busy?"

"Not too busy to listen," Layla said.

"That's a nice way of saying yes," Gloria said. "I'm sure we'll have plenty of time to talk up in Maine. Go get your work done."

"All right," Layla said. "But if you need to talk more, just call. I'll be here."

"Thanks," Gloria said, and hung up without saying goodbye. She was definitely not herself.

The second interruption came at four-fifteen, when Susan called and offered a greeting surprisingly similar to Gloria's.

"Hey, I saw your boy at the liquor store," she said.

Now that's a little bit less of a surprise.

"Oh yeah?" Layla said out loud. "What was he doing there?"

"Looked like he was buying a bottle of wine. I figured it was for the weekend or something."

"Hmm."

"Anyway, what's up?"

"Not too much," Layla said. "I'm kind of swamped. Standridge dumped all of this crap on me right before vacation, and now I'm going to be here all night and have to take work with me."

"Wow," Susan said. "Your new buddy?"

"My new buddy."

"That sucks."

"Yep."

"All right, then. Well, I'll let you get to work. I'm sure we'll see you up there, by the pool or something like that."

"Sounds good," Layla said, her eyes already shifting back to her computer screen. "Have a good trip."

"You too," Susan said.

It was after this conversation that Layla realized she'd better call Henry and tell him she would be late getting home from work. She did, and left a message.

About four hours later she was sitting at the kitchen table, not expecting anything, when Henry asked her, "Who's Ben?"

Whoa, she thought. This is going to be trouble.

Twenty

The question kind of hung there in the air, staring at her. Henry faded into the background, and all she could see was the question, which she pictured as that floating little green ghost from *Ghostbusters*—the one that dripped green slime and saliva, with a cigar sticking out of the side of its mouth.

Who's Ben? it asked over and over again, cackling in between each question. *Who's Ben? Hahahahahaha.*

She was caught. There was no way around it. Henry had looked her in the eye and asked a question she'd never seen coming, even though she should have. He'd run into both Gloria and Susan today—had either of them let it slip? Unlikely, but possible. They were both as hung over as she was. But they would have mentioned it when they called her, wouldn't they? No way that's how he found out.

Who's Ben? her green ghost asked again. *Hahahahaha-haha.*

Was it possible that he'd run into Ben? Could Ben have

stopped in at Starbucks with a friend and Henry overheard
him talking about his upcoming date with a girl with a very
unusual name? This was possible, and more likely than the
previous possibility, but still a long shot. Of all the Starbucks in all the world, etc., etc.

Who's Ben?

Hahahahahahahahahahahahahaha.

Was it possible that Ben had called the house? Had she
foolishly given him her home number instead of work? She
didn't think so, but she'd been pretty absentminded lately.

Who's Ben?

Hahahahahahahahahahahahahahahaha.

She noticed that Henry was still there, standing behind the
floating green goblin, leaning in the doorway to the kitchen,
his arms crossed over his chest. He looked as if he could wait
the rest of the year for an answer. He had the satisfied look
of someone who just realized he had the upper hand for the
first time.

She honestly did not know what to do. She could have
been straight with him, just fessed up and poured out the
whole story right there, with him standing in the doorway.
She could have made up something—lied and told him Ben
was somebody from work, somebody with whom she was
working on a project.

The problem was, she didn't know how much he knew.
She didn't know if he'd spoken to Ben. Didn't know if Ben
had left a message on the voice mail. Didn't know anything
about how Henry had found out, or what he believed was
going on. All she had was the chubby little green ghost, and
he wasn't giving up any information.

She decided to try and stall—to play innocent in the
hopes that Henry would give away something more. She
was aware that she'd hesitated too long to be believable,
but she had to see if she could gain another clue. It was her
only hope for survival.

"What do you mean?" she finally asked.

"Come on, Lay . . ." Henry said, as if she were a child who'd insisted she hadn't broken the lamp—or a favored horse who was beginning to fade in the homestretch.

"I don't understand the question," she said. "I need more information."

"What information?" he asked, starting to get testy. "I asked you, 'Who's Ben?' If you know somebody named Ben, then you can answer. If you don't, then you don't know what I'm talking about. But I can tell by the look on your face you know what I'm talking about. I hope you have a better poker face than this one when you're in court."

That one stung a little bit, but she figured he had the right to be as mean as he wanted to be. She sat and scanned what he'd said for clues. None. He was playing it pretty well. He had her cornered.

Now what?

"Sort of?" she offered.

"*Sort of?*" he shot back. He was agitated now, having sprung from the doorway and begun pacing along the tiled floor of the kitchen. He opened the refrigerator door, looked inside, shut the door without taking anything out, whirled to face her.

"*Sort of?*" he asked again. "Well, what the hell does that mean? Does it mean you *sort of* know what I'm talking about? Or does it mean you *sort of* know somebody named Ben? Or does it mean you're hoping to find a way out of a mess? Because I've known you a long time, Lay, and you sound to me like you're hoping to find a way out of a mess."

"Well, how big a mess are we talking about here?" Layla asked, figuring she might see about injecting a little levity into the discussion. Figuring she had little to lose at this point.

Figuring wrong.

Henry's fist came down on the kitchen counter—an uncharacteristically physical show of frustration for him. Layla had never been worried that Henry might raise his hand to her, and she wasn't now. But the fist on the Formica, that was a sign that he was truly pissed.

"That," he said, looking straight ahead at the microwave, "is a question you have to answer. For me. I'll be upstairs packing if you want to get anything off your chest. There's a message for you on the voice mail."

She didn't look at him as he left the room and headed upstairs to the bedroom, where he would begin packing for the weekend. She wondered how on earth they were going to ride up there together. She wondered if she should call Gloria and Susan to see about getting in their car. She wondered if Henry would ever speak to her again.

She checked the voice mail, heard what Henry had heard. Understood his confusion, his anger.

She looked up at the dripping green ghost, who just shrugged.

Right, she thought. This is my mess. And a big one.

Henry was stuffing piles of his own clothes into the large gray suitcase they always took on trips together. They were always proud when they could pack for a trip and only have to use this one suitcase between them. Of course, it helped that the thing was huge, and it helped when the trips were in the summer, when the clothes were less bulky. It also helped, in this case, that the tuxes and bridesmaid dresses were already in Maine.

Henry thought about the ring, sitting in its little red box, tucked into the breast pocket of the windbreaker that he'd planned to bring on the trip. Somebody had told him it got chilly at night there, even in June, and he figured he'd bring the windbreaker in the car. He'd left a note to remind himself, stuck it right over the hook where the keys hung.

But now he was wondering if he should bother to bring the ring at all. Now he was wondering if the guy at the jewelry store would take it back. What was the policy on that? He was sure it had happened before.

Henry was roughly stuffing handfuls of boxer shorts, socks, and T-shirts into corners of the suitcase. He'd asked Layla to lay out the clothes she wanted to bring in the morning, but she'd forgotten. So had he, actually, and for the same reason. They were both hung over. Now, though, he wanted her up here so he could bite her head off about forgetting to lay out her clothes. He wanted an excuse to have a screaming fight with her. He was getting angrier and angrier as he went into the bathroom and began chucking travel-sized shaving cream and toothpaste into a small leather bag.

He heard her coming up the stairs and braced himself. He was determined to be merciless. He'd had the bad feeling in his stomach all day that something would mess up his plans for this night, but never imagined it would be Layla who did it, never imagined it would get messed up so completely.

He wondered where that pain in his stomach had gone.

He came out of the bathroom and found Layla standing there, looking right at him. He couldn't tell what the look on her face was—contrition, embarrassment, something along those lines, he hoped. She said nothing at first. That gave him his opening.

"You going to lay out the clothes you want to bring?" he asked, rudely. "Or are you not coming now?"

"Of course I'm coming," she mumbled.

"Well, then let's get to it already!" he snapped. "I'd like to get a little sleep tonight before that drive."

Layla stood still another few moments before heading to her closet to start picking out clothes for the weekend. Henry shook his head. He hated this—how, when they'd fight, she would shut down and not say anything. He hated the fact that he always had to be the one to restart the conversation, as if, if he didn't say anything, they might never make up. It made no sense to him, and this time he was determined not to cave. It was her turn to say something. She had to make the next move.

They packed for a half hour in total silence. Occasionally their eyes would meet and she'd look at him hopefully, as if asking him to say something. He would turn his eyes quickly away, as if to tell her he had no interest in saying anything. Once, he held her gaze, hoping to convey a sense of expectation, hoping she'd get the message and start talking. She didn't. He went back to the packing.

When the packing was over, Henry zipped up the suitcase and walked it downstairs. He opened the hall closet and grabbed a sleeve of the windbreaker. But then he caught himself, and in an act of personal defiance, decided not to do it. He knew it meant risking forgetting the thing in the morning, but he had that note, right above the keys, to help prevent that. And besides, if Layla still had nothing to say by the morning, he didn't know if he wanted to bring the damn ring or not.

When he got back upstairs, she was dressed for bed and brushing her teeth. Henry sat on the edge of the bed and waited for her to finish. When she did, he got up, without looking at her, and walked into the bathroom. He shut the door, brushed his own teeth, washed his face, and walked back out into the bedroom. Layla was curled up under the covers. Her eyes were open, he could tell, but she was facing the other way. He undressed and slipped into bed alongside her. Without a word, he shut off the light.

They lay there in silence. Henry couldn't believe it.

Finally, out of nowhere, her voice came.

"Look . . ." she said.

But then she stopped right there, after only one word. *Look.*

Look? Henry thought. Look at what? It's dark.

Then, another surprise. She spoke again.

"This guy comes up to me out of nowhere in a bar. Gloria and Susan and I are sitting there together, talking, and he just comes over. He's talking to all three of us, but Gloria and Susan insist he came over to talk to me. I tell them they're being silly. Susan says, 'Hey, you could be single in a week.'"

"Hmm," Henry said. "So this was just last night this happened?"

"No, this was Sunday, when we went out to Tuxedo's to watch the Knick game."

"Aha," Henry said, determined not to help.

"So the next day, I'm in court, and I run into this same guy, Ben. And he asks me out. I can't remember the last time I got asked out."

"So you just jumped at it?"

"No, actually . . ." Layla said. She was staring up at the ceiling as she spoke. He was lying on his side, facing away from her in the dark. "Actually, I told him no. Actually, no, I told him I'd call him in a week. Figuring, you know, it kept an option open in case . . ."

And here she trailed off, maybe hoping he'd say something. He wasn't about to.

"Anyway, then we talked again a few days later," she said. "And I thought, what the hell? I could take him up on his offer, and if I'm single in a week, at least I'll have something to do. And if not, I can always cancel. I've canceled dates before. You can make up a reason. Doesn't even have to be true."

Henry still wasn't saying anything.

"I made a date I hoped to cancel," Layla finally said, repeating what she'd told her mother, hoping Henry would see it in the same light, doubting it. "I figured, who am I to say no? I mean, Susan could turn out to be right. Right?"

And Henry didn't say anything. As he lay in bed, he thought to himself that what she said made a pretty fair amount of sense, and that it was all probably true. It just raised so many other questions. Did she like this guy? Was he good-looking? Did she really want to get married after all, or had the thing with this Ben guy made her want to break up and start seeing other people all of a sudden?

He thought about the last few days—the haircut, all the new shoes, the giggly gossiping on the phone with her friends, the way Gloria wouldn't look him in the eye. He thought about the "girls' night out" and wondered if there were more to it than he was being led to believe.

Her explanation made sense, sure. And her practical streak was one of the things he loved about her—made him think that getting married to her might be a good thing for him, might help him keep the rest of his life in order. But this Ben thing, this had hit him pretty hard, and he still had to do a lot of thinking about it before he decided whether to let her off.

He lay there, facing away from her, staring at the shade pulled down in front of their bedroom window. She lay next to him, staring up at the dark blue of the ceiling in the dark, wondering if he was going to say anything.

Neither one of them spoke for the rest of the night.

PART VII

Friday

Twenty-one

"So, did you guys not talk at all, the whole trip?"

Susan was in a two-piece black bikini, sunning herself by the hotel pool, which was about fifteen feet from the beach but still proved the preferred alternative for most of the people staying at the hotel on this June weekend. The ocean water was still way too cold.

"Not that much," Layla said.

Layla was sitting on the side of the lounge chair next to Susan's, still wearing the shorts and T-shirt she'd worn on the drive up with Henry. She had plenty of work still to do, and needed to be in her hotel room doing it, but she had to talk to somebody about what had gone on the night before. She was chewing on the side of her thumbnail as she let Susan process the story she'd just told. She didn't care that she'd have to repeat it all for Gloria whenever she got there. She had to hear somebody's opinion.

"Did you talk about last night?"

"Only a little," Layla said. "About an hour into the trip I

asked him if we were going to talk about it. And he said, 'What do you want to talk about?' And I told him I wondered what he thought of my explanation from the night before."

"And what did he say?"

"Nothing, for a little while, and then he started going on about how many 'questions it raised' for him. Wanted to know all about Ben, whether I liked him, whether he was good-looking, whether there was any more he was going to find out that he didn't already know. I answered his questions, and I kept trying to tell him I wasn't out there looking for anybody. The guy approached me, and I figured it couldn't hurt to say yes. I could always cancel."

"Right," Susan said. "But think about if it happened the other way. If you got a call from some girl he'd made a date with for next week."

"True," Layla said. "But that's different."

"How so?"

"Well, I mean, I'm the one on record, wanting to get married. His opinion on the issue still has yet to be heard. If he reacted to the ultimatum by going out and making a date, I'd kind of have my answer, wouldn't I?"

"I can see you've thought a lot about this," Susan said.

"You tend to think a lot when you can't sleep."

"So, anyway, what did he say?"

"He went about another forty-five minutes without saying anything. I was wondering if it was okay to pull out some work I needed to do, but I didn't want him to think I wasn't into the conversation. So I just kind of stared out the window and watched the highway signs go by."

"Sounds like a country music song," Susan said.

"And then, he kind of gives this sigh, and he's still staring at the road, with his sunglasses on, driving, and he says, 'I don't know, Lay. I guess what I wonder is, do you want to get married, or don't you?'"

"Ha," Susan said flatly. "Not the proposal you were looking for."

"No," Layla said. "Not a proposal at all, really. More like he was saying, 'Maybe you should have had your own self figured out before you started throwing around crazy ultimatums and deadlines, you dumbass.'"

"Hmm," Susan said.

"Yeah, I know," Layla said. "I can kind of see his point."

"So, what did you say?"

"I told him of course I did. I told him this was just a strange coincidence, and that if the week turned out the way I wanted it to turn out, I'd never think about this guy again. That Ben was totally irrelevant—just a way to have something to look forward to if I got my heart broken."

Layla was looking over at the beach now. A young family was walking in the sand, barefoot. The parents were holding hands, and the daughter, maybe four years old, was dangling off her father's free hand, skipping out of his grasp periodically to grab at seashells.

"Did you cry?" Susan asked.

"I didn't cry," Layla said. "So far, I've kept my promise. I haven't cried all week."

"Are you crying now?" Susan asked, leaning up from her reclined position for the first time since the conversation had begun.

"A little," Layla said, dabbing at her left eye under her sunglasses.

"Oh, it's all right, Lay," Susan said, up now and lamely offering a corner of her towel. "It's all right. Hey, at least you guys are here together, right? You can talk it out. Something could still happen this weekend. There's no reason to be upset. Right?"

"I just wonder . . ." Layla said.

"Wonder what?"

"I just wonder, you know? I wonder what he was thinking before he heard that message. I mean, was he going to propose last night? What if he was going to propose last night?"

Susan didn't say anything, just sat there holding the towel in case Layla needed it, which so far she hadn't. Layla let a tear run down her cheek and drip onto the concrete. Then she forced a laugh.

"Maybe I didn't have the stomach for this after all," she said.

"Aw, Lay. Don't beat yourself up."

And then Gloria arrived, resplendent in a huge red straw hat.

"Hey guys," she said. "What's up?"

Henry was in a bad mood, and this was no time to be in a bad mood. He was the best man, after all, and this was Jack and Gina's big weekend. Nothing would do but constant smiles, and for Henry right now, they were all forced.

He and Layla had arrived shortly after one o'clock, after spending the final two and a half hours of their trip in horrible silence. Henry had no idea what he was supposed to do next, and all he wanted was to drive around a little bit and think about it. Instead, he had to go to the golf course, where the men of the wedding party were having a day-before-the-wedding golf outing in honor of the groom. Gina's father was the host, since it was his country club, and Henry and the rest of the guys were unable to spend a single penny. It was as if every employee of the place had each of their photographs on file and had been told not to take any money from them.

Henry tried to buy a fifty-cent bag of wooden golf tees. Actually put the two quarters on the glass counter.

"Oh, that's all right, sir," the golf pro said.

"What do you mean?" Henry asked.

"Everything's taken care of," the pro said, picking up his

two quarters and handing them back to him. "Mr. Cook is taking care of everything."

This annoyed Henry, but only because everything was annoying him today. He stuffed the small plastic bag of tees into his pocket without a thank-you and looked around the rest of the pro shop. He'd wanted to buy a new pair of socks, since the ones he brought had a hole in the right big toe, but he decided against having Gina's father buy him a pair of socks. Just didn't seem right. He barely knew the man.

"Somebody told me you're Henry," said a large voice, as a large hand clamped down on his right shoulder.

Henry turned and came face-to-face with a man he believed, instantly, to be Gina's father, the annoyingly generous Mr. Cook.

"Herb Cook," the man said, extending his other hand for shaking. Henry took it, shook it.

"Henry," he said. "Good to meet you, Mr. Cook. And thanks for—"

"Herb!" Mr. Cook barked. "Call me Herb. We're going to have a fun day. You're in the third group, with Jack and Pete and one of Gina's cousins. His name is Ed. Good guy. You'll have fun."

"Thanks," Henry mumbled, uncomfortable adding Gina's father's first name to his expression of gratitude.

And just like that, Herb Cook was spinning away from him and assaulting the shoulder of another groomsman. Henry turned his attention back to the hole in his right sock. It was going to annoy him all day. It seemed as if everything was.

Once they were out on the course, Henry actually managed to have a decent time. He was playing with Jack, one of his best friends since they were in first grade, and Pete, with whom he'd already played nine zany, drunken holes in New

Jersey earlier in the week. Their fourth was Ed, Gina's cousin, who seemed a decent fellow but kept fairly quiet in the presence of three men who'd known each other forever.

It took until the fifth hole for Pete to say the thing Henry had been hoping he wouldn't say. Henry hadn't wanted Jack to know about the situation with him and Layla. He felt it would be inappropriate, on the weekend of Jack's wedding, to involve him in his own loopy love life. And he knew that once Jack found out, he wouldn't be able to resist getting involved.

So he couldn't help cringing when Pete said, "Hey Henry, what'd you decide about Layla and the whole marriage thing?"

At this, Jack, who was off to the side of the fifth tee taking one-handed practice swings as he swigged beer from a can, perked up. Heck, at this, even Ed perked up. This was interesting stuff.

"What's this?" Jack asked.

"Thanks, Pete," Henry said.

"What?" Pete asked, spreading his arms, a beer can in his left hand, his driver in the right. "We're not supposed to talk about this?"

"I didn't want to make me and Layla the focal point of Jack and Gina's weekend."

"Whoa, whoa, whoa," Jack was saying, walking up to the tee now and toward Henry with a wide grin on his face. "Are you getting married, buddy?"

"Well," Henry said. "It's a little more complicated than that."

They were finished with the front nine, and they were sitting in their carts, eating free cheeseburgers off plastic plates as they waited for the group in front of them to tee off on the tenth. He and Jack were sharing a cart, and Jack was peppering him with questions. It had taken five holes for Henry to tell the story, mainly because he recounted the whole week, including everything from his destitute brother to ring shopping at Tiffany's to lunch with Layla's dad to the litany of Big John's wives. He talked about the phone message from Ben, and the fight, and the mainly silent car ride. He even filled Pete in on the surprise couple of hours he'd spent in the bar with Catherine—a part of the story that appeared to make Pete feel uncomfortable, which was fine with Henry. It wouldn't hurt Pete to keep his mouth shut for a few holes.

Jack loved the story, every bit of it. Henry thought it had a chance to replace *The Blues Brothers* as Jack's favorite. And Ed, a total stranger just two hours earlier, was so caught up in the telling that Henry wondered if he should be eating popcorn.

When Henry stopped talking, Jack wanted to know how it ended.

"So?" he asked. "What are you going to do? You going to propose to her tonight?"

"Well, like I said," Henry said. "I was going to propose to her last night, but then I find out she's got a date set up for next week and there's this guy in the picture and it's all a big freaking mess."

"Right," Jack said. He now knew about the flowers and the wine stashed away in the basement tool closet back in Jersey.

"So I don't know," Henry said. "I really don't know. And I'm all messed up about it, and the last thing I wanted to do was bother you with this on the weekend of your wedding."

"Well, that's your own fault," Jack said. "You should have called me a week ago and told me about this."

"I figured you were busy," Henry said.

"Busy as hell," Jack said. "But not too busy for something like this. This is big stuff, man. Big stuff."

Jack took a bite of his cheeseburger and stared off down the tenth fairway, where his prospective father-in-law was raking a sand trap.

"So, what do you think?" Henry finally asked.

"Sorry?" Jack said.

"I mean, what do you think? You're getting married tomorrow. What do you think about it? You ready for this?"

"Oh, right," Jack said, grinning again now. "That's the right kind of stuff for a best man to be asking the day before the wedding. I'm really glad I picked you, Henry. Really glad."

And he slapped Henry on the back and laughed. But Henry wasn't laughing. Henry was in a bad mood, and there was nothing Jack or anybody else could do about it.

"Have you not even had one beer?" Pete asked Henry as they marched up the hill from their carts to the fourteenth green.

"Nah," Henry said. "Don't feel like it."

"Man," Pete said. "You might want to think about it. It might loosen you up."

"That's okay," Jack said. "You'll get a nice treat out of it."

Henry didn't know what Jack meant. He raised his hands, palms upward, his putter dangling between two fingers on his right hand.

"If you're the only one who's sober, you can drive me to the tux shop," Jack said. "I got a new car."

"Oh yeah?" Henry asked. "What kind?"

"Oh, man," Jack said. "You're really in for a treat."

Henry was still moping when they got to the parking lot, but Jack looked like a little kid about to show his grandparents what he'd gotten for Christmas. He directed Henry to a little black Porsche convertible, and he stood next to it, beaming.

"This is your new car?" Henry asked, eyes widening.

"Yep," Jack said.

"Jesus, man," he said. "It's nice."

"Wait till you drive it," Jack said.

"Dude," Henry said. "I don't mean to pry, but . . ."

"How can I afford this on a cop's salary?"

"Yeah. That's what I wanted to ask."

Jack chuckled. "My new father-in-law is very wealthy," he said. "And very generous."

A few minutes later, as they were hugging sharp curves along the southern coastline of Maine with the top down and the engine bellowing, Henry wondered which was harder to believe—that Jack's prospective father-in-law had given him a sweet new black sports car as a wedding present, or that Jack was letting him drive it on the second day he owned it. It occurred to Henry that Jack was an awfully good and trusting friend—the kind for whom you got great joy out of being best man. Jack might be the guy he picked to be his best man. If he ever got married.

"Man," Henry said. "I really don't know what to do about this Layla thing."

Silence from the passenger seat. Henry shot a glance over at Jack, who was looking at him, grinning.

"I can't hear you!" Jack shouted with glee.

"Was that Henry and Jack in a convertible, doing about seventy?" Layla asked, staring up the road from the sidewalk where she and Gloria were finishing up their walk.

"Could be," Gloria said. "I heard Gina's dad bought Jack a sports car as a wedding present."

"He did not!" Layla said, still staring up the road.

"He did. Pretty generous guy, it seems."

"That's something," Layla said. "But would Jack let Henry drive it?"

"That's a good question," Gloria said. "But that sure looked like him."

"God," Layla said, almost in a whisper. "I hope he's sober."

Henry was, indeed, sober. Hadn't been this sober in almost a week. The rush he got from driving Jack's wedding present along the sleepy back roads was something, but having passed on beers throughout the afternoon, he was thinking clearly. His mind was producing question after question about the Layla situation. It was as if a seven-way debate, the kind you see in the presidential primary elections, was going on in his head, with issues flying all over the place. Did he love her? Did he want to marry her? Did he want to marry anybody, ever? Was the Ben thing as big a deal as he was making it out to be? What on earth was she thinking? What did she want? And why?

It was a good thing, Henry thought, that he hadn't been drinking. His mind was too cluttered already.

"Thanks, man," he said, handing Jack the keys as they stepped out of the car in the parking lot of the tux shop.

"Keep 'em," Jack said. "You might as well drive us back to the hotel too. We're not going to be here long enough for me to sober up."

"Hey!" they heard that large voice say. "You like it?"

It was Herb Cook, hopping down from the driver's seat of his massive black SUV.

"Wow," Henry said. "Really something, Mr. Cook. I mean . . . Herb. Really, some gift."

Henry wondered what Layla's father might get him as a wedding present, and whether it might have just a hint of carrot taste to it.

"Best part is, Jackie boy is a cop," Herb Cook said. "So he can drive it as fast as he wants."

"Is that true?" Henry asked.

"Well, not really," Jack said with his innocent smile. "I mean, if I'm out there doing a hundred twenty down the highway, they kind of have to bust me. But you know, once we get the police department plates on there, I'm sure I could get away with eighty, ninety on the highway, if it wasn't too crowded. We kind of stick together like that."

They all walked together up toward the tux shop, which sat on a hill overlooking the ocean. Seemed like everything here sat on a hill overlooking the ocean. This place was gorgeous.

"The views are incredible here," Henry said.

"Yeah," Jack said. "You might want to think about it for your own wedding."

"You getting married, Henry?" Herb Cook asked.

Henry looked at Jack, who was still grinning.

"It's a little more complicated than that, Herb," Henry said.

"Always is, isn't it?" Herb Cook said, and winked at Henry as he held the door open. "With women?"

The woman who was currently complicating Henry's life had finally gone back to her hotel room, which was a tough place to work. The sliding glass doors opened to look out over the ocean, and the sound of the seagulls chirping made Layla want to sit in the sun and drink something that had a little paper umbrella in it. It was almost six-thirty, which meant she had two hours before the rehearsal dinner. She had about twenty hours of work to do, but at least she had time to make some sort of dent in it.

The first thing she picked up off the pile was her organizer, and when she opened it, a small piece of paper fluttered to the floor. She picked it up and looked at it. It was the paper that had Ben's phone number on it. Layla groaned, crumpled the paper and threw it into the wastebasket.

Then she got up, stood over the wastebasket for a few minutes and stared into it. She worried that, if she left it there, Henry would find it, which was kind of absurd, since

Henry wasn't likely to go rooting around in the garbage looking for evidence to help him avoid marrying her. Then she thought she might want to pick it up and save it, since she really didn't know what Henry was thinking at the current moment.

Really, what would have helped was to know what the hell Henry was thinking at the current moment.

At that moment Henry was thinking, Is there a chance they can let this vest out enough so I won't suffocate tomorrow during the pictures?

"Looks a little tight on you, dude," Pete was saying.

"Yeah," Henry said. "Either they ordered the wrong size or I've been eating too much."

"Could be both," Pete said.

"Could be."

"Well, you might want to get it fixed," Pete said. "You wouldn't want to pop open a seam during your toast. That'd be embarrassing."

Henry froze, just for a second, but Pete saw it.

"Oh, man," Pete whispered, looking around to see if Jack was nearby. "Did you not write a toast?"

Henry didn't know what to say. In all the craziness of the past week—the stuff with Layla, the writer's block, all of the drunken golf with Big John—he'd completely forgotten that he would be expected to toast the bride and groom the next day.

"Shit," he said.

"Oh, man," Pete said, trying, unsuccessfully, to stifle a laugh. "What are you going to do?"

"I guess I can wing it," Henry said.

"Yeah, I guess," Pete said, with another drunken giggle. "But you're a *writer*, man. People are going to expect something great."

Pete was right. Henry knew it. And he was caught. Great.

Something else to spend the night worrying about.

"I think I can let this out enough," the tailor said, inspecting the sides and the back of Henry's vest. "Give me a few minutes."

Jack emerged from a nearby stall, dressed in his tuxedo shirt, pants, and jacket. He wore no shoes or socks.

"What do you think?" he asked, then noticed the expression on Pete's and Henry's faces. "Is something wrong?"

"Nah," Henry said quickly. "They need to fix my vest. No big deal."

The smile returned to Jack's face. This, Henry thought, was a guy who was happy to be getting married.

"So," Jack said again. "What do you guys think?"

"You look ready to me," Pete said, looking at Henry and smiling again. "Looks like everything's all set."

Twenty-two

The room was massive. The Cooks had rented out the dining room of their country club for a rehearsal dinner to which nearly one hundred people had been invited. The tables all had glittering golden tablecloths, and each one had an attentive-looking waiter standing next to it with a towel over his forearm and a look on his face that dared you to stump him.

Henry, walking in just behind Layla, let out a whistle.

"Yeah," Layla said.

"What's the actual wedding going to look like?" Henry whispered to her.

Layla giggled.

Around the room there were ten large, flat-screen TVs set up on tables, each one showing a continuous-loop video of Jack and Gina's vacation highlights. There they were in Cancún, swimming up to the bar that sat in the middle of their hotel's pool. The next minute there was a shot of Gina looking up at the Arc de Triomphe. Then a segue into a shot of Jack picking grapes off a vine at a northern California vineyard. In all of the scenes, Jack and Gina were smiling, happy as could be.

"They're like, the perfect couple," Layla said, then immediately wished she hadn't said it out loud.

Henry just looked at one of the TVs and smiled.

Gina was standing next to one of the front tables, gorgeous in a white floral print dress, chatting away with an older couple Henry and Layla didn't know. She continued chatting as Layla caught her eye, though she started shooting glances their way and smiling bigger and bigger.

Finally, Gina pulled herself away from the older couple and raced over to where Layla and Henry were checking out the seating chart.

"Hey!" she shouted, wrapping her arms around Layla's neck. "So good to see you guys! I'm so glad you made it!"

"Of course we made it," Layla said. "Don't be silly. Hey, this looks great."

"Yeah," Gina said, looking up at the ceiling, from which hung long white drapes, dotted with Christmas-tree-type lights. "I kept telling my dad it was too much, but he kept insisting. 'I only have one daughter,' he kept saying. 'I only get to do this once.'"

Gina hunched her shoulders for this last part, and affected a deep voice intended to mimic her father's. Then she broke down into a laugh, her mouth looking as if it would hurt if it kept smiling so much.

"So," she said. "What's going on with you guys? Anything interesting?"

She was talking to Layla but she was looking at Henry, and her smile had taken on a devious element. Jack told her, Henry thought. Of course he did. Jack tells her everything.

Layla, of course, didn't know how much he had told Jack on the golf course, so she was oblivious. She answered Gina's question straight—with the usual not muches and a comment about work being pretty busy. She mentioned that Henry was working on a new book, which was kind of true, he thought, and she made a little more small talk.

But while Layla spoke, Gina stared at Henry, sharing a look that would have made uninformed observers think they were having an affair. When he was fairly sure Layla wasn't about to turn her head and look at him, he quickly shot his right index finger to his lips, to tell Gina to cut it out. Gina, if it was possible, smiled harder.

"So, you know," Layla said, "same old."

Henry wondered how she did it. He had no idea how, with all of the crap that was going on in their life together, Layla could stand there and smile and make small talk as if the most major event of her life to that point wasn't scheduled for the next afternoon. Of course, he wondered the same thing about Gina, and about Jack, who was across the room gently shaking hands with an old woman he didn't appear to know.

He told himself it was silly to compare his own situation to Jack and Gina's, since they were actually taking the proverbial plunge—in less than twenty-four hours—and all he was doing was wrestling with a decision he should have made years earlier. But then he saw something that made him think he had more work to do than they did.

He watched Jack catch Gina's eye from across the room, watched the smile they shared with each other. It was simple, sweet and subtle, but Henry thought it looked as if, for one second, they felt they were the only two people in the room.

They know, he thought. They're sure.

There was nothing in that look that Jack and Gina shared but pure, perfect love and certainty. They knew for sure they were supposed to get married and spend the rest of their lives together. Henry figured he'd never before seen two people more sure of anything in his entire life.

* * *

It took about a half hour to get everybody seated, mainly because each of the nearly one hundred rehearsal-dinner guests had to be told individually that there was no need for them to go to the bar. Each table had its own waiter, after all, who would be delighted (they kept using the word "delighted") to get every person at the table the exact drink he or she needed. This attempt to impose order on such a large group would serve the next day's wedding well, Layla thought. But she worried about the two hundred or so people who weren't there, and wouldn't have had this practice session. She amused herself imagining a hall full of waiters with tazer guns, subduing unruly guests as they tried to make their way to the bar to refill their vodka-and-tonics.

"What's so funny, hon?" Henry asked, leaning in front of her right shoulder conspiratorially.

"Oh, nothing," she said, embarrassed. "Something I just thought of. Nothing big."

Henry went back to his discussion with Pete, the topic of which Layla thought could be anything from comic books to bridesmaids' legs. Layla liked Pete, in spite of herself, but her heart ached for Catherine, who was munching on a stalk of broccoli and staring straight in front of her, nobody to talk to at the table. Layla wondered what it was like to be married to a man determined to remain a child. She wondered if Catherine had really expected Pete to change, or if she'd married him knowing this was what it would be like—supermodel posters on the walls, Saturday morning cartoons on the TV.

Layla pushed her chair back from the table and caught Catherine's eye. Catherine understood the implied invitation and rose to join Layla on a trip to the ladies' room.

"Everything all right with you and Pete?" Layla asked once they were together in the bathroom.

Catherine sighed.

"Yeah," Layla said. "I kind of figured."

"I don't know, Lay," Catherine said. "I guess I just can't believe it's been all this time and he won't change even a little bit. I mean, you'd think, after a couple of years of marriage, he'd start to take you seriously. I mean, I really am allergic to that dog . . ."

Not knowing what to say, Layla checked her eyebrows in the mirror. She never felt like they looked quite right.

"Well," she finally said. "At least you got him to marry you. That's something I still haven't been able to pull off after six years."

"Yeah, but you've got a great thing with Henry, Lay," Catherine said, touching up her lipstick. "Don't you?"

Yeah, Layla thought. I kind of do.

When they got back to the party, they didn't go all the way back into the room. Layla and Catherine stood in the large doorway, watching Henry and Pete talk to each other. They were laughing like a couple of stoned teenagers watching *Beavis and Butthead*. Pete was pounding his fist on the table. They looked like they were having a great time.

Layla shook her head. "How do guys do it?" she asked.

"What do you mean?" Catherine said, still looking at Pete.

"They're just sitting there, having a great time. And you know they're talking about something totally ridiculous. They never have to worry about having these deep talks about their relationships and all that crap."

"I know," Catherine said. "What do you want to bet they're talking about some TV show, or some stupid thing they did together in college?"

Just then, Jack, who was roaming the room with his bride, took the seat next to Henry—the one that had been Layla's. Pete leaned over and said something to him, and suddenly Jack was laughing as if he'd been in the conversation the whole time.

"Definitely college now," Layla said.

"Must be nice," Catherine said.

"Hey," Layla said. "Can I tell you something, and you tell me what you think?"

Catherine looked her in the eyes. They'd never been all that close. It was one of the reasons Layla wanted to talk to her. A detached perspective and all that.

"Sure," Catherine said, both touched and intrigued.

And Layla proceeded to tell a story that had begun six days earlier, with French toast.

"So," Catherine said, her mouth agape. "You really don't know what he's going to do?"

"Nope," Layla said, sipping the vodka-tonic the waiter had brought her when he noticed they had no plans to leave the doorway anytime soon. Service in this place was pretty good. "He could have a ring in his pocket, for all I know. Or he could be planning to do nothing at all tomorrow. In which case I might need a ride home."

"You think he's messing with you?" Catherine asked.

"I really don't know what to think."

"You still want him to propose?" Catherine asked.

To that point, the only other person who'd asked her that question had been Henry, frustrated, that morning in the car. She hadn't considered it—not that directly.

She looked now, again, at Henry, who was wiping a tear from his eye as Jack got up from the table, his duties as groom preventing him from spending the rest of the dinner reminiscing with his old roommates. She thought about Henry, the way he'd been in college, when he brought those jokers over and sung to her outside her bedroom window. She thought about the crazy dates he used to make up because they had no money—taking her to the zoo but not going in, trying to count how many animals they could see from outside the fence before somebody chased them away.

She thought about the time they decided to move in together. She thought about house hunting. She remembered
the day he sold his first book, the day she passed the bar.
She thought about the way his hugs felt, and how he told
her he loved her as if it was the most important information anyone had ever shared with anyone else.

She thought too about the week that had just unfolded.
The tension, the alcohol, the arguments interspersed with
the sex and the sticky ice-cream kisses and the normal, ev-
eryday sweetness that had been such a part of her life for
so long that she sometimes didn't even pay it any attention
anymore. She thought about Ben, and how silly it was that
he'd become an issue. If she'd had that to do again. . .

She watched him take a break from Pete and look around
the room, and realized he was trying to spot her. He'd
looked around three times already since she and Catherine
walked back in, but it hadn't dawned on her until just now
that he was looking for her. She had been gone awhile, and
wouldn't you know, he was worried about her.

He spotted her this time, and smiled at her. She uncrossed
her arms long enough to give him a small wave and return
the smile. He noticed Catherine with her, nodded, and went
back to his conversation.

"Yeah," Layla finally told Catherine, in answer to a question she hadn't thought enough about all week. "I really
do."

Gina's father was banging his fork on the side of his water
glass for a long time. It took a while to get the attention of
a hundred eating, drinking, dinner guests, but Herb Cook
was determined. After a minute he stood up, holding the
water glass and still clinking it, a presence physically large
enough to attract the requisite attention. Seated to his right
was his wife, a tiny woman whose size explained Gina a
great deal better than Herb's did. Seated to his left was the

happy couple, Jack and Gina holding hands tightly, looking up at Herb, waiting to hear what he had to say.

"If I could take everybody's attention away from dessert for a second," Herb Cook said, drawing murmured laughs from a hundred mouths full of cake. "I'd just like to say a few words."

Henry was looking, again, at Jack and Gina. He was fascinated by them. He'd known for a while that Gina made his friend very happy, but it wasn't until this day, spent in the company of a fully contented Jack, that he'd realized what that really meant. Jack was all set now. He'd found the piece he needed to complete the puzzle. Gina was the only thing that had been missing from his life, and there they were now, together, whole. Henry was impressed at that more than anything else. The depth of the whole concept had never fully struck him before.

"When you have a daughter," Herb Cook began, "you worry a lot."

More laughs, these louder, cake-free.

"You worry about whether she'll make it to school all right. You worry when she starts to think she's ugly. You worry when you give her the car keys for the first time. You worry when she goes off to college, a little too sure that she doesn't need you anymore."

This is pretty good, Henry thought, and he knew he'd have to pull an all-nighter to write the speech Pete had so gleefully reminded him about at the tux shop.

I wonder if I should take notes?

"But you really worry when the boys start showing up at the front door," Herb said. "That's when you pretty much give up on sleeping. Forever."

More laughs. The guy was killing.

"And then one day . . ." Herb Cook said, pausing now, making everybody in the massive room wonder if it was possible that this huge man was about to cry. "And then one day, she calls and she says I'm bringing this guy home for Thanksgiving, is that okay? And you brace yourself, because what's it going to be? You don't know what the guy is going to look like, what kind of background he's going to have, what kind of family he's from. You don't know how he's going to treat her. You really hope she cares as much about that last part as you do."

Long pause here, as Herb Cook looked down at Jack, who was handing a tissue to his tearful daughter. By this point Herb was dabbing at his own eyes with the knuckle of his right index finger.

"Wow," he said. "Almost there."

More laughs. Nervous laughs.

"All I can say is, to the fathers out there who have daughters, or who will have daughters, I'm sorry. You're all on your own now. My little girl got the best one."

Jesus. Now Henry was worried *he* was going to start to cry. That was unbelievable.

The crowd said, *"Awwww,"* as one, and rose to applaud as Jack stood from his seat and wrapped Herb Cook in a bear hug. Herb slapped Jack on the back three times, and the two men embraced for a long time.

Layla, Henry noticed, was a mess, tears running down her cheeks as she smiled and laughed. He reached for her hand, squeezed it. She looked at him, looking surprised, then looked back at the head table. She and Henry sat down, still holding hands.

"Wow," Layla said.

"Yeah," Pete said, digging for another forkful of cake. "And you should see the car he got him."

The emotional workout brought on by Herb Cook's speech was over, and the room got to relax for about ten minutes before the telltale clink of fork on glass was heard again. This time, those turning to face the front saw that the hand clinking the fork belonged to the groom, who was rising for his own speech.

"Oh no," Layla said. "I don't know if I can take another one of these."

Henry smiled and squeezed her hand again. She leaned over, touching her left shoulder to his right. He kissed her on the top of the head.

"I'm sorry, but I'll be quick," Jack said. "Actually, after Herb's speech, I thought about just canceling mine, because I'm never going to look as good as he made me look."

Loud laughter from all corners. This had to be, Henry thought, the greatest rehearsal dinner of all time.

"First, I really want to thank Herb, not just for the kind words, but for all of this," Jack said, spreading his arms to indicate the room, the wedding, the weekend, the state of Maine. "I mean it. Thanks."

He began clapping, and two hundred hands joined him. It was doubtful that many of the people in attendance had expected to be treated quite this well this weekend. Each hotel room had come with a complimentary thirty minute massage, for goodness' sake. Henry didn't know if that was just for the wedding party or for all out of town guests, but either way . . .

"Now," Jack said, and let out a chuckle. "If I can get through this, I'd like to say a few words about the woman sitting to my right."

He looked down at Gina, who looked up at him as if she were a flower and he was the sun.

"I could tell you all about how beautiful she is," Jack said, drawing the requisite *awwwwws.* "I could tell you how smart she is, and how sweet she is, and how happy she makes me. I could tell you a lot about a person who works all day with kids, then spends two nights a week volunteering at a hospital, because she couldn't get to enough kids in the course of her workweek. I could talk about Gina all night."

He stopped and reached for Gina's hand. She gladly offered it.

"But instead of talking to all of you," he said, waving his drink in the direction of the crowd, "I'd like to say something to Gina."

Henry wondered if any group of one hundred people had ever been so quiet.

"My darling," Jack said. "Thank you. Thank you for coming on this adventure with me. I can't imagine living one single minute of the rest of my life without you in it."

At this point the room was a mess. Layla choked out a sob as Jack finished his last sentence, and Henry wondered if even Herb Cook could have made sure to have enough Kleenex on hand to accommodate the emotion of this event. As he had when he walked into the room two hours earlier, Henry wondered how on earth the wedding could possibly top this. He looked over, for some reason, at Pete, who had his arm around Catherine. Pete looked different, all of a sudden. Even Pete, the Friendly's regular who still stayed up late at night watching *Space Ghost* cartoons, was moved.

He looked now at Layla, who was staring at him, and he suddenly had a brand-new feeling. They hadn't stopped holding hands since the end of Herb Cook's speech, and it occurred to him all of a sudden that they shouldn't stop holding hands for a long, long time. Like, for the rest of their lives.

"All right," Jack said, when he and Gina were finished with their very long kiss. "All right. Enough of the cornball speeches. Enough! Let's dance."

And sure enough, out of nowhere, a twelve-man crew appeared in a far corner of the room, setting up a dance floor. And just as suddenly, a five-piece band appeared in that same corner and began setting up its instruments. And within minutes everybody was dancing—little kids bouncing around the floor in socks, old couples showing off moves that nobody bothered to learn anymore, an old lady in a walker, smiling as she swayed in the dead center of the floor.

Amid the fray, Henry and Layla embraced as they swayed to the slow songs and held hands as they swing-danced to the up-tempo numbers. They still hadn't said anything substantial to each other since the speeches, but they were having a blast, and he hoped he'd made it clear to Layla that she was off the hook for the night before. From the look on her face, he guessed she understood.

But he knew she still had to be wondering what would happen.

The clock on the wall said it was eleven-thirty. Henry did some quick math. The wedding was scheduled for twelve-thirty the next day, the reception for three o'clock. Figuring a four-hour reception (Jack had told him as much on the golf course), that put the bouquet toss at around six o'clock the next evening. That left a little over eighteen hours until Layla's deadline. Henry decided he didn't need to make her wait the whole time.

They danced together until midnight, and as they swayed to a slow song, he whispered into her ear, "You want to get out of here?"

She pulled back a little, looked up and him and said, "Yes."

It took them a while to find Jack and Gina, and then a little longer to find Herb Cook, who was accepting congratulations on his toast and generally looked as if he'd just conquered Australia. Once they said their good-byes, they left the country club and walked out into the cool New England night.

"It's nice," Layla said.

"Perfect," Henry said.

"You want to walk back to the hotel?"

"I guess," Henry said. "How far is it?"

"Shouldn't be more than about ten minutes," she said. "We walked out this way this afternoon, Gloria and I."

"How's Gloria holding up?" Henry asked.

"I don't know," Layla said. "You know her. She never says what she's really thinking. And she had this thing with this married guy and—"

"Married, wow," Henry said. "This the guy she met at Starbucks the other day?"

"Yeah," Layla said, kicking at a pebble. "I guess it's over now."

They walked along the beach, listening to the rush of the ocean as invisible waves crashed off to their right. Layla leaned into Henry's side.

"Actually, it's a little chilly," she said.

"Yeah," he said. "That wind coming off the ocean."

"Wish I'd brought a windbreaker or something," Layla said.

And Henry's heart thumped, and he stopped walking.

"Are you all right?" she asked, still clinging to his right arm.

The rush of the ocean had been replaced by a roaring in Henry's head. The word "windbreaker" had jarred something loose, and his thoughts suddenly soared off, way south down I-95, to a hall closet in Bergen County in which hung a windbreaker with a little red box in the breast pocket.

Oh, no, he thought.

"Henry," Layla said, sternly now. "Are you okay?"

He was not okay. He was in major trouble. He knew he should have laid out the windbreaker with the suitcase the night before. A flash of pettiness had cost him, and now, here he was in Maine, on a beach after midnight, with the woman he wanted to marry, and he had no ring to give her.

"Henry?"

"Sorry," he said, snapping out of it long enough to ease her worry. "Sorry. I just realized something."

"What is it?"

"Toast," Henry mumbled. "I forgot to write a toast for Jack and Gina."

"Is that all?" Layla said, whacking her hand softly against his shoulder. "Henry, you could bang out a toast in fifteen minutes."

"Yeah," he said, hoping his acting job was good. "Yeah. I just have to do it."

"Well, we'll be back in the room soon, and you can do it tonight before bed, right?"

"Right," Henry said. The feeling in his stomach was coming back.

Henry was uncommunicative for the rest of the walk to the hotel. As he slid the card key into the door of their room, Layla asked him again, "Are you all right?"

"Yeah," he said, without looking at her. "I'm fine. Why?"

"You seem like you're in a hurry or upset or something."

"I have to use the bathroom, is all," Henry said.

He did not have to use the bathroom, but he desperately had to be inside of the bathroom, with a door separating himself from Layla. He needed to lean both fists on the vanity and shout whispered profanities at himself in the mirror. He would have loved to tear the shower curtain off and crumple it into the garbage, he was so mad at himself, but that might alert Layla to a crisis. And he didn't want to do that. Not now when he felt like he had everything figured out.

Think. He had to think.

It was one o'clock in the morning. Could he drive home and back in time? Was it even possible? The ceremony began in eleven and a half hours. It had taken almost six to get here. Six hours down, six back, would make him late, and he was the best man. Couldn't do it. He didn't have a car fast enough to pull it off.

Didn't have a car fast enough to . . .

Wait a minute.

He might not have a car fast enough to pull it off. But he knew somebody who did.

PART VIII

Very Early Saturday

Twenty-three

Henry wasn't too worried about knocking on Jack's hotel room door at one o'clock in the morning. Jack was the one guy in the hotel that he was certain was sleeping alone on this night. As he rode the elevator up to the eighth floor, the thing he was more worried about was Layla.

She hadn't understood why he was leaving all of a sudden. When he came out of the bathroom, she was lying on the bed, still in her dress from the party, looking as if she might want sex. Truth was, a half hour earlier he had wanted sex too, and was pretty sure he was going to have it. But now it was out of the question, much as it pained him to look at Layla stretched out on the bed and realize this. Now he needed a way out.

"Hey," he'd said. "I don't really know how to tell you this, but I have to go."

Layla sat straight up. It was possible that this came as a bigger surprise than anything else that had happened all week.

"What do you mean, you have to go?"

"It's an emergency, Lay. A best man thing," Henry said.

"A best man thing?"

"Yeah," he said. "Jack called my cell while I was in there. He said he needs somebody to hang out with tonight."

Layla curled her mouth into a wanton smile.

"Can't he wait a little while?" she said, rubbing her bare feet together and rolling slightly toward him.

This was physically painful.

"I'm sorry," he said. "Man, if you only knew how much I wish I could stay."

She stuck out her lower lip, like she would when pretending to be hurt. But Henry could tell she was putting a happy face on the thing. She really was hurt, and she likely would call Susan and/or Gloria as soon as he left to try and figure out what was going on in his head.

But he had no time to worry about that, so he gave her a nice, full, sexy kiss that promised more to come, and said, "I'll wake you if I make it back before morning."

"Before morning?" she asked. "Hey, is this some kind of bachelor party thing you don't want to tell me about?"

"No, I promise," Henry said. "Just me and Jack, hanging out. I'll be there as long as he needs me. It's a best man thing."

"All right," Layla said, in that way she had of saying it without allowing him to believe it. "Whatever you need to do."

She wasn't looking at him anymore. She was looking at her pile from work.

"Oh, come on," he said. "Don't do this."

"Do what?"

Again he had no time.

"I'm sorry," he said. "I gotta go."

"Go," she said. "I'm really all right."

And so he left, and now here he was, hopping out of the

elevator and making his way to Room 818, which he knew was Jack's, and knocking on the door.

Jack answered the door still in his shirt and jacket from the dinner, but otherwise wearing only his boxer shorts.

"Oh, geez," Henry said. "I'm so sorry. Is . . . is Gina in here or something?"

"What?" Jack asked, looking confused. "No. No. I'm just getting undressed. Come in, come in."

"Sorry to bug you, man," Henry said. "You're going to think I'm the worst best man of all time."

"I seriously doubt that," Jack said. "Although this is a questionable move. What'd you think of the party?"

"Absolutely incredible," Henry said. "And I mean that."

"What's wrong, Henry? You look very upset."

"I did a dumb thing," Henry said. "And I need to borrow your car."

"The new car? You've got to be kidding me. I've had it for two days."

"I know, I know," Henry said. "And if you say no, I'll understand. But here's the thing. I bought Layla an engagement ring, and I was going to give it to her tonight, but I forgot it."

"You forgot it," Jack said.

"Yeah," Henry said. "In Jersey."

"Wow," Jack said.

"Yeah. That about sums it up."

"You sure that's where it is?"

"Positive," Henry said. "It's in the inside pocket of a black windbreaker that's hanging in our hall closet. I forgot to bring the jacket."

"Wow," Jack said. "So, what? You want to drive down there, get the ring and drive back in time for the wedding? You'll never make it."

"That's why I'm asking for the car."

Jack looked very serious, and he thought about the situation for a while.

"Can't it wait until you get back?" he asked. "I mean, she'd understand, right?"

"In your experience—and tell me, because you have more experience with this than I do," Henry said, "but based on your experience, do you think she'll understand? More importantly, do you think she'll be happy about it?"

"You're right," Jack said. "How long is the drive?"

"Took me six hours today, in the middle of the day."

Jack looked at his watch and did some math in his head. He looked back at Henry.

"We can make it," he said.

"Sweet!" Henry said. "You have no idea how much . . . wait. *We?*"

"Hell yeah, man," Jack said, sliding back into his pants. "I'm coming with you."

PART IX

Saturday
(Deadline Day)

Twenty-four

Henry's protests were fervent, but brief. There was, after all, little time to waste.

The basic point he tried to make was that Jack was the groom, and thus a vital part of the wedding ceremony. Should something terrible (a car accident, say) or something mildly annoying (serious road construction on the Mass Pike) happen, and Jack not be on time for his own wedding, it could cause him serious problems.

"It's not worth the risk," Henry said.

"It's no risk," Jack said, snatching the keys from the desk in his hotel room. "We'll make it in plenty of time. I've been wanting to open this thing up on the highway anyway and see what it's got."

They were in the hallway now, heading to the elevator bank.

"All right," Henry said. "Let me try it this way. If you're not worried about your own ass, what about mine?"

"Come again?" Jack asked, still sporting the same goofy smile he'd had on his face all day.

"Well, I'm the best man. Technically, it's my responsibility to make sure you make it to the wedding in one piece. If you don't, Gina might forgive you, but she'd almost certainly kill me."

"She would," Jack said, pressing the Down button again, impatiently. "She definitely would. I wonder how she'd do it. She's not big on guns . . ."

"Laugh if you want, man," Henry said. "I'm glad you think this is funny."

"Hey," Jack said as the elevator arrived. "Here's the thing. There are three reasons I'm coming with you."

"Okay," Henry said warily as they got into the elevator.

"No, four. There are four reasons."

"Okay, okay," Henry said as the elevator descended. "What are they?"

"One," Jack said, holding up a finger. "It's my car. And there's a big difference between me letting you drive it around some cheesy little beach town and letting you take it out for a twelve-hour spin on the interstate."

"All right," Henry said.

"Two," Jack said, holding up two fingers. "I'm your friend. And you shouldn't have to go on a mission like this alone."

"Well, I appreciate that," Henry said, holding the door for his friend.

"Three," Jack said, holding up three fingers as they rushed out of the lobby and into the parking lot. "I wasn't going to sleep anyway. I'm getting married tomorrow."

"So you say," Henry said.

"And four," Jack said, whacking Henry on the left shoulder with his right hand as he pointed the electronic key chain at the car and actually started the ignition with it from fifteen feet away. "What are they going to do? Start without me?"

* * *

Their first obstacle came less than twenty minutes into their trip, when they arrived at the New Hampshire toll-booth at which Henry and Layla had spent a full silent hour that afternoon. It was still backed way up, both ways, even at one-thirty in the morning.

"No EZ-Pass," Henry said, squirming in the passenger seat.

"It's unbelievable," Jack said. "I could drive all the way from Maine to the tip of Florida, and the only tollbooth I have to wait at is this one."

"Why won't they put the EZ-Pass in?" Henry asked.

"Stubborn New Englanders, what do you want me to tell you?"

"Come on!" Henry barked toward the windshield.

"Hey," Jack said, still, somehow, smiling. "We'll be all right."

They cleared the tollbooth at one-fifty and tore off down I-95 into the black New England night. They were silent for a while, listening to the roar of the monster engine as it pushed the gleaming new car down the highway at ninety-five miles an hour.

"Rides pretty good," Henry said.

"It makes you wonder how you ever drove any other car," Jack said.

"So," Henry said. "You're pretty close with your father-in-law."

Jack's grin widened. "What gave you that idea?" he asked.

"You mean other than the car and the tearful speech about how you were the perfect guy?"

"Yeah," Jack said. "Other than that."

"How'd you trick him?"

"Ah, he's a good guy. Funny guy. Always all emotional, always gushing. I think he would have liked any guy who came in and treated Gina right. He's just a great big generous guy who loves his family."

"There are worse things," Henry said, nibbling on the nail of his right pinky as he looked out the window at a New Hampshire State liquor store.

"Yeah," Jack said. "And for me, it's been great. You know, this is a tough thing to go through when your own parents aren't around. I think a lot about my mom and dad, and how much fun they'd be having this weekend."

Henry had nothing to say to that. He nodded, looking straight ahead, and figured his friend's grin had probably taken a few seconds off.

"But things are good," Jack said. "Things are great. Gina's great, and I can't wait to see her in this dress I've heard so much about."

"That's great, man," Henry said. "It's good to see you so happy."

They crossed the border into Massachusetts and faced their first big decision.

"What do you think?" Jack asked. "Take 95 or the Mass Pike?"

"I always come up the Pike," Henry said. "You never know about 95. There always seems to be some construction."

"Which way is less likely to have cops?" Jack asked.

"Ha!" Henry said. "I thought that didn't matter."

"Well, it wouldn't, if we had the police department plates on the car," Jack said. "But we don't. Still too new. So my guess is, we'll get stopped and have to talk our way out of it."

"Hmm," Henry said, glancing at his watch. It was nearing two-thirty. The wedding started in ten hours. This was nuts. "This is nuts."

"Yeah," Jack said, grinning. "It's great. I had no idea how I was going to spend my last night as a single man, and this is cooler than anything I ever pictured."

"Glad you're having fun," Henry said, nibbling on the nail again.

"What's the matter?" Jack asked. "You're not?"

"I don't know," Henry said. "This is kind of a big deal, isn't it? I mean, if we're driving to New Jersey and back in the middle of the night to pick up an engagement ring, that kind of makes me feel like I'm probably about to get engaged."

"I'd say that's a fair assessment," Jack said.

"So I don't know," Henry said. "Heavy stuff."

"It is," Jack said. "It is. Are you not sure?"

"Not sure?"

"Are you not sure you want to do it?"

"No, I'm sure," Henry said. "Finally, I'm sure."

Silence for a little while.

"Anything you want to talk out?" Jack asked. "I mean, we have some time."

"I don't know," Henry said. "I guess I never pictured myself as the family type. Wife, kids, house, all that stuff."

"Right," Jack said.

"But then I think a lot of that is just guy crap, you know? Just some clutter in your head—the kind of stuff you're supposed to say to yourself when you're a single guy who likes being single. I think sometimes that's too easy."

"Okay," Jack said, both hands on the wheel, staring straight ahead, blinking.

"You all right?" Henry asked. "You want me to take over?"

"Nice try," Jack said. "I think a bug flew in my eye. I'm fine. Keep talking. I love the confessional thing."

"Well, the thing is," Henry said, "it's her, you know? I mean, it's not about the other stuff. It's not really about how I pictured my own life working out, or whether I thought I wanted kids, or anything like that. It's about her. You know what I'm talking about?"

"I'm pretty sure I do," Jack said.

"There's this guy I met on the golf course last week, one of these big, bellowing type of guys, great big handshake, slaps you on the back, you know the kind of guy I'm talking about?" Henry asked.

"Sure," Jack said.

"Well, this guy's been married five times."

"Five times?"

"Five times," Henry said. "To five different women, and he's not currently married to any of them."

"Wow," Jack said. "And this is the guy you've been getting your advice from this week?"

"Kind of, in a weird way," Henry said.

"You really should have called me," Jack said.

"No, I don't know," Henry said. "I think, in the end, this guy actually helped me make up my mind."

"Oh yeah?"

"Yeah. I mean, he's going on and on about marriage and what a pain women are and how they boss you around and how, in South America, you don't have to get married for life."

"Come again?"

"Forget it," Henry said. "You don't want to get into all of that right now."

"Sure," Jack said. "Maybe I'll get back to you in a couple of years."

"Anyway," Henry said. "I'm listening to this guy, and I'm watching him, and I was actually playing with him and Pete the other day, and all of a sudden it dawned on me. This guy's a mess. A total mess. He's this great, big, confident-sounding guy, but he's really totally lost. He's spent his whole life looking for something, he doesn't know what it is, and he hasn't been able to find it yet."

"And?" Jack said.

"And I already have it."

"Awwwww," Jack said.

"It's her," Henry said again. "Ever since she's been in my life, I've been happy. So really, none of the other stuff matters. It's about me and her, together. So the ring, when you think about it, is overdue."

"Awww," Jack said. "That's really sweet, man."

"All right, all right," Henry said. "Enough out of you. I sat through your sappy speech. I know you're a softie."

"Sappy?" Jack said, feigning hurt. "You thought it was sappy?"

"Put it this way," Henry said. "I didn't think my shirt was going to survive the dinner, Layla was crying so much."

"Wow," Jack said. "So you really screwed up."

"What do you mean?"

"Well, if you hadn't forgot the ring, and had to drive all the way back to New Jersey, it sounds like you probably would have got lucky tonight."

"All right," Henry said. "Now, that's really enough out of you. Take the Pike."

"You got it," Jack said, downshifting and swinging out onto I-695, heading west into Nowhere, Massachusetts.

The State Highway Patrol in Maine, New Hampshire, and Massachusetts let them pass without a whimper. Jack was maintaining between ninety and ninety-five miles an hour, and they hadn't seen a single flashing blue light. By three-fifteen in the morning they were in Connecticut, and feeling good.

"Uh-oh," Jack said.

Henry, who had begun to doze, looked up. Jack was looking in the rearview mirror. Henry craned his neck and saw the police car coming up behind them.

"Uh-oh," Henry said. "Is that for us?"

"Think so," Jack said.

Jack slid over to the side of the road, and the police car slid onto the shoulder behind them. Henry felt that sick, final disappointment you feel when your last hope is gone—when you'd known the sirens were for you but you still had been hoping the cop would speed on up the road after someone else at the last minute. He wondered if Jack ever got that feeling.

It took a few minutes for the cop to get out of his car. Henry checked his watch three times, mainly for lack of anything better to do.

"It's really going to be all right," Jack said, staring straight ahead with both hands on the wheel, the way they tell you to do it. "We'll be back on the road pretty quick."

"If you say so," Henry said.

The officer looked extremely young. Looked like a teenager, really. It occurred to Henry that this might be a problem—that a new-to-the-force, by-the-book highway patrolman might be less likely to do a favor for a fellow officer of the law. Henry was fretting a lot on this trip, and he was likely to fret until they were back in Maine, safely parked at the hotel with the ring in hand.

"Connecticut State Police," the officer said. "May I see your license and registration and proof of insurance, please?"

Jack reached into his back pocket and handed the kid a flipped-open leather case that included his badge and police department ID.

"Oh, I'm sorry, Detective," the officer said immediately.

"Don't be," Jack said. "How could you have known?"

"Bergen County, huh?" the young officer said, still holding the badge in his hand. "I grew up in Oradell."

"No kidding?"

"Yeah, we moved to Connecticut when I was fourteen. My dad got a job up here. I always figured I'd be a cop in Jersey. Still seems like it'd be more exciting than Connecticut."

"It has its moments," Jack said as the kid handed his badge back to him.

"So," the Connecticut officer said. "Is there some problem?"

"What do you mean?" Jack asked.

"Well, you were, you know, going kind of fast."

"Oh, right," Jack said. "Sorry."

"So, is there something you need some help with or something?"

"Well," Jack said, "I'm getting married up in Maine in about nine hours."

"You're going the wrong direction, sir," the officer said.

"Yes, I know," Jack said. "But I'm not running away, don't worry. My best man here, he has to propose to his own girlfriend by the end of my wedding, or she's ditching him."

Henry leaned forward and waved at the young officer, who looked confused and waved back.

"Only problem is," Jack continued, "he left the engagement ring at home down in Ridgewood."

"In Jersey?" the young cop asked.

"Yup," Henry said, looking at his hands.

"Wow," the young cop said. "So you're going to get it?"

"Yup," Henry said.

Jack was grinning like a little kid. He turned back to the Connecticut cop.

"So, as you can imagine, we're in a little bit of a hurry," Jack said.

"Sure," the young officer said. "Me, I don't see the big deal. I mean, I know I'll never get married."

Jack and Henry shared a small smile here, Henry still a little worried about making the kid mad.

"But," the kid went on, "if you're in a hurry, don't let me keep you. How you planning to get there?"

"We were going to take the Merritt to the Hutch to the Tappan Zee, then down the Garden State Parkway."

"Well, the Merritt's clear tonight," the cop said. "No delays. And I'll radio ahead with your description, so nobody else will bother you. Just do me a favor, though, will you?"

"Sure," Jack said. "What is it?"

"Maybe just don't go over ninety?"

"You got it," Jack said. "And thanks. Good luck to you."

"Hey, good luck to you—and to you."

This last part was for Henry, who acknowledged it with another wave.

"Thanks again, officer," Jack said.

"No problem," the officer said. "Nice car, by the way. How's it drive?"

"You really wouldn't believe it."

"I'm sure. Have a good night, now."

And he went back to his car, and Jack turned to Henry with a huge grin.

"So, what do you think?" Jack asked.

"If people knew about that, man, they'd hate cops even more than they do," Henry said.

"Funny," Jack said, easing the car back out onto the highway. "See the next time I do a favor for you."

"Did he call you 'Detective'?" Henry asked all of a sudden.

"Oh yeah," Jack said. "Forgot to tell you. I got a promotion."

"Geez," Henry said. "You're kind of on a roll, aren't you?"

The Merritt Parkway was poorly lit, and it was raining when they got there, so it slowed them down to around seventy-five miles an hour. Henry began looking at his watch again. They were racing past Greenwich, Connecticut, and it was five-fifteen in the morning. The sky off to their left was starting to show the slightest bit of light, but not much. They hadn't seen another car, let alone a police car, for more than an hour.

"So, what made you decide?" Jack asked.

"You mean about Layla?"

"Yeah," Jack said. "We were playing golf this afternoon, or yesterday afternoon or whatever, I've lost track, and you still didn't know. And now, well, here we are. What changed? Was it my sappy speech?"

"Nothing changed, man," Henry said. "It was just a matter of making my way through all that crap we talked about, you know? And the thing with her and this Ben guy didn't help either. Remember, I would have given her the ring last night, or Thursday night, or whenever, if not for the whole 'Ben' thing."

"Hey," Jack said. "That would have thrown me off too, I'm sure."

"Yeah, but I don't know," Henry said. "I figure, what am I supposed to expect? She's a good-looking girl. I see the way guys look at her. I'm surprised she doesn't get asked out more. And it was a messed-up week, so you can see what she was probably thinking. And it's not like she actually went out with him."

"All true," Jack said. "But I wonder how many guys would be so level-headed about it."

"Well, it helps that I went a couple of days without getting drunk on a golf course."

"Sure," Jack said.

"And besides, we're talking about the rest of my life, right? I've been with Layla for six years, and I've been happy the whole time. I'm going to kick her out and spend my life alone because some guy calls the house one time in six years? This is bigger than all that."

Jack was smiling again.

"What?" Henry asked. "I'm wrong?"

"Oh, no," Jack said. "I think you sound great. I think our little Henry's all growned up."

"Man," Henry said, shaking his head. "If this wasn't your car . . ."

Just before six A.M. they got pulled over again, on the Garden State Parkway. This time, when the cop got to the front window, he leaned in and said, "Jack?"

Henry figured that meant it was going to be all right.

"Hey, George," Jack said. "Morning."

"Morning, Jack," George said. "Where's the fire? You all right?"

"I'm all right," Jack said. "No time to explain, though. We're stopping in Ridgewood to pick something up and heading right back up this way. We'll be out of your hair soon."

"Sure, no problem," George said. "Sorry to keep you. What's with the car?"

"You like it?" Jack asked, infuriating Henry with his propensity for small talk in the face of a rapidly ticking clock. "I guess I'm moving up in the world. Don't tell anybody."

"You got it," George said, straightening up. "Hey, aren't you getting married soon?"

Jack let out a laugh. "Yeah," he said. "Real soon."

"Well, congratulations, if I don't see you, and good luck."

"Thanks," Jack said, and rolled the window back up.

"Yeah," Henry said. "This is giving me a really high opinion of law enforcement."

"Easy there," Jack said. "We have enough problems with all of you lawless schmucks. We have to stick together."

It was six-eighteen A.M. when Jack pulled his bug-splattered new car up to Henry's house.

"You mind if I come in?" Jack asked. "I've been holding it in since around Hartford."

"Sure," Henry said, unfolding himself and sliding his legs out of the car. "I mean, we're in a huge rush, but it's your wedding. If you're not worried, why should I be?"

Once inside the house, Henry went right to the closet and grabbed the windbreaker. He reached inside the breast pocket and found the red box. He took it out, opened it, saw the ring and exhaled.

"Nice," Jack said. "Nice work by you. She'll go nuts."

"Thanks," Henry said. "Now we just have to get it to her."

"Not going to be a problem," Jack said. "I'll just make my wee-wee and we'll get back on the road."

"Wee-wee?" Henry said. "What are you, getting ready for kids?"

"What are you, my mother-in-law?"

They stopped to get gas (had to buy it in Jersey, where prices were always considerably lower than anywhere else) and tore back up the parkway. Around the Montvale exit they saw George writing out a ticket for a guy in a red Dodge Viper. George waved as they went by. Jack honked his horn. Henry figured the guy in the Viper hated them all.

"You hungry?" Jack asked.

"Oh yeah," Henry said. He was feeling a great deal more relaxed now that he had the ring. He still kept looking at his watch, but he believed that if they didn't run into any more stops, and if the New Hampshire toll plaza was reasonable, they'd make it with plenty of time to put on their tuxes and get to the ceremony before anybody knew they were gone.

Anybody except Layla, that is. He wondered if she'd been back to sleep, and whether she was worried about him.

His stomach growled.

"Burger King work for you?" Jack asked.

"About all we have time for."

"B.K. it is," Jack said, and pulled into a rest stop. "Let's make it quick, though. I have a wedding to get to."

They were back in the car by 6:55, stuffing greasy breakfast sandwiches and little round hash browns into their mouths and not speaking. Henry was doing a few calculations in his head.

They'd left the hotel parking lot a little after one A.M., and with the toll delay and two traffic stops, the trip had taken them just a few minutes over five hours. This being a Saturday morning in the summer, there were likely to be a lot more cars on the road for the trip back. If it took them an hour at the New Hampshire toll plaza, as it had the day before, they'd get back by noon.

"What time are you supposed to be at the ceremony?" Henry asked with a mouthful of egg, cheese, and bacon.

"Eleven-thirty," Jack said.

"Going to be close."

"Yup," Jack said, shifting with his greasy right hand and sliding into the left lane. "We're going to need a little bit of good luck."

"Why didn't you say that before?" Henry asked, suddenly panicked again.

"I didn't want you to worry," Jack said.

"You ever think it's possible to be too good a friend?" Henry asked.

"Not until this morning I didn't," Jack said.

Henry looked over and saw that Jack was smiling. He wondered if his brother would be upset if he asked Jack to be his best man.

Henry's cell phone rang at five minutes after eight, as the car was speeding past a small food mart/gas station combo on the side of the Merritt Parkway.

"That Layla?" Jack asked.

"Yeah," Henry said, checking the caller ID.

"You going to answer it?"

"Just trying to figure out what to say," Henry said.

"Ha!" Jack barked. "Good point."

Henry answered the phone.

"Hey," he said.

"Hey," Layla said on the other end. He could tell she was trying to be calm but wasn't. "I was worried about you. Where are you?"

"Well," Henry said, looking for a road sign that might help him answer that question. "I'm not really at liberty to say."

"Okay . . ." Layla said. Henry couldn't tell if she was annoyed or just confused. "Are you coming back at some point?"

"Oh, sure," Henry said, trying to project as much confidence as possible. "We'll be back."

"In time for the wedding?" Layla asked.

"Of course," Henry said. "What kind of best man do you think I am?"

"Right now, an absent one," Layla said. "Pete told Catherine he couldn't find you guys."

"Well, Pete can't be that worried," Henry said. "He hasn't called."

From the driver's seat, Jack said, "You got a speakerphone on that thing?"

"Yeah," Henry said.

"What?" Layla asked.

"Turn it on," Jack said.

"I was talking to Jack," Henry said. "Hold on."

"Okay," Layla said.

"I'm putting you on speaker. I think Jack wants to talk to you."

"Okay," she said again, with the tone of someone who had no idea what was going on but was powerless to fight it.

Henry pressed the speakerphone button.

"Layla?" Jack asked.

"Yeah?"

"It's Jack."

"Hi, Jack," Layla said, sounding much sweeter all of a sudden than she had on the phone with Henry three seconds earlier. "How you feeling? All ready for your big day?"

She never failed to astound Henry with her ability to make small talk.

"Sure," Jack said. "Weather looks perfect, doesn't it?"

Henry looked at Jack, who shrugged at him. Neither one of them knew what the weather looked like in Maine at that moment.

They both tried not to laugh.

"Oh, it's gorgeous," Layla said. "You guys got so lucky."

Henry put a hand over his mouth as Jack pumped his fist in celebration of his good guess.

"Hey, Layla, I need you to do me a favor, all right?" Jack asked.

"Sure, Jack. Anything."

"Are you with the rest of the bridesmaids?"

"Yeah, I'm outside the hair salon. They're all inside, with Gina."

"All right," Jack said. "I guess Henry said something about Pete looking for us?"

"Yeah, he told Catherine he couldn't find you guys," she said.

"All right," Jack said. "If anybody in there sounds like they're worried, I need you to tell them you talked to Henry, and that he and I are just taking the car out for a spin around town to help kill the morning. Can you do that?"

"Um . . . sure," Layla said. "I'll make sure Gina doesn't worry."

"Thanks," Jack said.

"Is it true?" Layla asked.

"What's that?" Jack asked.

"I mean, is it true? Is that where you guys are?"

Jack looked at Henry. Henry shook his head.

"We're not really at liberty to say," Jack said.

"All right," she said. "Enough of that. Could you put Henry back on?"

And Henry hit the speaker button again and put the phone back up to his ear.

"What's up?" he asked.

"Are you sure you're all right?" she asked. "I don't think I'm any less worried than I was before I called."

"We're fine," Henry said. "Don't worry about a thing. We'll see you at the ceremony."

"All right," she said. "If you say so."

"I love you, babe," he said.

"I love you too," she said. And they hung up.

It was ten o'clock, and they were making unbelievable time, having already crossed the border from Massachusetts into New Hampshire. Not one member of any state's police force had seen fit to disrupt their morning, and the weekend summer commuters must have been behind them, since they didn't hit much traffic at all. The car was humming up I–95 at ninety miles an hour. They were less than an hour from the hotel, maybe an hour and a half with a reasonable delay at the toll plaza.

Jack was relaxed, and he was talking about Pete and Catherine.

"I wonder what's going to happen with them," he said.

"What do you mean?" Henry asked.

"Well, she really wants to have kids."

"How do you know that?"

"Catherine told Gina yesterday."

"I didn't think Catherine and Gina were close," Henry said.

"They're not," Jack said.

"Oh," Henry said.

"Yeah."

"I wonder what they're going to do. I mean, Pete basically told me at Friendly's the other day that it was out of the question, and he thought she understood."

"Friendly's?" Jack asked. "He's still having lunch there?"

"Every single day."

"Sheesh," Jack said. "I wonder what's going to happen to those two."

The toll plaza was a parking lot. They came to a dead stop well before the point at which Henry and Layla had hit their delay the day before. Henry guessed it would be an hour and a half, a guess backed up by the traffic report they put on the radio when they hit the blockage. It was ten-fifteen. They had an hour and fifteen minutes to get to the ceremony, and they weren't dressed.

"This is a problem," Henry said.

"Yeah," Jack said, still somehow looking relaxed. "I didn't want to have to do this."

"Do what?" Henry asked.

Jack was reaching behind the driver's seat with his right hand, digging for something. Henry hoped to hell it wasn't a gun. Jack had seemed far too relaxed.

After a few seconds of rummaging, Jack found what he was looking for. A little red cherry light. Henry's jaw dropped. This was like a movie. Jack rolled down his window, reached up to the top of the car and sat the light right there on the soft convertible top.

"Will it stay up there?" Henry asked, trying to play it cool.

"I guess we'll find out," Jack said. "Hold on."

He flipped a switch, a siren went off, and the ocean of cars quickly began to part in front of them. As the lane opened up, Jack drove through it, through one of the tollbooths without paying, and took off up the very open road on the other side. Henry craned his neck to look at the speedometer. The car was going 135 miles an hour.

Jack, of course, was smiling.

"I'm not really supposed to do that," he said.

Twenty-five

When she hung up, it struck Layla as odd that she wasn't all that worried.

Yes, of course there was plenty about which she could justifiably be worried. There was the issue of where Henry was, and whether he was safe. He said he was, but it was unlikely that he'd tell her the absolute truth if it would have worried her.

There was the issue of Jack, the groom, and whether Henry felt the appropriate amount of responsibility for making sure he got Jack to the wedding on time. Again, she figured he did, but the two of them had disappeared at one in the morning and hadn't been heard from since.

And of course there was the issue of her deadline, now one week old and only hours from expiration. As she lay in bed the night before, alone and not sleeping, she resolved not to say anything to Henry about the deadline today. He obviously knew about it, and obviously was approaching it in his own, maddening way, and she didn't want to do anything that might screw anything up. The Ben thing had already done enough of that.

When she hung up with Henry, she looked in through the front window of the hair salon. Her turn was a ways off. She dialed Gloria, who sounded as if she was just waking up.

"You all right?" Gloria said.

"I think so," Layla said.

"How did last night go?"

"Not . . . exactly the way I expected it to go," Layla said.

"Oh, I'm sorry, Lay," Gloria said.

"No, it's okay," Layla told her. "At least, I kind of sort of think it is."

And she recounted the story of the walk back, and the brief thrill she'd felt when Henry stiffened nervously and acted as if he might drop to one knee and pop the question there on the beach. And how he suddenly started acting very strange and ran off into the night with Jack, and that she had no idea where they were.

"Oh, and don't tell anybody that last part," she added. "We don't want to worry the bride."

"My lips are sealed," Gloria said.

"So, anyway, I don't know what's going on," Layla said. "I really didn't think he'd drag it all the way out until the end."

"Oh no? That's not the way he does things?"

Layla thought of Henry's unfinished manuscript and smiled.

"Actually . . ." she said.

"Hang in there, Lay," Gloria said. "You've still got a little bit of time."

From the other end of the phone, Layla heard a deep groan.

"Holy crap," Layla said. "You're not alone?"

She heard a lot of rustling around on the other end, as if

Gloria was racing out of bed to find a quiet place to talk, which is exactly what she was doing.

"Yeah," Gloria finally said. "It's this guy Ed. I think he's one of Gina's cousins or something."

"All right," Layla said, thinking she sounded like the same old Gloria again, wondering if that was a good thing or a bad thing.

"Hang in there," Gloria said as Layla heard a crashing sound in the background. "I think I have to go now."

Pete was pacing nervously in his tuxedo when the bridesmaids arrived at the church—one of the little white steeple churches that you find every couple hundred yards or so in certain parts of New England. He looked as if he was waiting for somebody, and she wasn't it.

"You all right?" Layla asked. Her car had arrived first, ahead of the one carrying Catherine. Gina and her parents were coming in the limo in a half hour. The bell in the steeple was ringing out noon.

"Ah, yeah," Pete said. "Me? Yeah. I'm fine."

"Looked like something was the matter," Layla said.

"Yeah, well . . . we don't know where Jack and Henry are."

Layla felt something in her stomach, like a small fist punching away at her insides, once, then again. She struggled to remember Jack's instructions. She thought she had them right.

"Oh, I talked to those guys a little while ago," she said, thinking, Like, four hours ago. "They're fine. They're up to something, but I'm sure they'll be here."

"Yeah," Pete said. "I'm glad you're sure. The minister has decided to take this out on me. He says they were supposed to be here at eleven-thirty."

"I'm sure it'll be fine," Layla said, forcing her broad smile to stay on as best she could. "But I think it would be best if you went back inside and acted like nothing was happening. The worst thing we could do right now would be to worry Gina if she got here early."

"Okay," Pete said. "Nobody else here, so you're the boss."

And he turned on the heel of his patent leather loafer and headed back in through the heavy white wooden door of the church. As soon as he was gone, Layla whirled around and looked up the road for some sign of Henry and Jack. She was listening for the roar of a monster sports car engine. The bell had stopped clanging. It was very, very quiet.

It had not been in her plans to start greeting guests, but she was out in front of the church when they all arrived at once. Literally.

Jack and Gina (or, more likely, Herb) had arranged for all of the guests to be picked up at the hotel and taken to the church in trolley cars—the kind they used for quaint little tours of the town. The dual purpose of this maneuver was (a) to skirt what could have been a major parking problem at the church if everyone had driven their own cars, and (b) to give the guests something to do in the time between the ceremony and the reception, while the bridal party was having its pictures taken. The plan was for the guests to load back onto the trolleys and go on a quaint little tour of the town, eventually stopping back at the country club for the reception. It was a nice idea, Layla thought, but it resulted in everybody getting there at once, and her having to act like a hostess in a silly ruby red dress on the front steps of the church.

"Great day, isn't it?" somebody asked her at least six hundred times.

"Perfect," she said every time, wondering if her smile looked as fake as it felt.

She was elated to see Gloria and Susan, because she knew she didn't have to smile for them, and because she just had to tell somebody what she knew. She pulled the two of them off to the side of the church steps.

"Nice dress," Gloria said, smirking behind huge sunglasses.

"No it's not," Layla said. "Shut up. I have something to tell you."

"Ooh," Susan said. "Sounds juicy."

"Jack and Henry aren't here yet," Layla said.

Susan and Gloria looked at their wrists. Neither was wearing a watch.

"What time is it?" they both asked at the same time.

"It's ten after twelve. The ceremony's supposed to start in twenty minutes. The bride could be here any minute. And there's no groom."

"Have you tried calling them?" Susan asked.

"I left my cell phone at the hotel. Figured I wouldn't need it. I had no place to carry it anyway. No pockets in this stupid thing."

She slapped the sides of her dress with her hands. Behind her, a long line of guests was streaming down the front steps of the church and out onto the sidewalk. Inside the church, four frantic ushers were trying to seat everybody as quickly as possible without forgoing any of the required take-the-lady's-arm-while-the-guy-walks-behind-you etiquette of their task. It was a circus. It led Layla to believe that they had more time than they thought. But she still would have felt better if she'd seen Henry. Or at least Jack.

"I have my phone," Gloria said, reaching into her purse. "You want to try calling them?"

"Yes!" Layla said. "Thank you!"

She reached for Gloria's phone, grabbed it and began dialing. Susan put a hand on her wrist.

"I think I've found them," she said.

Layla looked up. Susan was pointing around the side of the church, where two mischievous-looking faces were sticking out of some bushes. Henry and Jack were smiling as if they were Tom Sawyer and Huck Finn on the lam.

Layla didn't know whether to kiss him or kill him.

"Hey!" Henry said in a loud whisper. "We need your help!"

Layla shook her head, thanked Gloria as she handed her the phone, and rushed over to where Jack and Henry were hiding in the bushes. They were both in tuxedos. Their bow ties were not tied. Henry held a small pad of paper with the hotel's logo and a pen in his right hand.

Layla looked at the paper.

"Working on my toast," Henry said.

"Yeah," Jack said. "Wasn't it nice of him to put so much advance thought into it?"

"Are you guys crazy?" she asked, looking around as if Gina were about to sneak up on them. "Where have you been?"

"There's just no way we can tell you that, hon," Henry said. "I wish we could, but I'm afraid we'll have to take it to our graves."

Jack was laughing.

"Are you guys drunk?" Layla asked.

"Oh, God, no," Jack said. "Oh, please, no, don't tell Gina I'm drunk. We're not drunk at all. Haven't had a sip since the rehearsal dinner."

"A little tired, maybe," Henry said.

"Yeah," Jack said. "A little tired. But not drunk."

"You're really not going to tell me where you were all night, are you?" she asked.

"I wish I could, but I can't," Henry said, smiling as he held up his hands, palms facing upward.

"So what do you need me for?" she asked.

"Huh?" Henry said.

"You said you needed my help."

"Oh yeah," Henry said. "Neither one of us knows how to tie a bow tie."

And they couldn't take it anymore. Punchy and exhausted, Jack and Henry started laughing out loud, right there in the bushes. Layla shook her head and got to work on Jack's tie.

"His is more important," she explained.

"Damn straight," Henry said through his cackles. "I'm just here to make sure he makes it to the church on time."

"Hell of a job with that, by the way," Jack said, laughing harder now.

"Thanks," Henry said.

"Hold still," Layla said, sounding annoyed but smiling herself. "Seriously, I'm glad you guys had so much fun."

Fifteen minutes later you would never have known anything had been wrong. Layla was walking very slowly, very deliberately, up the aisle of the church, all eyes on her. She'd always hated this part of being a bridesmaid. For one minute all of the guests are focusing their attention on you, and you're not the bride. You're the bride's friend, in an ugly dress. Why should anyone pay attention to you?

Anyway, to avoid thinking about it, she looked to the front of the church, where Jack was at the head of a line of handsome, tuxedoed men. He stood tall and straight, with the same huge, warm smile he'd worn all the previous day. He caught Layla's eye and put two hands up to his bow tie. She smiled back at him.

Next to Jack was Henry, who was staring at her. She'd been annoyed with him a moment earlier, when Catherine was walking up the aisle and he pulled the pen and paper out of his pocket to jot down some idea he'd had for the toast. But now he was staring straight at her, with a look on his face like he had some big secret. There was no doubt he was acting strange, and Layla's mind raced with possibilities, but she didn't want to get all messed up in maybes and make some kind of scene at Jack and Gina's wedding. Not the ceremony, at least.

She wondered what Henry was thinking.

* * *

At that very moment Henry was thinking, I don't think I've ever had this much jewelry on me at any one time. In the right front pocket of his pants, where he could touch it with his hand six or seven times a minute to make sure it was still there, was the little red box that housed Layla's engagement ring. Henry had been proud of himself for not giving anything away in the bushes, and he credited the intense exhaustion he felt for his success in that endeavor.

In the left breast pocket of his tuxedo jacket, there were two more rings—Jack and Gina's wedding rings. The reason they'd been so late to the church was that they'd driven halfway there before Jack realized he'd forgotten to give the rings to Henry.

"Where are they?" Henry had asked, now driving the car because Jack said he was too tired and too nervous all of a sudden.

"They're probably on the desk in my hotel room," Jack said.

And after they'd done a horribly illegal but incredibly fun U-turn in the middle of a back road, driven back to the hotel, ridden the elevator, and barged into Jack's room while it was being cleaned, they'd found out that he was right. The rings were right there, across the room from a startled maid who was frozen in the act of changing the sheets. She composed herself long enough to ask Jack to slide his key card in the door, just to make sure it was his room and they were his rings. He'd done it, the little green light went on, and she smiled and wished them luck.

Now, here they were. Henry had three rings in his pockets along with some notes for a half-written best man toast on a pad of paper. He was tired, and hungry in spite of the greasy Burger King breakfast, but he felt good. He felt energized by the night, by the time he'd spent with his best friend—a time they'd never forget. He felt energized by the secret he was keeping from Layla—the one he believed would give her a day she'd never forget. And he was very pleased with the plan he'd devised for meeting her deadline.

He smiled so broadly at her as she walked up the aisle that she had to look away, or else she would laugh. He loved that he could make her do that.

The ceremony was sweet, and the pictures took forever, but Henry and Layla spent as much time together during them as they could. Layla was determined to cross-examine Henry about his night, and Henry was determined to give up nothing.

"Did you guys go to a strip bar?" she asked.

"I really can't say," he said.

"Henry!"

"All right. I can tell you that we didn't go to a strip bar," he said.

"Good," she said.

"We looked, but there aren't any around here," he said with a grin.

She punched him in the shoulder. He rubbed his shoulder and laughed, but it actually did kind of hurt.

"So you didn't drink, and you didn't go to a strip bar, and still there's some reason you can't tell me what you did," she said. "Do I even want to know?"

Henry shrugged and smiled. The photographer yelled, "Bridesmaids!"

"That's you, babe," he said.

She made a move to punch his shoulder again. He twisted out of the way.

The guests, in their trolleys, were arriving at the country club, where the reception would be held. The bridal party already had been there awhile, since many of the pictures were taken at the club. So they all had drinks in their hands and relieved smiles on their faces when the guests who were not beholden to the whims of a perfectionist photographer arrived en masse. There was a receiving line, but only for Jack and Gina and Gina's family, so the bridal party got to do what it wanted.

Henry and Layla were the only two people seated at a table for twelve in the middle of a room so large it could have been used to build the space station. Around them, waiters and waitresses buzzed, while the guests who had been the first off the trolleys studied a huge seating chart. Henry was busily writing his toast out on scraps of small hotel-room paper. Layla was still trying to get information out of him.

"Did you drive the car around?" she asked. "Did you go somewhere? Did you go to Niagara Falls or something?"

"Does that even make any sense?" Henry asked.

"I don't know. You won't tell me anything."

"I told you about the strip club," he said.

"True."

"I'm sorry, babe. I really have to work on this toast."

"Okay, okay," she said. But she didn't get up to leave. She was thinking of her next question.

There were the introductions, and there was a first dance. And then there was some more dancing, as the bridal party was invited to join in the first dance. Layla never liked that one either. She thought the bride and groom's first dance should be all alone, in the middle of the floor, just them as the center of each other's universe. But no one had asked her.

Henry was a decent dancer, though he never seemed to believe it. Layla enjoyed dancing with him, mainly holding him through a slow song. She liked how strong he felt. She liked how comfortable she felt in his arms. She wondered when she'd stopped worrying about the deadline.

Then she wondered how much time there really was until the deadline. And if, at this point, if he blew it, she'd have the heart to go through with her ultimatum. At this point, things seemed pretty well decided.

Didn't they?

The dance segued into another, and some of the bridal party left the floor. Jack walked Gina over to where Henry and Layla were standing. Henry saw them coming and said, "Oh, right. Gina?"

And he took Gina's arm and danced away with her. Jack, left standing with Layla, offered his arm, and she took it. They began to dance, but Layla was watching Henry and Gina together. Henry was doing a lot of talking. Gina was doing a lot of listening.

"Are they plotting something?" Layla asked.

"I have no idea," Jack said, unconvincingly.

Gina began to laugh and nod her head vigorously. Henry looked over at Layla and smiled.

Layla shook her head.

"What?" Jack asked.

"I don't believe you," she said.

"May we have the best man up at the front of the room, please?" the band's lead singer said into his microphone.

There was some tepid applause and some loud moving of chairs as Henry crossed the dance floor and took the microphone. He slid the hotel-room pad out of his pocket and shuffled some of the pages that had come loose.

"As you can tell, this toast was painstakingly prepared," he said into his microphone.

The room laughed.

"Thanks, buddy!" Jack shouted, holding Gina's hand in his left and a champagne glass in his right. "I appreciate that!"

The room laughed louder.

"All right," Henry said. "Anyway, I'm Henry, and, well, here goes."

He heaved a sigh, looked at the first piece of paper, then looked back at the crowd.

"When Jack was eight years old, he broke his leg jumping off his front porch," Henry said.

The room laughed again. This was a good start.

"He had tied a towel around his neck and was attempting to fly. But he landed funny on the bottom step, twisted his leg and broke it. It was about the most disgusting thing I've ever seen in my life."

The room was laughing out loud. Henry had to wait to continue. He looked back at the pad.

"So I'm eight years old, nobody's parents are home, and I have to figure out what to do with this friend of mine who just snapped his leg being a dummy and trying to fly. Well, I remember what I did. I went into the garage, found an old wooden sled, put Jack on the sled and started pulling him up the street."

More laughter.

"Now, this was the middle of the summer, and it's hard to pull a sled when there's no snow on the ground. But still, I would say I made it about, oh, I don't know . . . maybe fifty or sixty feet."

Louder laughter.

"Fifty or sixty feet until, thank God, Jack's father's car came around the corner. I remember Jack's father bouncing out of the car and shouting, wondering what the hell we were doing . . ."

He trailed off here, because much of the room was laughing, and Jack, while smiling, was looking down at the floor. He missed his father.

"I remember Jack's father thanking me for my help. 'I'll take it from here,' he said, as if I'd dragged his son fifty miles through the desert and now all he had to do was load him into the ambulance. But I remember feeling proud, because I'd helped my friend. I'd helped Jack out."

Silence in the room. Henry looked again at the pad.

"And ever since then, I've been the screwup and Jack's been the one helping me out."

Laughter again.

"Jack's the kind of guy you like to go on an adventure with. In fact, we kind of just got back from one this morning."

Gina looked at Jack and gave him a playful whack on the arm. Jack shrugged. Henry caught Layla's eye. Her expression was a curious one.

"But something Jack said last night got me thinking about adventures, and what a real one must be like."

Now the room was silent again. They sensed the serious, mushy part of the toast. Henry looked at his notes for the last time. He looked back out at the crowd, in search of Layla. He didn't speak until he made eye contact with her. He didn't break eye contact until he was finished speaking.

"The adventures Jack and I had when we were eight were fun. We got to be superheroes, policemen . . . well, all right, I guess some of it wasn't make-believe."

A little laughter, not much.

"We were astronauts, whatever. And we had adventures on our bikes, exploring the woods behind our houses, getting into trouble, all that good stuff. We had some adventures in college, but we're not going to get into that here. Mixed company."

Good, solid burst of laughter.

"But the real adventure, that's this thing Jack and Gina are taking right now. They're heading into the real part of their lives—the one where they take on the world together. No matter what happens the rest of their lives, they're going to be there, side by side, facing it together. They wouldn't want it any other way."

Layla was looking right back at him. Very seriously now.

"It's almost like Jack was killing time, knowing he had to go on this big adventure, but waiting until his partner showed up. And when she got here, man, did he know it."

Layla looked at the floor for a second, then right back into Henry's eyes.

"The way Jack talks about Gina makes you realize what life and love and marriage are all about. He doesn't want to do anything—have kids, buy a house, buy a car, mow the lawn—doesn't want to do any of it without her there next to him, cheering for him, helping him out. This is a guy who hasn't needed anybody's help since he was eight years old and broke his leg, and he's found somebody he just can't wait to lean on. That's special. That's really special."

Layla was crying now. Not a shock. Henry took a deep breath and gathered himself for the finale.

"So," he said, raising his champagne glass. "If you'll join me in raising a glass to Jack and Gina. Wish them luck on their greatest adventure, and congratulate them for finding each other."

The room broke into shouts of "Hear! Hear!" and clinking glasses. Jack and Gina rushed to the front of the room to offer hugs to Henry. The whole time, he kept looking at Layla, who was clapping and wiping tears out of her eyes.

He smiled a knowing smile.

What must she be thinking? he asked himself.

At that moment, Layla was thinking, So, is he going to do it, or what?

She wondered if he'd do it during the toast, but he hadn't, and when she thought about it, she was glad. Now that the toast was over, she wondered if he'd ask her to go somewhere alone with him, and do it in private. She was clapping, staring at him as he embraced the bride and groom, when Susan sneaked up behind her.

"Sweetheart," Susan said. "If you don't marry that guy, I will."

Layla laughed. "He still hasn't asked!" she said.

Henry came back to her, finally, and asked, "What did you think?"

"It was great," Layla said. "So great. I can't believe you wrote it this morning."

"Well, I was kind of winging it, really," Henry said. "Didn't use that much of what I wrote."

"Well, it sounded great."

"Thanks, babe," he said, and he kissed her. They both turned around to watch Jack and Gina go into another dance.

Henry didn't say another word.

There was dinner, and a cake-cutting, and then there was cake for everyone. And the reception wore on into its fourth hour. Layla and Henry were flushed from dancing, and she was starting to wonder again. The time was coming for the bouquet toss, and the end of the reception. And then what? Would she have to stick to her word? Would there be a fight if he forgot? She didn't want to fight with him, not after all of this.

"May we have all the single ladies on the dance floor, please?" the lead singer said.

Layla looked at Henry, and her guard collapsed. She showed panic. He noticed. He looked at her as if worried, and then he stepped back.

"Oh, man," he said. "The bouquet toss."

"Henry?" she asked.

"That's my deadline, isn't it?"

Layla didn't know what to say. Gina came and pushed her onto the dance floor. Layla kept staring at Henry, who was smiling but doing nothing. This was it. This was the moment when he was supposed to do something, and he was doing nothing. He was just smiling, as if it was all a big joke.

She wasn't about to get upset and make a scene in the middle of Jack and Gina's wedding reception. So, after one more long look at Henry's smiling face, she turned toward the front of the room, where Gina was turning her back. She wasn't sure, but she thought she saw Gina smile at Henry, and Henry wink at Gina.

She was about to lose her mind.

The band struck up a drumroll and counted, "One! Two! Three!"

And Gina turned around and walked the bouquet over to Layla.

Stunned, Layla looked up at Gina, who giggled and looked to her left. Out of the corner of her eye Layla saw Henry walking toward her. When he got there, he dropped to one knee.

She gasped.

Something else caught her eye. A twinkle. She looked at the bouquet. And there, sticking up out of the middle of it, tied to green wire, was a beautiful diamond engagement ring.

She gasped again, looked around the room. Looked at Jack and Gina, who were beaming. Looked at Gloria, who was stunned. Looked at Susan, who was clapping. Looked at the cake.

Finally, she looked down at Henry, who took her free hand.

"Layla," he said. "Will you marry me?"

DAN GRAZIANO is a sportswriter for *The Newark Star-Ledger*. He writes baseball stories and columns for the paper. This is his second novel. He lives in New Jersey with his wife and two sons. He may be reached on the internet at www.dangraziano.com.

Dan Graziano